706508 328

HUNGRY FLAMES

and other
Black South African
Short Stories

HUNGRY FLAMES

and other
Black South African
Short Stories

edited and with an introduction by
MBULELO VIZIKHUNGO MZAMANE

Longman

Longman Group Limited
Longman House
Burnt Mill, Harlow,
Essex CM20 2JE, England
and Associated Companies
throughout the World

© Mbulelo Mzamane 1986

First published 1986

Produced by Longman Group (FE) Ltd
Printed in Hong Kong

For Can von Themba and Casey 'The Kid' Motsisi:

The sons of a bitch had no business to die!

And for Nombulelo and Mncedisi:

Lala ngoxolo mza, nawe mfo'.

And for Mam' uAlbertina Sisulu, Winnie Mandela,
and all the persecuted mothers of our land:

We suck the milk of fortitude from your breasts;
You who are the heroines of continuance.

And for Jigsaw:

You hold the future in the palm of your hand, mzala.

Look closely, those lines are screaming to be heard.

Shakong!

Thanks for your abiding faith, chom.

Mduduzi ka Mbele!

Nawe phela, mngane!

And you Kos-kos, Tam-tam, and Vuvu.

Nthoana!

Acknowledgements

We are grateful to the following for permission to reproduce short stories:

George Allen & Unwin and Kraus-Thomson Organisation Ltd for 'S'ciety' by Peter Abrahams in *Dark Testament* (1942); BLAC Publishing House for 'The Park' by James Matthews in *The Park and Other Stories* (1974); Dr T. Couzens for 'Juwawa' by R. Dhlomo in *English in Africa* Vol. 2 No. 1, ed. Dr T. Couzens (1975); the author, Bessie Head for 'The Prisoner who wore Glasses'; the author, Professor E. Mphahlele for 'Grieg on a Stolen Piano' in *Modern African Stories* ed. E. Mphahlele and E. Komey (1964); and author, M Mzamane and Longman Group Ltd for 'The Day of the Riots' in *The Children of Soweto* (1982); Ravan Press (Pty.) for 'Mita' by Casey Motsisi in *Casey & Co: Selected Writings of Casey 'Kid' Motsisi* ed. Mothobi Mutloatse (1978), and 'Riva' by Richard Rive, 'The Music of the Violin' by N. S. Ndebele, 'Call Me Not a Man' by M. Matshoba, 'The Promise' by Gladys Thomas from *Staffrider* Vol. 2 No. 1 (March 1979), Vol. 3 No. 3 (Sep./Oct. 1980), Vol. 1 No. 3 (1978), Vol. 4 No. 1 (April/May 1981); Dr T. Vincent, on behalf of *Black Orpheus* for 'Tattoo Marks and Nails' by Alex La Guma in *A Walk in the Night & Other Stories* (1967).

We have been unable to trace the copyright holders of 'Hungry Flames' by J. A. Maimane in *New Classics V* ed. S. Sepamla (1978), 'The Dignity of Beginning' by B. Modisane in *Come Back, Africa: Short Stories from South Africa* ed. H. L. Shore and M. Shore-Bos (1968), 'The Urchin' by Can Themba in *The Will to Die* ed. D. Stuart and R. Holland (1972), and we would appreciate any information that would enable us to do so.

Contents

Introduction

'Although it is bursting with life, the short story in Africa is a neglected genre', Wilfried Feuser reminds us. 'Critics have paid scant attention to the short story and have treated it as a footnote to the novel. And yet short story writers were deeply involved in the genesis of African writing in European languages.'[1] Nowhere on the continent are these general truths better illustrated than in South Africa.

The short story tradition in South Africa is as old as the Xhosa *intsomi*, the Zulu *inganekwane*, the Sotho *tsomo* and other indigenous oral narrative forms. In addition, there are many excellent White exponents of the short story form in South Africa such as Charles Herman Bosman and Nadine Gordimer. They are, however, adequately represented in numerous anthologies and individual collections. This selection is limited to modern short stories in English by Black writers of South African origin—'Black', as understood by the new generation in South Africa, refers to the darker races of acknowledged African, Asian and mixed descent, who constitute the vast majority of the disadvantaged and oppressed in South Africa. The selections in this anthology demonstrate the springs of Black South African literature in English, its themes and techniques, in the period since 1930. The anthology provides a wide-ranging introduction to, or an opportunity to renew acquintance with, an art form in which many South African authors have distinguished themselves. Fifteen authors have been selected, with the aim of producing a collection as representative as possible of all the characteristics, qualities and diversities of mood that co-exist in the genre.

Unlike their counterparts in other parts of Africa, with few exceptions, South African writers have not turned to tradition for their inspiration. This is not so much because three centuries of European occupation and cultural dominance have cut them off from their traditional roots—African cultures have proved their resilience and adaptability on that score—but because, under the harsh conditions of settler colonialism experienced in South Africa, for Black writers to dwell on the beauty of traditional culture would be a hollow exercise performed at the expense of more vital issues.

The authors represented in this anthology are concerned with the immediacy of life, as perceived by the disadvantaged and oppressed people of South Africa. Their themes range from the hardships of the working place to what Can Themba has described as 'the swarming, cacophonous, strutting, brawling, vibrating life' of the townships.[2]

South African literature is closely tied to political developments, which it largely mirrors and which can either retard or advance its growth. An appreciation of South African literature at any stage in its development requires some degree of familiarity with the corresponding political events. Each generation of writers responds to the central political and human questions of its age. The stories point out a real world and the following survey is intended to demonstrate the structures and operations of that world while, at the same time, placing each author's work within its historical context.

The Pioneers

R.R.R. Dhlomo achieved distinction as the first Black South African to publish a novel in English, *An African Tragedy*, which appeared in 1928. It was actually written after Sol Plaatje's *Mhudi*, which Plaatje completed around 1917 though it was not published until 1930. Dhlomo also wrote poems and short stories, some of which appeared in contemporary newspapers and journals such as *Ilanga lase Natal*, *Sjambok* and the *Bantu World*. His stories inaugurated the modern short story tradition among Blacks in South Africa.

Tim Couzens explains the significance of Dhlomo's work in the following terms: 'Any definitive histories, even assessments, of Black South African literature cannot fail to take the writings of R.R.R. Dhlomo into account. Many of the themes he raised are "universal" to the Black South African condition and foreshadow the concerns of present-day African writers.' A number of Dhlomo's stories are set in the gold mines of the Witwatersrand, where he worked as a mine clerk before turning to journalism. 'It is this first hand experience of life in the mines which is so clearly evident in his mine-orientated stories, producing an authenticity which surpasses that of Peter Abrahams in his later novel *Mine Boy*.'[3]

Dhlomo's story, 'Juwawa', which opens this anthology, was first published in *Sjambok* (22 August 1930). The story depicts the merciless exploitation of African mine workers. In their desperation, they craftily resort to covert resistance, employing every physical and psychological weapon at their disposal. Constantly beaten by his White overseer, 'a bitter flood of invective and hatred, born of a vicious desire for vengeance' wells in the heart of the African miner, Juwawa, the Shangaan (a member of a despised ethnic group, even within the ranks of the dispossessed and exploited Africans). Dhlomo employs bitter irony to convey the acrimony engendered by oppression and exploitation. He does not only recreate the oppressive and exploitative conditions under which Africans live and work but also suggests a way of fighting back. He depicts the working class as the vanguard of the African liberation struggle. In his class analysis and consciousness, Dhlomo is more revolutionary than many of his successors.

Peter Abrahams, who followed in Dhlomo's footsteps, made his literary debut in 1936 in the *Bantu World* as a poet. In some ways, along with B.W. Vilakazi, H.I.E. Dhlomo and A.C. Jordan, he is the precursor of the Black Consciousness poets. Two recurring themes in Black Consciousness literature appear in Abrahams' earliest work: Black pride and the need for solidarity among the oppressed. Both themes emerge again in his first published work in prose fiction, the short story collection, *Dark Testament* (1942), and in his first two novels, *Song of the City* (1945) and *Mine Boy* (1946).

'S'ciety', one of the best realised stories from *Dark Testament*, demonstrates how the traditional mode of story-telling is transplanted to the new environment of the cities. The gang gather in the evenings, as they might have done in the villages around the communal fire, to spin tall yarns which serve the same purpose as the traditional tale; the 'stories' impart to the group the basic facts of life necessary for survival in the hostile world of South Africa's segregated ghettoes. Uncle Joe in 'S'ciety', a fine fellow in his heyday who is destroyed by alcohol, is the prototype of Daddy in *Mine Boy*. Finding life unbearable, both characters 'freak out' but are looked after by the community in which no one is ever regarded as an outcast. In some respects, 'S'ciety' is a tribute to the communal spirit that holds ghetto societies together. Though life and death are uncomfortably juxtaposed in the story, in a manner that is reminiscent of Steinbeck's work, it is life that triumphs: 'Yes, the name of S'ciety must be kept up.'

In 'S'ciety', pathos and humour (in essentially morbid situations) are mixed delicately to good effect, as in real life among ghetto communities, where the people must look beyond the life-denying aspects of their existence in order to survive their 'deprivation, severance, loss'.[4] In the story, Abrahams comes across more subtly than in his novels. Like Mphahlele, La Guma, Modisane and other subtler exponents of the art form, he does not force down his readers' throats the staple diet of politics which we have come to expect from South African literature. However, the didactic, political element, which forms the backdrop to the action in 'S'ciety', emerges without interfering unduly with the natural development of events in the story and without stretching our credulity, as often happens in his novels. We also see in the story the emergence in South African literature of a 'Coloured' English, a process carried forward by La Guma in *A Walk in the Night and Other Stories* (1962).

Ezekiel Mphahlele emerged soon after the Second World War. *Man Must Live and Other Stories*, his first collection, was published in 1946. After the establishment of *Drum* magazine in 1951, he became one of its most regular and distinguished contributors and was the first African appointed to its panel of judges for its annual short story competition. In 1956, following his dismissal from teaching for organising protests against Bantu education, an inferior system of education designed for Africans, he became the literary editor of *Drum*. He continued to churn out short stories for the magazine in the form of serialization of his 'Lesane' stories. He eschewed crime and cheap romance, sensational and escapist stuff of which *Drum* was inordinately fond; as were the other magazines aimed at Black readers which emerged in the period such as *Drum's* sister magazines, *Zonk* and *Afrika* (later *Post*). However, his more accomplished stories, of which 'Greig on a Stolen Piano' is an example, were written after his departure in 1957 from South Africa. Cultural syncretism, alienation wrought upon the individual by apartheid and the attendant struggle for survival in the cities are prominent themes in Mphahlele's stories.

In 'Grieg on a Stolen Piano', the central figure of Uncle personifies Mphahlele's 'African paradox' — detribalised, urbanised and Westernised, but still African.[5] There is an Uncle 'a synthesis of the traditional and the westernised African'. He plays Mohapeloa's 'Leba', a song by the Mosotho composer which fuses traditional Basotho rhythms with European classical music, and Grieg's piano concertos with equal deftness. He is a self-made man who, despite having reached the top in his profession, finds difficulties making ends meet, unless he supplements his meagre income from his salary by some other means, mostly illegal. His primary concern is survival in the face of underpayment and deprivation experienced by Blacks in South Africa, where the concept of equal pay for equal work is suppressed in the interests of maintaining White political and economic supremacy.

The English spoken by Mphahlele's characters demonstrates how Africans have fused African and Western culture in their persons. 'The African writer', he explains, 'listens to the speech of his people, to the ring of dialogue in his home language and struggles to find an approximation of the English equivalent.'[6] The arguments advanced by some critics that Black South African writers use English in a completely orthodox fashion notwithstanding, we see in Mphahlele an attempt to employ transliteration to bridge the two cultures.[7]

The 'Drum' era

The 1950s produced an unprecedented spate of literary activity among Blacks in South Africa which received its greatest impetus from the establishment of *Drum*. The writers who emerged during this period received their literary apprenticeship as journalists either with *Drum* or its sister Sunday newspaper, *Golden City Post*, *Zonk* and *Bona*; and the more politically oriented papers such as *Torch*, *Fighting Talk* and *New Age*. The other new crop of writers from this era who were not journalists were, nonetheless, associated with *Drum* or with one or the other of the periodicals, either as occasional contributors of short stories or of articles on a variety of social, cultural and political subjects. Sophiatown on the Witwatersrand and District Six in the Western Cape, both of which have since been demolished under the Group Areas Act, were designed to promote residential segregation. They became the great centres of literary, artistic, musical and other artistic activity. A distinctive 'Drum' school came into being: urban oriented; employing the imagery, the racy idiom and the staccato speech cadences of the ghetto, liberally spiced with Americanisms picked up from the movies, American comic strips, blues records and writers of the Harlem renaissance; and occupied, in the main, with social issues, with only writers from District Six showing an inclination to tackle political subjects headlong. *The Classic*, founded in 1963 by Nat Nakasa, Can

Themba and others, became the finishing school for writers of the 'Drum' generation. They form the majority of contributors to this anthology because they come from an age during which the short story tradition in South Africa produced its most distinguished exponents.

The Sophiatown Renaissance

Bloke Modisane's delightful satire, 'The Dignity of Begging', first appeared in *Drum* in 1951. Modisane's work resembles Mphahlele's in the sense that both writers are concerned with the affront of human dignity under apartheid and the struggle for survival in a hostile socio-political environment. As in Mphahlele, Modisane's characters take up the challenge of having to help 'balance the family budget' and, in so doing, evolve a new ethical code of survival to counteract their deprivation and compensate for their disabilities. 'The Dignity of Begging' asserts the right even among the lowest of Blacks, the beggar class (a position to which every Black person in South Africa has been relegated) to lead decent lives. The story is an indictment of White justice. Against the views propagated by Alan Paton in *Cry, the Beloved Country* (1948), views which were gaining wide currency in South African liberal circles, about the impartiality of the South African judiciary, Modisane gives the opposite point of view that the judiciary is part of the system and is implicated in upholding apartheid.

Nathaniel Mokgomare, the crippled beggar in the story, is trapped in the system in which a beggar, in as far as he is Black, can expect to receive neither mercy nor sympathy from the White courts. The law enforcement agents connive with the social workers, sometimes with lowdown criminal elements, against the beggars, who need a strong trade union to facilitate collective bargaining. Modisane's political message, indirectly rendered, is that Blacks need a strong organisation on a countrywide scale to effectively counteract the oppressive and exploitative forces. This oppressive network is so complex that even the families of the beggars exploit the situation and become exploiters in their own right. Nathaniel Mokgomare is saved by his resourcefulness and his indomitable will to live. In this, he embodies the *chakijane* or *mmutlanyane* (Brer' rabbit) motif found in traditional Southern African folktales. *Chakijane* or *mmutlanyane* is the Anansy figure of traditional Southern African folklore. The story is about the tactics of survival in which *chakijane* excels. Modisane writes with a total lack of self-pity and a subtle touch rarely equalled by his contemporaries.

In Can Themba, we encounter 'an extreme cultural "underworldism" of the African township'. Widely regarded as the poet laureate of Sophiatown, his work celebrates the robust, raucous life of the township. That is not to say Can Themba wished 'for the continuance of slum conditions in order to engender a spurious vitality' but, as Lewis Nkosi explains:

> For Can Themba, the African township represented the strength and the will to survive by ordinary masses of the African people. In its own quiet way the township represented a dogged defiance against official persecution, for in the township the moments of splendour were very splendid indeed, surpassing anything White Johannesburg could offer. It is true that Can Themba's romanticism drove him in the end to admire more and more the ingenious methods of that survival — the illicit shebeens and illicit traffic, the lawlessness, the everyday street drama in which violence was enacted as a supreme test that one was willing to gamble one's life for one moment of truth . . . In this respect he echoed Ernest Hemingway's romanticism of violence.[8]

Each of the elements described above is present in 'The Urchin', which contains scenes of young township ruffians at work, scenes that are as finely observed and as psychologically penetrating as Graham Greene's descriptions of anarchy and wilful destruction among London's youth in the World War II period. Can Themba writes about the underworld life of Sophiatown in a highly evocative manner and with unrivalled authenticity, 'because he himself was the supreme intellectual *tsotsi* [street urchin] of them all, always, in the words of the blues singer, "raising hell in the neighbourhood" '. Lewis Nkosi adds that Can Themba evinces 'a mind both vigorous and informed, shaped by the city as few other minds are in the rest of Africa'.

Arthur Maimane was one of *Drum*'s most prolific contributors of short stories in the 1950s. He created the first Black private detective in a serial which ran for several months. 'Hungry Flames' pursues the subject and theme of Can Themba's story. Juvenile delinquency is rife in South Africa's urban ghettoes. Baragwanath

Hospital in Soweto probably treats more cases of stabbings by *tsotsis* in the streets than any other hospital in the world; and Johannesburg's courts are kept perpetually busy trying cases of mugging, rape, murder and other serious crimes of violence. In Maimane's story, the juvenile 'delinquent' is treated more compassionately than he can ever hope to be in South Africa's courts, which have the reputation of dispensing justice swifter than a Baragwanath dispenser. Maimane laments the disintegration of family life which exacerbates the problem.

Casey Motsisi carved himself a reputation as a humorist in *Drum* and subsequently as a columnist in the *Golden City Post, World, Weekend World* and the Johannesburg *Star.* But he also had his serious side and, like every other sensitive South African not yet brutalised by the system, he deplored the senseless and fratricidal violence of Blacks in the townships. In his work, he portrays township folk in their rounds of giving birth, making love, drinking, brawling and dying. 'Mita' captures the flavour of life in the Sophiatown that Motsisi, like Can Themba, dearly loved, those personal tragedies that go to make up township life. Motsisi popularised street culture and 'created a fictional world based on the "shebeen" culture of Johannesburg'.[9] He also resembled Can Themba in the way he could transform tired English words and employ them in a fresh manner all his own. He fused the patois of the townships, also called *Tsotsitaal*, into English more effectively than any other writer.

Casey Motsisi was the last major writer of the 'Drum' generation to emerge before Sharpeville. He stayed on in South Africa until his death in 1977 and provided the vital link, along with Richard Rive and James Matthews, between writers of his generation and writers of the Black Consciousness era.

The District Six School

While their contemporaries of the Sophiatown renaissance were primarily concerned with social issues and only indirectly with political affairs, writers of the 'District Six school' turned more directly to political subjects. They were chiefly responsible in the 1950s for sustaining the protest tradition in Black South African literature, a tradition which goes back to the emergence of Xhosa literature in the nineteenth century. Their work, as exemplified by Richard Rive and James Matthews, mirrors the political preoccupations of the 1950s, manifested in such crusades as the Defiance Campaign against segregation, bus boycotts against the increase of bus fares, potato boycotts against the use of African convict labour on White farms and other similar civil rights campaigns.

The setting of Richard Rive's story, 'Riva', is Cape Town in the 1950s, when Rive was an undergraduate at the University of Cape Town. In the story, Paul, a 'Coloured' undergraduate and the author's *alter ego*, feels sore about segregated amenities, illustrated in the provision of separate Mountain Clubs for Whites and 'Coloureds'. In this respect, Paul betrays a predilection for the bourgeois cultural values of the society that persistently regards him as a social *pariah*—Mountain Clubs are hardly likely to appeal to the majority of Blacks, who climb mountains as a matter of course, often in the line of duty as caretakers of mountain resorts or porters to those who climb mountains for the sake of adventure and relaxation. But Paul's reaction to Whites is also conditioned by what he construes as their imposing attitude and superior airs. He, in turn, erects a barrier between himself and every White person he encounters, as a defensive mechanism against insults, real or imagined, to his racial ego. In the final analysis, his extreme sensitivity appears no more than racism in reverse, a malady from which Paul is suffering and which is subsequently exorcised through his encounter with Riva, an eccentric Jewish woman jeweller who is a member of the White section of the Mountain Club. Her persistence in treating 'Coloureds' in the same peremptory fashion in which she treats everyone initially irritates and, when he gets to know her better, finally discomposes Paul by exposing his 'inverted racialism'.[10] Richard Rive regrets the fact that South African society has not produced more bridge figures like Riva, who is untainted by any racial antipathy or consciousness.

'The Park' by James Matthews is a moving indictment of apartheid, more specifically, the Separate Amenities Act. Prior to the take-over of the government in 1948 by the ruling National Party, segregation in public places in South Africa, as in the United States of America, had been based more on custom than having its foundation in law. The discretion, previously vested in the courts, to rule on the suitability or otherwise of public amenities for Blacks was removed from the courts. According to the new law, there was no need for public amenities for people of different races to be 'substantially similar to or of the same character, standard, extent or quality [as] those set aside for other races'.[11] As Edward Roux explains, this was not merely an invitation to exclude Blacks from using facilities reserved for Whites, but it was actually a means of sanctioning the erection of inferior amenities for them. In many instances, as in the story, the authorities never bothered to provide alternative recreational facilities for Blacks excluded from using White facilities. Matthews brings out the inhumanity in the practice by showing its effects on a young 'Coloured' boy who is prevented from playing on the swings in a park that is reserved for Europeans. The spirit of the Defiance Campaign catches on as the boy steals to the park by night, defies the 'Coloured' caretaker frightened for his job, and swings with a frenzy that startles the caretaker, who decides to let sleeping dogs lie.

The 'Sharpeville' Era

The era of passive resistance and civil rights campaigns came to an abrupt end in 1960 and gave way to underground resistance, as the government crackdown after Sharpeville broke overt political opposition to the regime. In March 1960 the government moved onto a war footing by declaring a state of emergency as a result of the Sharpeville crisis, sparked off by country-wide anti-apartheid demonstrations during which the police shot dead sixty-seven people at the African township of Sharpeville. These political developments brought about a shift in literature from the largely social concerns which had preoccupied most writers of the 'Drum' era to pressing contemporary political issues. The tendency evinced by most writers in the 1950s, with the exception of writers of the 'District Six school', to let politics take a back seat was superseded by a fierce political commitment. As the political element, which is never totally absent from South African literature, gained ascendance, all the leading literary figures of the period suffered imprisonment for political offences, exile, banishment, intimidation, censorship or death by suicide.

Between 1960 and 1966, the government made a desperate bid to wipe out the literary achievements of the preceding decades. A Government Gazette of 1966 named forty-six exiles as 'statutory communists'—among them Abrahams, Mphahlele, Modisane, Themba, Maimane and La Guma, all of whom could neither be read nor quoted in South Africa. Prose fiction within South Africa declined sharply as Black South African literature came to flourish in exile. In this exile literature, a further shift occurred from protest to the politics of challenge. Alex La Guma and Bessie Head, who made their mark as creative writers during the Sharpeville era, offer examples of the 'prison' literature produced in exile and the new radicalism in literature brought about by the government's frantic efforts to eliminate extra-parliamentary opposition, however mild and from whichever source.

Alex La Guma comes from the 'District Six school'. His outstanding characteristics as a writer are his use of the language of the *skollies*, the Cape 'Coloured' proletariat, to capture the socio-economic milieu in which his work is set; his sharp eye for significant detail, however minute; his 'ability to choose a core idea or situation and work it out in the tightest, most organic way'; and his preference for commonplace situations, treated in a low-key fashion, in the lives of his characters. He never raises his voice or waves his fists. As Adriaan Roscoe further points out, 'La Guma resembles Ngugi in so far as his politics—frankly Marxist—seem as if they have grown out of a shocked response, an intrinsic response, to human suffering and not from either library or lecture hall. The human condition is sense, examined, and understood; then a politics is embraced to cure the seen ills.'[12] He has successfully reconciled his creative impulse with his political creed as few South African writers have managed to do. In his work, prison is seen as a microcosm of life in South Africa, as in the poetry of Dennis Brutus.

'Tattoo Marks and Nails' shows the dehumanising effects of oppression. The narrator in the story is sucked into the decadent world of his fellow prisoners. He assimilates their speech habits and disposition, a love for violent drama. The brutalising prison environment unleashes violence in which the stronger turn against their weaker inmates. Roscoe makes the following penetrating assessment of La Guma's work:

> His special artistic qualities, such as his power of transcending stereotype to grasp the rich variety of human character and experience, have produced a body of work broader than the cramping fences of political theory can contain and larger than anything one might remotely consider parochial. At his best, which means in his short stories, La Guma not only ranks with the finest in Africa; he can hold his head high among the finest writers in English anywhere.

His work refutes 'the misleading logic of the view that because South African conditions are inimical to the growth of good writing, none has in fact appeared'.[13]

Lewis Nkosi's following remarks about Bessie Head are couched in half-truths and unsubstantiated generalisations: 'She has none of the showy glitter that the fast paced life of Johannesburg can impose on the prose style of someone like Carim; none of the quickness of mind that is so evident in the writing of Can Themba, nor has she the same rigorous political commitment of a writer like La Guma; indeed, for most of the time Bessie Head seems politically ignorant.'[14] Nkosi's remarks are based on the novels, which Bessie Head has intentionally set in Botswana in order to explore life in a politically healthier environment where, to use her own expression, people are just people. It is not as though she is not aware of South Africa's racial malady; on the contrary, she has suffered from South Africa's abnormal obsession with race in an intensely personal way. Nkosi's observations are not all borne out by the evidence of her 'political' stories with a South African setting such as 'The Coming of the Christ-Child', based on the life of Robert Mangaliso Sobukwe, founder-President of the Pan Africanist Congress of Azania, to which Bessie Head belonged. A comparison with La Guma refutes the suggestion that she is 'politically ignorant' or naïve.

Whereas, with the exception of *In the Fog of the Season's End* (1972), La Guma's prison stories centre around 'petty-thieves, gangsters, murderers, rapists, burglars, thugs, drunks, brawlers, dope-peddlars'; 'The Prisoner who wore Glasses' by Bessie Head deals with political prisoners who pit their resources against the system and engage their White prison warder in a war of nerves he can never win. They display the kind of unsagging spirit and group solidarity that are often lacking in La Guma's prisoners. Her story, like La Guma's work in general, illustrates the double-edged effect of apartheid, whereby the oppressor becomes a victim of the same vicious and malevolent forces he has helped unleash upon society. Bessie Head was the last major writer of prose fiction to emerge from South Africa before the advent of Black Consciousness.

The 'Soweto' era

Black Consciousness and the literature it inspired emerged in the midst of political and cultural repression after Sharpeville. The new wave of writers who emerged in South Africa after 1967 appeared to shy away at first from the more explicit medium of prose and took up poetry, after the manner of more established literary figures such as James Matthews. Prose fiction appeared to lag behind as publishers, magazine editors and critics gave their attention to the nascent poetic tradition. Between 1967 and 1974 the cultural renaissance which accompanied the rise of Black Consciousness produced, at an unprecedented rate in the literary history of South Africa, many outstanding poets of the calibre of Dollar Brand (Abdullah Ibrahim), Oswald Mbuyiseni Mtshali, Mongane Wally Serote, Sipho Sepamla, Mafika Gwala, Mafika Mbuli, Mandlenkosi Langa and Njabulo Ndebele. However, by the mid-1970s the gravitation towards poetry had begun to have a bandwagon effect, as some jolly riders with no special aptitude for poetry and others whose talents were better suited to prose fiction took to poetry.

After the 1976-77 student and workers' revolt, which broke out in Soweto and spread to other Black residential areas, prose fiction picked up again with a political vengeance. The banning of Black Consciousness organisations in October 1977, the death in police custody of some leading figures of the Black Consciousness Movement such as Mapetla Mohapi and Steve Bantu Biko, the banishment and the imprisonment without trial of many others, far from suppressing opposition to the regime or forcing the majority of leading literary figures of the Black Consciousness era into exile, as had been the case after Sharpeville, only intensified such opposition and led to more outspoken criticism against apartheid. After Soweto, writing by Blacks in South Africa became charged with a fresh vigour and political fervour that is best captured in Mtutuzeli Matshoba's stories. Developments after 1976 also encouraged poets such as Gladys Thomas and Njabulo Ndebele to take up short story writing, while others such as Mongane Serote and Sipho Sepamla even turned novelists. By the close of the decade the tradition of story-telling had been revived again.

Njabulo Ndebele emerged in 1969 as the most methodical and literary conscious poet of the Black Consciousness era, in his quest for an appropriate medium to reflect his African personality and convey a genuinely African response to African phenomena. As Ursula Barnett points out, he initiated a movement back to tradition and advocated the use of African imagery. He upheld the view that poets could draw their inspiration from their environment, as well as from American myths, beliefs and moral codes; and he demonstrated his theories in his poetry, particularly in its symbolism. Then came several years of soul-searching silence after 1973. When he ultimately resumed writing he turned to prose fiction, though he did not drop poetry altogether. 'The Music of the Violin' is one of twelve stories he presented for his doctorate at the University of Denver. 'I am still playing a lot with technique,' he says, explaining his artistic purpose. 'I am experimenting a lot with point of view, flashback, and levels of reality; at the same time I want to retain the traditional story-telling technique in which there is a core of suspense. I toyed a lot with the technique of flashback as a device of suspense in my story, ''The Music of the Violin''.'[15] The story first appeared in *Staffrider*, 3, no. 3 (1980) and effectively marked Ndebele's return to the world of writing and publishing. The version of the story in this anthology is the final version in which the story appears in Noma Award-winning *Fools and Other Stories*.

Glady Thomas first attracted public attention as a poet in a joint publication, *Cry Rage* (1972), with James Matthews. Towards the close of the decade, after several years of silence, she too switched over from poetry to prose fiction. In her fiction, as in her poetry, we encounter the concerns of underprivileged Black women, who suffer multiple oppression as members of a despised race, an exploited class and a downtrodden sex. 'The Promise' is written with touching simplicity and delicacy; it is handled with an artist's skill for portraying convincing characters and depicting pathetic situations credibly and in a dignified manner, without yielding to the temptations a sob-story of this kind dangles before the writer to indulge the base emotions. Maria Klaasen, the central figure in the story, is a victim of broken promises and exploitative practices of every description. Her tragedy lies in her unfulfilled dreams for self-realisation. Besides raising, from a woman's point of view, some pressing social questions pertaining to the plight of women in society, Gladys Thomas also highlights the plight of rural folk, a subject rarely touched upon by her predecessors. The lingering impression we get from reading Gladys Thomas's story is of the humiliation and the affront to human dignity exploitation under apartheid brings about. 'The Promise' was first published in *Staffrider*, 4, no. 1 (1981), though written several months earlier.

Mtutuzeli Matshoba's work first appeared in *Staffrider*, the magazine founded in March 1978 that best represents the new writers' movement which grew up after Soweto. He soon emerged as the most prolific contributor of short stories to the magazine. The publication of his stories had the effect of giving some lead in the direction of taking up short stories again. Mike Kirkwood, director of Ravan Press, publishers of *Staffrider* and Matshoba's collection, *Call Me Not A Man* (1979), describes Matshoba's most striking attributes as a writer in the following terms:

> I confess that I find it difficult, as I read Matshoba's stories, not to see him in front of me. It is the polar opposite of James Joyce paring his fingernails behind the complete and self-sufficient artwork. And these aren't 'short stories' because the short story suggests deliberate artifice to me, pre-eminently among prose-forms. Neither are they stories in the traditional sense. Yet Matshoba seems to me the story-teller come to life, all the same. His narrator is a participant. He carries the function of the story-teller into the midst of the fractured lives of the prisoners of apartheid. He is the sympathetic listener who tells the stories of others, but sometimes he will advise, and maybe a crucial juncture he will act (as in the title story). He looks for the continuities hidden under the oppressed, face of the land.[16]

'The Day of the Riots', like Matshoba's 'Call Me Not a Man', is set in the Soweto era. Brian Willan summarises the author's preoccupations as follows:

> 'The Day of the Riots' explores the remarkable escalation of the students' resistance to Bantu Education, as the community as a whole comes to be mobilised, with the inspiration and leadership of the students pitted against the South African government. The events of June 16 1976 are explored from several different perspectives, and the author deals with the dilemma of a White man caught in Soweto and fearful for his life, and the position of the Black Urban Bantu Council (commonly known as the UBC, Useless Boys' Club) members, regarded as government stooges.[17]

Brian Willan further points out that, in a way, the events dealt with in the story, as in Matshoba's, were so remarkable that the need to fictionalise does not arise. Both writers concentrate on reconstructing the activities, the perceptions, the dialogue of those involved against a background of real characters and events. 'The Day of the Riots' attempts to convey, in a way that the several accounts of the Soweto uprising written by journalists and academics do not, what it felt like to be one of those involved or caught up in the crisis and how life in Soweto was transformed in its response to the call of the students. The story, the second in a trilogy of 'Soweto' stories published as *The Children of Soweto* (1982), was written to preserve the memory of the events of 16 June 1976, as seen from the inside. In a situation where history is forever being distorted by writers whose interests are often diametrically opposed to those of the community they describe, and who impose a world-view that is alien to the people whose lives they seek to portray, the creative writer is called upon to combine the functions of his craft with those of the historian and, both as creator and historical witness, to reveal more than the historian's selective 'truth'. The story illustrates the proposition, considered largely axiomatic by men and women of vision in South Africa, that the Black person is the soul of the White person and any White person who rejects the complementary nature of the relationship does so to the detriment of his or her own soul and the souls of his or her progeny.

No doubt, certain names some readers would have wished to see included have been left out. To keep the selection within certain limits so that the book can be reasonably priced and not overly long, we have omitted such well-known writers as Lewis Nkosi, whose talents appear to us better suited to literary criticism; and other contributors to *Drum* and *Zonk* such as Peter Clarke, Arthur Mogale, Dyke Sentso, Duke Ngcobo, Fred J. Hawkins and Chicks Nkosi; as well as writers of the Black Consciousness era such as Webster Makaza, Meshack Hlongwane, Ahmed Essop, Moteane Melamu, Miriam Tlali, Mothobi Mutloatse, Achmat Dangor, Sipho Sepamla, Mongane Serote, Mafika Gwala and a host of others. In a field so teeming with talent, the task of paring down has been a painful one. Nevertheless, the anthology is representative enough.

The short story in South Africa may not possess the rich variety in themes and styles that national literatures in other parts of the world possess. But it boasts an unsurpassed tradition of political commitment, emotional intensity, high seriousness, freedom from pretentiousness, simplicity, and an almost unpremeditated craftsmanship and closeness to life—endearing qualities which should recommend this book to many readers in all walks of life.

Notes

1 Wilfried F. Feuser (ed.), *Jazz and Palm Wine*, Harlow, Longman, 1981, p.1

2 Quoted from 'The Obituary of Can Themba', Lewis Nkosi, in Can Themba's *The Will to Die*, selected by Donald Stuart and Roy Holland, London, Heinemann, 1972, pp.vii-xi (p.viii)

3 Tim Couzens, *English in Africa* (Special 'Dhlomo' issue), 2, no.1, 1975, pp.1-2; published by the Institute for the Study of English in Africa, Rhodes University, Grahamstown.

4 Dennis Brutus, 'Somehow We Survive', *Sirens Knuckles Boots*, Ibadan, Mbari Publications, 1963.

5 Ezekiel Mphahlele, *The African Image*, London, Faber, 1962, p.66

6 Ezekiel Mphahlele, 'The Language of African Literature', *Harvard Educational Review*, 34, no.2, 1964, pp.298-305 (p.303)

7 See, for instance, Jean Marquard's 'Some Racial Stereotypes in South African Writing', a paper presented at the Conference on Literature and Society in Southern Africa, Centre for Southern African Studies, University of York, 8-11 September 1981

8 Nkosi, 'Obituary of Can Themba' pp.viii-xi

9 Quoted from the blurb of Casey Motsisi's collection, *Casey and Co*, selected by Mothobi Mutloatse, Johannesburg, Ravan Press, 1978

10 Richard Rive (ed.), *Modern African Prose*, London, Heinemann, 1964, p.xiii

11 Edward Roux, *Time Longer than Rope: A History of the Blackman's Struggle in South Africa*, Madison, University of Wisconsin Press, 1964, p.389

12 Adriaan Roscoe, *Uhuru's Fire: African Literature East to South*, Cambridge, Cambridge University Press, 1977, p.258

13 *ibid* p.258

14 Lewis Nkosi, *Tasks and Masks: Themes and Styles of African Literature*, Harlow, Longman, 1981, p.99

15 Njabulo Ndebele, Letter to M.V. Mzamane, 16 December 1980

16 Mike Kirkwood, Letter to M.V. Mzamane, 17 March 1980

17 Brian Willan, Extract from his reader's report for Longman, February 1981

Mbulelo Vizikhungo Mzamane
Department of English
Ahmadu Bello University
Zaria
Nigeria

Juwawa

R.R.R. DHLOMO

The group of surveyors sat lolling about in the drawing office, eating their sandwich lunches, and chatting idly on those interesting little problems and experiences which so often occur in the work of underground men.

Raikes, the Chief Surveyor, had just finished an account of an accident on 12 Level West, involving the deaths of a miner and two natives. A solid slab of rock had fallen without warning—fallen from what had appeared smoothing, perfectly safe hanging, and as Raikes said, 'You never can tell what may happen underground. One minute a place looks as safe as a house, the next the darned thing is clattering about your ears—if you aren't killed, you are buried alive, so either way you get it in the neck! If I could afford it, I'd chuck mining to-morrow and start a poultry farm, or buy a cart and horse and sell fish door-to-door. A friend of mine started that way and he's worth a fortune now! Yes, mining is no game for a gentleman.'

A shout went up from the others—the idea of Raikes selling fish from door-to-door struck them as funny.

'Where's Garwin?' asked Raikes. 'He's late, isn't he?'

'Not up yet—he was still busy giving them a line on 6 when I came up,' said Alf Martin, a friend of Garwin's. Raikes sat thinking for a while, then,

'Say, Alf, you're a pal of his, what's this I hear of Garwin knocking his boys about? I haven't said anything to him yet, as I want to be sure it's true. What's the trouble?'

'Well,' said Martin hesitatingly. 'Well I suppose it is true enough, Mr Raikes, but—well, the fact is George can't speak their language, and they pretend they don't understand either English or Dutch, and so whatever suits them. As a matter of fact, he was knocking blazes out of his Boss-boy Juwawa when I passed him on 6 this morning. I've told him often enough to cut it out, but he wont take any notice.'

'Hm, I see—it's a pity. Well I'll speak to him when he comes in. Meanwhile, what about some work. This office does nothing but eat all day!'

That night George Garwin lay tossing restlessly in bed, trying desperately to get to sleep, and as is usually the case when we try, failing dismally. Certain sentences in his conversation with Raikes that afternoon kept recurring to him —

'George, you've got to understand your boys. They are like a bunch of big kids, and must be handled as such!'

And again,

'A good thing for any miner to remember—never, if it possibly can be avoided, HIT ANY of YOUR OWN BOYS: hit any one else's, if you like, but not your own. SOME DARNED QUEER THINGS HAPPEN UNDERGROUND!'

In a sheltered spot at the foot of a towering waste-dump Juwawa the boss-boy, one eye badly swollen and a large lump disfiguring his forehead, stood facing an aged, blanketed figure, known in every Compound as 'Keleti, the shangaan Witchdoctor.'

The aged one, seated on a low boulder, was idly tossing the bones into a small circle traced in the dust before him. From the filthy folds of a piece of knotted linen which he had at last succeeded in untying, Juwawa now withdrew a gold 10s. coin. Dropping it into the circle where it lay glittering besides the bones, he stood eagerly watching the wizard.

The old man reached forth a wrinkled, skinny hand, picked up the coin, and being assured of its genuineness, at once secreted it somewhere in the dim interior of his blanket.

In silence, the low murmur of the distant, gigantic stamp batteries up at the Mill, like waves breaking on a seashore, drifted along on the dust-laden breeze.

From the lips of the boss-boy there poured, on a sudden, a torrent of language, a bitter flood of invective and hatred, born of a devouring, vicious desire for vengeance. The old man held up a hand. Juwawa stuttered, endeavoured to continue, was silent. A thin smile came fleeting to the lips of the wizard, as he quietly contemplated the inflamed eye and quivering anger of the man before him.

Taking up his bones from their bed of dust, he held them tight-clenched in one hand, while the other covered his face. Slowly he started swaying, back and forth, side to side, and as he swayed he chanted softly. The purport of his chant was at first barely audible to Juwawa's straining ears, but as the voice grew louder, a look

2

of cunning satisfaction crept into his face. Eagerly he strained forward, that no word might be lost; and when the old man suddenly broke off and with a sharp cry dashed the bones into the circle, examining their layout with aged, critical eyes, Juwawa stood breathlessly awaiting his verdict.

Completely satisfied—with his course of action now clearly settled in his mind, Juwawa turned and hastened back to the Compound.

Early the following Saturday morning, Cowan, Mine Captain, No.2 Shaft, walked hurriedly into the Survey Office and enquired for Raikes.

'Been an accident Raikes—awfully sorry, but it's one of your men, Garwin; yes, killed outright—a jumper fell on his neck! Will you notify his parents? Yes, the ambulance has just been for him. I'm off to see the Manager, see you later.'

An enquiry was held. Death, it appeared, was due to a terrific blow from an iron crowbar (jumper) which, falling from the top of a stope, had hit the deceased on the back of the skull.

Much suspicion attached to the boss-boy, one Juwawa, a Shangaan, who while working above, had probably (in evidence he denied this, though admitting the 'Possibility') dislodged the implement, when endeavouring to change his position in a confined space.

The Commission discharged him, however, as there was insufficient evidence to warrant a change of Manslaughter being brought, despite the presence of a motive—revenge.

The Mine sacked him, he was paid off, and steps were taken to ensure that no further employment be granted him in any local Mine.

On his way to the Railway Station he sang; the atmosphere of his song, triumphant, and in the words a singular sentiment. 'Ya, Keleti! Ya, Keleti, that was good advice!' sang Juwawa, the savage.

S'ciety

PETER ABRAHAMS

He was a fine fellow, was Uncle Joe, in the days when he was still young. The trouble was booze. He loved booze. He lived with it. He courted it. Johnny Stone, who died last year, told him it was going to kill him. But he wouldn't listen. He was a hard nut, that ol' bastard. And it did kill him. Not like Johnny said. But it did.

The trouble with us coloured folks is that we are too quick to say a person is good for nothin'. We dont ask why he is good for nothin'. He *is* just good for nothin'. Then we shake our heads like Saint Jesus, and tell each other how this one or that goes boozin' to hell. Sometimes we say singin'. Sometimes we say dancin'. Sometimes fightin'. But 'most always boozin'.

We're too quick, us folks. We don't care 'bout the whys and wherefores. We just says: 'He's good for nothin' and he goes boozin to hell.' Just like that. But us others that knows the inside of the case are not so quick with out tongues. We just leave these imitation whites to sing their songs of hell, and we chews our pipes. Of a night we come together and talk 'about these fellows. There won't be no light in the room. Just the glow of the pipes and cigarettes, and the white teeth and the bright eyes. An' mebbe some one will heave a heavy sigh; most likely ol' Matt. He likes to start the ball rollin'. Always he begins the same:

'Jeez, when ah thinks of the good ol' days, my heart would fair burst!' He had been in America a long time when he was still young. He liked to show off 'bout it when he spoke. He had run away from a boat when he got to New York, and stayed there for more'n six years. He said Noo Yurk. Just so. But us others didn't mind. We was fond of ol' Matt's lyin', an', the b—— knew it. When he said 'Jeez,' one-eyed Joe would hit him hard on the back so that he coughed and said: 'Go it, ol' boy, we are alistenin'!' He would say, 'Damn you,' to ol' one-eyed, but he'd start. Then he'd tell 'bout all the tarts he knew. What he did to them. How they liked it. Then there'd be a quarrel about what nationality can give it best. And who had had the most nations. And what white nation was the most decent. For my part I loves the Irish. I dunno why. I just loves them. But after a while we'd all turn serious. Then we'd talk sad.

4

Then we are ol' men, broken ol' men. Then the laughter goes out of our eyes. Then you can see them feeling tired. Then we look and see who's missin' from the ol' crowd. Armless Hick would ask, 'Where is de gennelmen?' He spoke just like a darky, old Hick. Then I'd shake my head and say: 'Didn't you hear 'bout it?' Then Johnny who died last year's brother would say: 'Sure. The ol' toff died three weeks back. He was walkin' across the road with his ol' stick from Paree when some bigger toff in a shining car knocked him down. There was a decent bloke for you, the toff. Never worried nobody, even when he was tight. Always white collar and tie, even though his pants was not ironed sometimes. His hands was fine too, just like a s'ciety dame's. Did youse see them?' Then everybody'd say something good 'bout the toff. Then Johnny who died last year's brother would go on: 'Darn cops didnt do anything to the blighter who knocked him down and killed him. Said he was drunk and such things. The b—— got off scot-free. Now ol' toff's gone!' Then we would all curse the b—— and say what's happening to Sith Africa, and how they treat us coloureds just like dogs.

Ol' Art would cough, and the pipe would go up to where his mouth is supposed to be. He left half his face in France. D'you know 'bout ol' Uncle Joe? His voice was soft. Like a girl's when she starts lookin' for fellows. Then he'd cough some more and clear his throat. Someone would say, 'No, tell us.' Others would say, 'Yes, do.' Ol' Art was known for politeness, and we'd be all politeness. There'd be all quiet. Like when orders has been given in the trenches to be quiet before a big attack. Only the lights would glow in the darkness. The lights of cigarette and pipes. Then ol' Art would take the pipe out of his mouth and look at it, and then he would look at us to see if all is lookin' at him. He was a school teacher once, long ago. Now he treated us all like his school kids. Poor ol' Art. He had some tough times, but he is a fine blighter. A little horsey, but fine.

If all are ready he'd begin. He spoke soft, just like I said: 'Well, friends, ol' Uncle Joe has passed away.' We'd all say something 'bout our sorrow. And we *was* sorry. Our crowd was gettin' small. I pity the poor blighter who would go last. He'd be mighty lonesome with none to talk to. Out of over a dozen we was just five left. But ol' Art would go on: 'They took him to his ol' wife from jail, and I must say this for her, she did not turn his poor body away. The funeral is tomorrow; that's what I want to talk about, the funeral.'

He stopped, and felt for the ninepenny bottle of stout in front of him. Every night when we met we would put all we had on the table. We always had enough for five bottles. A bottle for each man. He held the bottle to his throat, and we could all hear the sound of the stout going down. That made us all want to have a drink. So we all had one. When we was finished he went on: 'Well, we all know, gentlemen (we liked that about him), that good intentions are not enough.' (Cockeyed Joe asked me what intentions was; I tol' him; ol' Art stared as us, but said nothing.) 'The widow intend good, but it is our duty to try and help her with the expense.' Some put their hands into their pockets, but he stopped them. 'Not yet, gentlemen. Let me first tell the story of Uncle Joe so that you can know what you are givin' your money for'. We all said, 'Yes, do.' he said, 'Yes, the name of the S'ciety must be kept up.'

'Well, we all know that the late Uncle Joe was a fine fellow when he was young. There was some that say that he was bad because he drank. We all here know it is not so. When we was young I had the honour to meet Joe on the boat going over.' (Ol' Lamm, who had a fightin' chest, coughed, so he waited until that was over.) 'He was a fine lad, and told me all about the trouble at his home, and why he had run away. How his father used to beat him and his mother. How there was nothin' in the house to eat most of the time, and how his father would drink away all his wages on Friday night and come home and beat him up. All these he tol' on that trip over.' He stopped and looked at us for a while. He lit his pipe, then he went on: 'Well, then he was lost to me for some years. When I met him again it was here. He tol' me about how well he had been goin' on, and about his wife and is two little children, and took me to his home. He was happy. We were together for six weeks; then I left him to go to one of the many ports of the world. I made two trips back. On the second I met him. He was changed. He had been boozin'. I tried to speak to him, but he would not listen. Later he tol' about his wife, and how she ran away with the children and another man, and took all his money with her. He took me to a little room where he lived with his present widow. It was terrible. But the woman looked after him. I must say that for her. I left him there. I did not see him for five years. Then I heard that he had found his wife and the man with whom she had run away, and killed them in drunken moment. You all know the rest of the story.

6

'It is the duty of this S'ciety to show our respect and broadness. Do not listen to these imitation whites. Let them say what they like. The S'ciety will not forget its duty.'

He stopped, and there was a long silence. Ol' Art put his hand into his pocket and took out two coppers. Someone struck a match and lit the stub of candle. Two more and a ha'penny were thrown with it. But the promises made it two shillings and one ha'penny.

We then finished our stout, and one by one we went out. Each wondering who would leave the S'ciety next.

Grieg on a Stolen Piano

EZEKIEL MPHAHLELE

Those were the days of terror when, at the age of fifteen, he ran away from home and made his way towards Pietersburg town. Driven by hunger and loneliness and fear he took up employment on an Afrikaner's farm at ten shillings a month plus salted mealie-meal porridge and an occasional piece of meat. There were the long scorching hours when a posse of horsemen looked for him and three other labourers while they were trying to escape. The next morning at dawn the white men caught up with them.

Those were the savage days when the whole white family came and sat on the stoep to watch, for their own amusement, African labourers put under the whip. Whack! Whack! Whack! And while the leather whip was still in the air for the fourth stroke on the buttocks, he yelled *Ma-oeeee!* As the arm came down, he flew up from the crude bench he was lying on, and, in a manner that he could never explain afterwards, hooked the white foreman's arm with his two, so that for a few seconds he dangled a few feet from the ground. Amid peals of laughter from the small pavilion, the foreman shook him off as a man does a disgusting insect that creeps on his arm.

Those were the days when, in a solo flight again towards Pietersburg, terror clawed at his heart as he travelled through thick bush. He remembered the stories he had so often listened to at the communal fireplace; tales of huge snakes that chased a man on the ground or leapt from tree to tree; tales of the giant snake that came to the river at night to drink, breaking trees in its path, and before which helpless people lay flat on their stomachs wherever they might be at the time; none dared to move as the snake mercifully lifted its body above them, bent over, drank water and then, mercifully again, turned over back-wards, belly facing up, rolling away from the people; stories that explained many mysteries, like the reason why the owl and the bat moved in the dark. Always the theme was that of man, helpless as he himself was in the bush or on a tree or in a rock cave on a hill, who was unable to ward off danger, to escape a terrible power that was everywhere around him. Something seemed to be stalking him all the time, waiting for the proper moment to pounce upon him.

But he walked on, begged and stole food and lifts on lorries, until he reached Thswane—Pretoria.

There was the brief time in 'the kitchens', as houses of white people are called where one does domestic work, as if the white suburbs were simply a collection of kitchens. There were the brutal Sundays when he joined the Pietersburg youth, then working in the kitchens, on their wild march to the open ground just outside Bantule location for a sport of bare fisticuffs. They marched in white shorts on broad slabs of feet in tennis shoes and vaseline-smeared legs; now crouching, now straightening up, now wielding their fists wrapped in white handerkerchiefs. One hankerchief dangled out of a trouser pocket, just for show. The brutal fisticuffs: mouths flushed with blood; then the white mounted police who herded them back to the kitchens; the stampede of horses' hooves as the police chased after them, for fun . . .

Those were the days when chance lifted him like a crane out of the kitchens and out of the boxing arena, and deposited him in Silvertown location. This was when his aunt, having been alerted by her brother, had tracked him down.

There was regular schooling again. At twenty he began teacher-training at Kilnerton Institution nearby. There were the teaching days, during which he studied privately for a junior secondary school certificate.

Those were the days, when, as the first black man in the province to write an examination for, he timidly entered a government office for the first paper. The whites stared at him until he had disappeared into the room where he would write in isolation. And those were the days when a black man had to take off his hat as soon as he saw a white man approach; when the black man had to keep clear of street pavements.

Then the return home—the first time in seven years—as a hero, a teacher. The parents bubbled over with pride. Then the feast . . .

It was one of those hot sub-tropical nights when Pretoria seems to lie in its valley, battered to insensibility by the day's heat; the night when a great friend of his was tarred and feathered by white students of the local university at Church Square: Mr Lambeth, a British musician who had come to teach at Kilnerton and there discovered this black young man's musical talent. He had given his time free to teach him piano. Many were the afternoons, the nights, the weekends that followed of intensive, untiring work at the instrument. What else had Mr Lambeth done wrong? he asked himself several times after the incident. The Englishman had many friends among African teachers whom he visited in their locations: he adjudicated at their music competitions.

This black young man was my uncle. He is actually a cousin of my late father's. So, according to custom, my father had referred to him as 'my brother'. As my father had no blood brothers, I was glad to avail myself of an uncle. When my father died, he charged my uncle with the responsibility of 'helping me to become a man'. It meant that I had someone nearby who would give me advice on a number of things concerned with the problem of growing up. My mother had died shortly after. Uncle has seven childen, all but one of whom are earning their living independently. The last-born is still in school.

Uncle is black as a train engine; so black that his face often gives the illusion of being bluish. His gums are a deep red which blazes forth when he smiles, overwhelming the dull rusty colour of his teeth. He is tall and walks upright. His head is always close-shaven, because, at sixty, he thinks he is prematurely greying, although his hair began to show grey at thirty. He keeps his head completely bald because he does not want a single grey hair to show.

His blackness has often led him into big-big trouble with the whites, as he often tells us.

'Hei! Jy!'

Uncle walks straight on, pretending not to see the bunch of them leaning against a fence. He is with a friend, a classmate.

'Hei! Jy! die pikswart een, die bobbejaan!'—the pitch-black one, the baboon.

One of them comes towards the two and pushes his way between them, standing in front. They stop dead.

A juvenile guffaw behind sends a shiver through Uncle. He breaks through his timidity and lunges at the white boy. He pommels him. In Pietersburg boxing style he sends the body down with a knee that gets him on a strategic place in the jaw. The others are soon upon them. The Africans take to their heels . . .

A new white clerk is busy arranging postal orders and recording them. The queue stretches out, out of the post office building. The people are making a number of clicking noises to indicate their impatience. They crane their necks or step out of the queue in order

10

to see what is happening at the counter.

Uncle is at the head of the queue.

'Excuse me,' he ventures, 'playtime will soon be over and my class will be waiting for me, can you serve us, please?'

The clerk raises his head.

'Look here,' he says aggressively, 'I'm not only here to serve Kaffirs, I'm here to work!'

Uncle looks at him steadily. The clerk goes back to his postal orders. After about fifteen minutes he leaves them. He goes to a cupboard and all the eyes in the queue follow each movement of his. When he comes back to the counter, he looks at the man at the head of the queue, who in turn fixes his stare on him. The white man seems to recoil at the sight of Uncle's face. Then, as if to fall back on the last mode of defence, he shouts, 'What are you? What are you?—just a black Kaffir, a Kaffir monkey, black as tar. Now any more from you and I'll bloody well refuse to serve the whole bloody lot of you. Teacher—teacher, teacher *to hell!*'

Irritation and impatience can be heard to hiss and sigh down the queue.

Uncle realizes he's being driven into a corner and wonders if he can contain the situation. Something tells him it is beyond him. The supervisor of posts comes in just then, evidently called in by his junior's shout.

'*Ja?*' he asks. '*Wat is dit?*'

'Your clerk has been insulting me—calling me a Kaffir monkey.'

The clerk opens his mouth to speak, but his superior leads him round a cubicle. After a few moments the clerk comes back, ready to serve but sulky and mute.

Uncle says that throughout, the white clerk seemed to feel insulted at the sudden confrontation of such articulate human blackness as thrust itself through the wire mesh of the counter.

This time, Uncle had the satisfaction of causing the removal of the white clerk after a colleague, who had been an eye-witness of the incident in the post office, had obtained support from fellow-teachers at Silverton to petition a higher postal authority against the clerk.

'Can you see that happening today?' he asked. 'No, man, I'd have been fired at once on a mere allegation out of the clerk's important mouth.'

Years later, Uncle was promoted to the post of junior inspector of African schools (the white man being always senior). He went to live in the western Transvaal. This is where his wife died while giving birth. He really hit the bottom of depression after this. The affection he had for his wife found a perverse expression in drink and he took to his music with a deeper and savage passion which, as he puts it, was a kind of hot fomentation to help burst the boil of grief inside him. He kept his children with him, though. Each one had the opportunity to go to an institution of higher education. Here he was lucky. For although all of them were mediocre, they used what they had profitably and efficiently. One did a degree in science; another played the saxophone in a band; another was a teacher and 'pop singer'; another became a librarian for an institute of research into race relations; one daughter went in for nursing, and a son and a daughter were still in secondary school.

There were nights of sheer terror when their father failed to return home, and they knew he must be in some drinking orgy somewhere. Then they got to know that he was doing illicit diamond-buying. As he visited schools in his circuit, he sold or bought small stones. But he was always skating near the edge. Once he had the bitter experience of discovering that he had bought a few fakes for £50 from an African agent.

Then there was the day he says he'll never forget as long as he lives. The C.I.D. after crossing his path several times and picking up and losing trails, finally came to the converging point—Uncle. They found him in a train from Johannesburg to Kimberley. They took him to the luggage van and questioned him. Nothing was found on him and he wouldn't talk. When eventually they realized they might have a corpse on their hands, they put him out on a station platform, battered, bleeding and dazed. His suitcase was thrown in his direction.

Uncle was transferred to Johannesburg, but not without incident. A white educational officer wanted him to carry his typewriter—heavy table model—to his car outide. Uncle told him he wouldn't. He had before refused to wash the official's car when asked to do so. As the educational authorities had a high opinion of his work, after serving several years in the department, they engineered a transfer for him. If you ask him how he managed to keep his post, he will tell you, 'I made more or less sure I don't slip up that side, and besides whites don't like a correct black man, because they are so corrupt themselves.'

Each time after some verbal tiff with a white man Uncle says he felt his extra blackness must have been regarded as an insult by those who found themselves working in the shadow it seemed to cast around him.

His arrival in Johannesburg was like surfacing. He went slow on his drinks, and even became a lay preacher in the Methodist church at Orlando. But he started to go to the races and threw himself into this kind of gambling with such passion that he resigned as preacher.

'I can't keep up the lies,' he said. 'There are people who can mix religion with gambling and the other things, but I can't. And gamble I must. As Christ never explained what a black man should do in order to earn a decent living in this country, we can only follow our instincts. And if I cannot understand the connection, it is not right for me to stand in the pulpit and pretend to know the answers.'

The 'other things' were illicit diamond dealing and trading as a travelling salesman, buying and selling soft goods, mostly stolen by some African gang or other that operated in the city. There were also workers who systematically stole articles from their employers' shops and sold them to suburban domestic servants and location customers. While he was visiting schools, he would call this man and that man round the corner or into some private room to do business.

Uncle married again. He was now living with three of his children, two of whom were still in secondary school. A cloud descended upon his life again. His wife was an unpleasant, sour woman. But Uncle woke up to it too late. She sat on the stoep like a dumpling and said little beyond smiling briefly a word of greeting and giving concise answers to questions. The children could not quarrel with her, because she said little that could offend anyone. But her ant-heap appearance was most irritating, because she invited no one's co-operation and gave none beyond fulfilling the routine duties of a wife. She did not seem to like mothering anyone.

Once she succeeded, perhaps in all innocence, in raising a furore in the house.

'You must find out more about the choir practice your daughter keeps going to every week,' she said to Uncle in the presence of the other children. They had stopped calling her 'Ma' because she insisted on referring to them as 'your daughter' or 'your son' when she talked to their father about them.

'It'a a choir practice,' Uncle said brusquely.

'*Wai-i-i!* I know much about choir practices, me. A man's daughter can go to them without stopping and one-two-three the next time you look at her she has a big choir practice in her stomach.'

The girl ran into her bedroom, crying. Soon tongues were let loose upon her. But she continued to sit like an ant-heap, her large body seeming to spread wider and wider like an overgrown pumpkin. Her attitude seemed to suggest much Uncle would have liked to know. What *was* she hiding?

'What do you do with such a woman?' Uncle sighed when he told me about the incident.

He was prepared to go through with the 'companionship', to live with her to the end of his days. 'I promised I'd do so in church,' he remarked. 'And I was in my full senses, no one forced me into the thing.'

Another time he threatened, 'One day I'll get so angry, Neph', I'll send her away to her people. And at her station I'll put her on a wheelbarrow like a sack of mealies and wheel her right into her people's house if I've to bind her with a rope.'

I knew he was never going to do it.

Uncle could only take dramatic decisions which were not going to leave him any need to exercise responsibility either to revoke them or fall back on them. He made decisions as a man makes a gamble: once made, you won or lost, and the matter rested there. It was the same with his second marriage, I think. He met the woman during a church conference, when he was by chance accommodated in her house in Randfontein together with two other delegates, according to the arrangements of the local branch. His wife had been dead twelve years. He had decided that his children were big enough not to look so helpless if a second marriage soured the home atmosphere by any chance. His personal Christian belief would not permit him to get out of a marriage contract. This was the kind of responsibility he would want to avoid. If there was a likely chance that he might have to decide to revoke a step later, he did not take it.

There was in Uncle a synthesis of the traditional and the western-ised African. At various periods in his life he felt that ill luck was stalking him, because misfortune seemed to pour down on him in torrents, particularly in money matters, family relations, and

14

relations with white educational authorities. At times like these, Uncle went and bought a goat, slaughtered it, and called relations to come and eat the meat and mealie-meal porridge with their bare hands, sitting on the floor. He then buried the bones in the yard. At such times his mind searched the mystery of fate, groping in some imagined world where the spirits of his ancestors and that of his dead wife must be living, for a point of contact, for a line of communion.

After the feast, he felt peace settle inside him and fill his whole being until it seemed to ooze from the pores of his body as the tensions in him thawed ... Then he would face the world with renewed courage or with the reinforced secure knowledge that he was at peace with his relations, without whom he considered he would be a nonentity, a withered twig that has broken off from its tree.

Twice, when I was ill, Uncle called in an African medical doctor. But when my migraine began and often seemed to hurl me into the den of a savage beast, he called in an African herbalist and witchdoctor. The man said he could divine from his bones that I had once – it didn't matter when or where – inhaled fumes that had been meant to drive me insane, prepared by an enemy. So he in turn burned a few sticks of a herb and made me inhale the smoke. It shot up my nasal cavity, hit the back of my skull, seeming to scrape or burn its path from the forehead to the nape of my neck. Each time, after repeated refusals to be seen by a witch-doctor my resistance broke down. I felt temporary relief each time.

So he was going to keep his wife, rain or shine. When her behaviour or her sullenness depressed him, he went back to his whisky. Then he played excerpts from Grieg's piano concerto or a Chopin nocturne, or his own arrangement of Mohapeloa's *Chuchumakhala* (the train) or *Leba* (the dove) and others, vocalizing passages the while with his deep voice. He loved to evoke from his instrument the sound of the train's siren *Oi – oi-i-i* while he puffed *chu-chu, chu-chu.*

'If she knew this piano was lifted out of a shop,' he thought often, 'this dumpling would just let off steam about the fact, simply to annoy me, to make me feel I'm a failure beacuse she knows I'm not a failure and she wants to eat me up and swallow me up raw the way she did her first husband.'

He had lately disposed of his twenty-year-old piano.

The keyboard felt the impact of these passionate moments and resounded plaintively and savagely. Self-pity, defiance, despite, endurance, all these and others, played musical chairs in his being.

'Look, Neph', Uncle said one day when he was his cheerful, exuberant self again, 'look, here's an advertisement of an African beauty contest in *Afric.*'

'Oh, there is such a rash of beauty contests these days we're all sick of them. It's the racket in every big town these days. Haven't they learned that a woman is as beautiful as your eyes make her?'

'You're just too educated, that's all. You know nothing, my boy, wait till I tell you.'

'Is it a new money-catching thing again? Don't tell me you're going to run a gambling game around the winning number.'

Uncle and beauty queens simply did not dovetail in my mind. What was behind that volume of blackness that frightened so many whites? I was curious to know.

'Better than that, Neph'. If you want to co-operate.'

'In what?'

'Now look at the prizes: £500, £250, £150 and consolation prizes. One of these can be ours.'

'But this is a beauty contest, not a muscle show.'

'Don't be so stupid. Now, here. I know a lovely girl we can enter for this contest.'

I felt my curiosity petering out.

'I go and fetch the girl – she's a friend's daughter living in the western Transvaal, in a village. Just the right kind of body, face, but she needs to be brought up to market standard. The contest is nine months away still, and we've time.'

'But——'

'Now listen. You put in £25, me the same. We can keep the girl in my house – no, your aunt will curdle again – not let me think – yes, in my friend Tau's house: his wife has a beautiful heart. The money will go to feeding her and paying for her lessons at Joe's gym. Your job will be to take her out, teach her how to smile when she's introduced; how to sit – not like a brooding hen; how to stand in public – not like an Afrikaner cow. You've got to cultivate her in her sense of public attention. Leave the body work to Joe. If she wins, we give her £100, and split £400.'

Joe was one of these people who know just when to come in for profit. He set up his gym in a hired hall with the express aim of putting candidates through 'body work'.

For my part, I simply did not like the idea at all. Beauty on a platform; beauty advertised, beauty mixed up with money; that is how the thing seemed to me, a person with the simple tastes of a lawyer's clerk. To what extent Uncle had assimilated these jazzy urban habits, I couldn't tell.

'Thought about it yet, Neph'? We can't wait too long, you know.'

'Yes, Unc', but I just don't see the point of it. Why don't we leave beauty queens to the – er – experts?' I actually meant something much lower than experts. 'Like Joe, for instance.'

'Joe's just a spiv,' Uncle replied. 'He just loves to rub shoulders with top dogs, that's all. We are investing.'

'But I've only £30 in the post office savings; if I take out £25 I shall be almost completley out.'

'A black man never starves if he lives among his people, unless there is famine: If the worst comes to the worst, you would have to be content with simply having food, a roof over your head, and clothing.'

'That's rural thinking. The extra things a man wants in the city I can't afford.'

'Two hundred pounds can give you the extras.'

I paused to think.

'No, Unc', gambling is for the rich, for those who can afford to lose, not for people like us.'

'You think I'm rich? Don't be silly, you mean to say all those hunchbacked, dried-up, yellow-coloured whites you see at the races and betting booths are rich?'

I relented after a good deal of badgering. Who knows, I thought, we may just win. What couldn't I do with £200 if it came to me!

What a girl!

Her face was well shaped all right: every organ on it was in place, although she had a dry mouth and an unpleasant complexion. She could not have been well fed in the western Transvaal. Her bones stuck out at the elbows, and her buttocks needed plumping a good deal.

'What is your name?' I asked her.

'Tryphina.' I almost giggled, thinking: what names people have!

'That name won't do, Unc', I said to him at the house, affecting a tough showmanship. 'I can't imagine the name coming out of the mouth of the M.C. when he calls it out.'

17

'Call her 'Try' or 'Phina' or 'Tryph', he said indifferently.

'No, they sound like syllables in a kindergarten reading class. Just as bad as 'Jemima' or 'Judida' or 'Hermina' or 'Stephina'.'

'Let's use her Sesotho name, she should have one I'm sure.'

'Torofina,' she said.

'No, not the school name spoken in Sesotho, I mean your real Sotho name. You see, in things like a beauty competition, people like an easy name that is smooth on the tongue (I meant *sweet to the ear*). They may even fail you for having a difficult name.'

Didn't I loathe *Afric's* cheap, slick, noisy journalism!

'Oh, Kefahliloe,' she said sweetly, which means 'something has got into my eye'. 'That is what they call me at home.'

'Nice,' I commented, meaning nothing of the sort. 'But you don't have a shorter Sesotho name?'

'No.' She was still all innocence and patience.

'Well – er – may be you can – er – think of an English name. Just for the contest, you see, and for the newspapers and magazines. Your picture is going to appear in all the papers. We'll call you Kefahiloe – a person's name is her name, and there's nothing wrong in it. Do not hurry, you can tell us the name you've chosen later. Is it all right?' She nodded. Things never seemed all wrong with her. Sometimes there was something pathetic about her pliability, sometimes irritating.

The next day she gave it to us, with a take-it-over-leave-it tone: Mary-Jane.

The first three months showed a slight improvement. Her weight was going up, her paleness was disappearing, the lips moistening and softening, her small eyes taking on a new liveliness and self-confidence. Joe was doing the body work efficiently. I felt then, and Uncle agreed, like one who had known it all along, that there was something latent in the girl which we were going to draw out in the next few months.

She had finished her primary schooling and done part of secondary school, so she was all right on that side.

I took her to the bioscope on certain Saturdays, especially musicals, which appealed to her more than straight drama or bang-bang movies. I took her to Dorkay House in Eloff Street where African musicians go each Saturday afternoon for jazz improvisations. There we found other boys and girls listening eagerly, ripples

18

of excitement visibly travelling through the audience as now and again they whistled and clapped hands. The girls were the type called in township slang 'rubber-necks', the ostentatiously jazz type. We found the same type at parties.

Mary-Jane was drinking it all in, I noticed.

I invited her to my room to listen to my collection of jazz records. She took in small doses at a time, and seemed to digest it and her bodily movements were taking on a city rhythm.

Uncle and I shared entertainment expenses equally. We went for cheap but good entertainment.

After six months, Uncle and I knew we were going to deliver a presentable article of good healthy flesh, comportment, and luscious charm. Charm? Strange. Through all this I did not notice the transformation that was taking place in this direction. She was close on twenty-one, and at the end of the next six months, I was struck by the charm that was creeping out of her, seeming to wait for a time, not far off, when it would burst into blossom. She was filling up, but her weight was in no danger of overshooting the mark. Her tongue was loosening up.

I was becoming aware of myself. I felt a twinge of guilt at treating her like an article that should be ready against a deadline. Before I could realise fully what was happening, the storm set in.

The thing was too delicate; I would have to go about it carefully. Particularly so because I had sensed that she was innocent and untutored in a rustic manner about things like love. And one didn't want the bird to take fright because one had dived into the bush instead of carefully burrowing in. Besides, I am a timid fellow, not unlike my uncle in other things.

Uncle had expensive photographs taken of Mary-Jane for the press. Publicity blazed across the African newspapers, and the air was thick with talk about *Afric's* beauty contest at which Miss Johannesburg would be selected; who was going to be the £500 consignment of beauty dynamite? the journal screamed...

I heard a snatch of conversation in the train one morning amid the continuous din of talking voices, peals of laughter and door-slamming.

'Hey man, see dat girl's picture in *Afric*?'

'Which?'

'De one called Mary-Jen – er – Tumelo?'

'Ja-man, Jesus, she's reely top, ech!'

'God, de body, hmm, de curves, de waist, dis t'ings!' (Indicating the area of the breasts).

'Ach, man, dat's number one true's God jealous down.'

I warmed up towards the boys and wished they could continue.

'I've seen the three judges,' Uncle said.

'The judges? But *Afric* hasn't published the names!'

'They don't *do* such things, you backward boy.'

'How did you know them?'

'I've my contacts.'

'But we don't do such things, Uncle!' I gasped.

'What things?'

'Talking to judges about a competition in which you have vested interests.'

'Don't talk so pompously. You're talking English. Let's talk Sesotho. Now all I did is took photographs of Mary-Jane to each one at his house, paid me respects with a bottle of whisky and asked them if they didn't think she's a beautiful girl. What's wrong with just talking?'

'What did they think?'

'What are you talking, Neph'! Each one almost jumped out of his pants with excitement.'

I wanted badly to laugh, but wanted also to show him that I disapproved.

'I didn't suggest anything to them. I just said she is my niece and I was proud to see her entering the contest. They swore they hadn't seen such beauty so well photographed among all the pictures they had seen in the papers. We're near the winning-post, Neph'. I can see the other side of September the fifteenth already – it's bright. Those judges caught my hint.'

I continued to sit with my eyes fixed on the floor, wondering whether I should feel happy or alarmed.

'By the way, Neph', do you realise you have got yourself a wife, home-grown and fresh? Anything going on between you two?'

'What do you mean?' I asked, without wanting an answer. His eyes told me he was impressed by my affectation. He waited for me to crawl out of it.

'I haven't thought of it,' I lied. After a pause, 'Was this also on your mind when you thought of her as a beauty queen, Uncle?'

'Yes, Neph'. I got to liking her very much while I visited her people during my inspection trips. It was sad to think that such a bright pretty girl would merely become another villager's wife and join the rest who are scratching the soil like chickens for what good there still remains in those desolate places. Her father and me are like twin brothers, we were at school together.'

'But the contest? Surely you could obtain a husband for her without it? And you're not so sure she'll win, either.'

He was silent.

'Nor are we sure she'll like me for a husband.'

'Her father knows my plans. He has told her since she came here.'

'But the contest, why that?'

Silence.

'It's too difficult to explain. All I ask you is to trust me enough to know that I'm not simply playing a game with Mary-Jane for my own amusement.'

During the next few days vanity blew me up. I abstracted the whole sequence of events from their setting and the characters who acted them out. Gradually I built up a picture of myself as someone who needs to be independnet and around whom a hedge was being set up, a victim of a plot. I regarded myself as a sophisticate who couldn't willingly let others choose a sweetheart or wife for me. But in fact I sensed that the real reason for my resentment was that I was actually in love with Mary-Jane but could not face the prospect of living with someone I had presumed to raise to a level of sophistication for reasons of money. I had often been moved by films in which the hero eventually married the less-privileged, artless and modest girl rather than the articulate, urbanised girl who goes out to get her man. Now I had the opportunity of doing the same thing, and I couldn't. In either case, I realise now, one saw a different version of male vanity at work.

Another disturbing element was my uncle's motive for doing what he did by throwing Mary-Jane into a beauty contest when he could arrive at his other objective without going into all the trouble. Although he declined to say it, I think it was his gambling urge that pushed him to it. I wondered what Mary-Jane herself thought about all this; the manner in which she was simply brought to the city and put through a machine to prepare her for a beauty competition, probably without her opinion being asked. Did she perhaps take it that this was how townspeople did things, or one of the things country people were bound to do when they came to the city? I still wonder.

Mary-Jane had to enter the competition in spite of our vanities. She looked forward to it with zest and a certain vivacity which one would not have guessed she was capable of about nine months before. Yes, she was charming, too. How I wished I had found her like this or it had arrived as if through someone else's efforts and planning!

Uncle himself infected me with his high spirits. We decided to have an Indian dinner at the Crescent, after the event.

That night came.

The lights went on full beam, washing out every bit of shade from every corner of the hall. The Jazz Dazzlers struck up 'September in the Rain'. Masses of faces in the packed hall looked up towards the rostrum. The music stopped. The M.C.'s voice cut through the noise in the hall and the people held their breaths, unfinished words and sentences trailing off in a sigh.

It came to me with a metallic mockery – the announcement that *Afric* had decided that this was going to be a you-pick-the-winner show. The queen and the other two prize-winners would be chosen by popular vote. There were hilarious applause and whistling from the crowd of what must have been about two thousand people. The M.C. explained that as the people filed out of the hall after the contest, each person would, in the presence of supervisors at the door, drop two tickets each into a box fixed at every one of the four exits. One ticket would bear the numbers of the winners of the three prizes in evening dress, and the other card numbers in beach attire. The categories were indicated on the cards. These and pencils were distributed while the band played.

I looked at Uncle next to me. He kept saying, 'Stupid! Hoodlums! Cheats! Burn the bloody *Afric*! Nothing ever goes right in things organised by the Press. You take my word for it, Neph'. Ah!'

'Anything happens in beauty conpetitions,' I said, for lack of a stronger remark to match my sagging mood.

'Anyway, Neph',' Uncle said his face cheering up, 'two thousand people looking with two eyes each must be better than three men looking with two eyes each, with the possibility of a squint in one of them.'

This really tickled me in spite of myself. It gave me hope: who could be sure that all these judges knew a lovely bust from the back of a bus or a bag of mealies? We could at least enjoy our Indian dinner and leave the rest in the hands of fate.

What use would it be to describe Mary-Jane's superb performance?

We had two couples – friends – with us at dinner. Mary-Jane was most relaxed. Her ingenuous abandon and air of self-assurance went to my head. The dinner proved worth waiting for. That went to my stomach and made me feel what a glorious thing it is to have a healthy receptacle for such exquisite food.

During our twelve-mile trip by car to Orlando, I felt the warm plush body of Mary-Jane press against me slightly, and I was glad to have things in contact like that. She, in turn, seemed to respond to something of what was radiating from me.

'Are you worried about the results?' I ventured to ask, merely for the sake of saying something to relieve the drowsy full-bellied silence in the car.

'No,' she replied warmly. 'Not a bit. But I'm glad it's all over.'

We lost.

Mary-Jane wasn't in the least worried. Uncle regarded it simply as a match that was lost and couldn't be replayed. For my part, I suspected that I had often heard a faint whisper within me telling that I should be better off if we lost. So I did not know what I ought to feel.

On a Sunday I went to Uncle's house for a casual visit. I found his wife in one of her sour moods. She greeted me with the impatience of one who waves off a fly that hovers the face and hinders conversation. She was actually talking alone, in a querilous mood. Her right elbow was resting on her huge breast and in the cup of the left hand, the right hand stroking her cheek and nose.

I passed hastily on to the room where Uncle played and sang an excerpt from Grieg's piano concerto. He saw me as I went to seat myself but continued to play. At the end of a passage he said, casually, 'She is gone,' and continued playing. I shrugged my shoulders, thinking, 'That's beyond me.'

'She left me a note,' he said. 'Did you receive one?'

His eyes told me that he had just visited his whisky cupboard. I realised that he wasn't talking about his wife.

'Who? Are you talking about Mary-Jane?'

He nodded. 'Who do you think I mean – Vasco da Gama's daughter-in-law?' Then he shouted, *'Ja.* Gone with Joe!'

He went back to some *crescendo* passages of Grieg, picking them up and dropping them in turn. Then he suddenly stopped and came to sit by me.

'How's everybody in the house?' I asked.

'Still well. Except your aunt. That stupid native boy who sold me this piano comes here and finds your aunt and tells her this is a stolen piano. Just showing off, the clever fool. *Setlatla sa mafelelo* – fool of the last order. His mother never taught him not to confide everything in woman. Kind of lesson you suck from your brother's breast. The native! Now your aunt thinks all the house money goes out for the piano. Nothing can convince her that I'm paying £30 only, and in bits, too. So you see she's staging one of her boycotts.'

Uncle did not even pretend to lower his voice. Has it gone this far – no bother about what she thinks? I asked myself. No, he did care. He was too sensitive not to care. Always, when he told me about her, he spoke with a sense of hurt. Not such as a henpecked husband displays. Uncle had tremendous inner resources and plenty of diversions and could not buckle up under his wife's policy of non-collaboration, the way a henpecked man would do. This 'speaking up' was just a bit of defiance.

'She worries about a stolen piano.' Uncle continued, lying back on the divan, his eyes looking at the ceiling, his thumb playing up and down under his braces. 'She forgets she sleeps between stolen sheets; every bit of cutlery that goes into her mouth was stolen by the boys from whom I bought it; her blouses are stolen goods, her stockings.' And then, looking at me he said, 'Don't we steal from each other, lie to each other every day and know it, us and the whites?'

I said, '*Ja*,' and looked at my tie and shoes. But I considered this superfluous explanation.

'You know, Neph',' he continued in rambling fashion, 'a few days ago I had a sickening experience involving a school I've been inspecting. A colleague of mine – let's call him J.M. – has been visiting the school for oral tests. At no time when his white superior calls him or asks him a question does J.M. fail to say "Yes, baas," or "No, baas," or "I'll get it for you, baas." Now, during lunch break, some of the staff say to him in the staff-room, they feel disgraced when a black man like him says, "baas, baas" to the white man. They say they hope he'll stop it – just a nice brotherly talk, you see. Guess what J.M. goes and does? He goes and tells his white superior that the staff members of such-and-such school don't want him to call him "baas"! Guess what the white man does? He comes and complains to me about the bad conduct of those teachers. Now I ask you; what chance do you or I stand against idiots like these two who have so much power? We don't all have the liver to join the Congress Movement. So we keep stealing from the white man and lying to him and he does the same. This way we can still feel some pride.'

As I rose to go, I said, 'So Mary-Jane's gone off with Joe, eh!' as though her image had not been hovering over me all the time since Uncle had announced her 'flight'.

'Yes, because I've a stupid timid nephew. Are you going to wait till horns grow on your head before you marry?'

I laughed.

'Any country girl who starts off with Joe had made a real start in town-living, Neph'.'

As I went out, the woman in the lounge was saying: 'Kiriki, Kiriki – who do they say he is – Kiriki with the stolen piano. Me, I cannot eat Kiriki, I want money for food. He can take the Kirikinyana and Mohapeloanyana of his, put them in the lavatory bucket.'

By saying 'He can take...' she clearly wanted me to listen. The use of the diminutive form for the names of the musicians was meant for his ears.

'What do you do with your aunt, Neph', if she does not understand Grieg and cannot like Mohapeloa?'

If you had picked me with a pin as I was going out, I should have punctured, letting out a loud bawl of laughter which I could hardly keep back in my stomach.

The Dignity of Begging

BLOKE MODISANE

The Magistrate raises his eyes above the documents and plunges them like daggers into my heart. His blue eyes are keen: my heart pounds like the bass of a boogie-woogie.

'I'm sick to death of you . . . heartily sick. There's not a native beggar on the streets whose full story I don't know,' the Magistrate says. 'I've watched some of you grow up. There isn't one I haven't tried to rehabilitate many times. Some I was forced to send to goal, but they always come back . . . they come back to the goose that lays the golden egg.'

These are fighting words. The Magistrate sounds as though he's going to put us away for a few weeks. My only regret is that Richard Serurubele has to share my fate. If only the Magistrate knew that he is not a parasite like the rest of us, that he's what is called an exploited beggar. He was crippled by an automobile accident, and since then his parents have made capital out of it. They use him to beg so they can balance the family budget. They never show him the comfort of love. Relentlessly they drive him, like an animal that has to work for its keep and feed. He is twenty-one. Dragging one foot along, he is an abject sight who had all the sadness of the world in his face. He looks many times older than my mother-in-law.

'You beggars make it difficult for me to do my duty, and in spite of my failure to rehabilitate you, I always believe in giving you another change . . . A fresh start, you might call it.

But I'm almost certain that you'll be back here in a few days.'

The Magistrate is getting soft, I can see my freedom at a distance of an arm's stretch. Here is my chance to put on my act. A look of deep compunction and a few well-chosen words can do the trick. I clear my throat and squeeze out a tear or two.

'Your Honour, most of us beg because we've been ostracised by our families; they treat us as though we were lepers,' I say, wiping off a tear. 'They want us to look up to them for all the things we need. They never encourage us to earn our own keep. Nobody wants to employ us, people are more willing to offer us alms rather than give us jobs. All they do is show us pity . . . We dont want

26

to be pitied, we want to be given a chance to prove that we're as good as anybody else.'

I can see from the silence in the court that everybody is deceived . . . Everybody is filled with a sense of self-reproach. The Magistrate is as mute as the undertaker's parlour. I can read pity on the faces of all the people in the court; perhaps the most pathetic is my own. I am magnificent . . . an answer to every film director's dream. I know I have said enough . . . enough to let us out, that is.

'I understand you have matriculated, your name is Nathaniel, isn't it?' He turns a page of the report prepared by a worker in the Non-European Affairs Department. 'Yes, here we are, Nathaniel Mokgomare, the department recommends that you be sent to a place where you will be taught some useful trade. I want you to report to Room 14 at the department's building tomorrow morning.'

This is not what I had bargained for; my brilliant idea has boomeranged. Why must I take a job when I can earn twice a normal wage begging? After all, what will horses do if I take a job. I *must* uphold the dignity of begging. Professional ethics forbid all beggars from working.

'As for you, Richard Serurubele, I'll let you go this time, but mark my words: the next time you appear before me, I'll have you sent to the Bantu Refuge. Now get out of here, both of you'

If the Magistrate had seen the big grin on my face as we leave the court, he would have thrown my deformed carcass in gaol and deliberately lost the key. He does not see it though.

With the exception of a few loose ends everything has gone according to schedule, but my friend Serurubele is just about the most miserable man on earth. The trouble with him is he lacks imagination, but then of course, not everybody is as bright as I am. He always seems to be looking at the dull side of life, a vice coupled with an appalling brand of honesty most bishops would swear didn't exist.

'One of these days, I'm going to kill myself,' Serurubele says. 'I can't go on like this, I'm tired of living off other people. Why did this have to happen to me? Tell me, Nathan. Why?'

How this man expects me to answer a question like this is beyond me. For one unguarded moment I almost tell him to send his Maker a telegram and ask Him all about it, but my gentler nature sees the harm such an answer might do.

27

'I don't know,' I say, abruptly. 'Things like this just happen; it's not in us to question why. Nature has a way of doing things, but even then she gives something in return . . . at least I think so . . . But how should I know, anyway?'

This is the one time I cannot find something concrete to say; I want to show him that there is compensation for his disability, but I just cannot lay my hands on it. This, I remember, is what made me leave home.

I left because my parents did not understand. They almost made a neurotic out of me; but today I wonder if it wasn't my own sensitivity which gave their actions then their seemingly absurd proportions. They seemed afraid to walk about freely; everybody sat down as if the house was full of cripples. I was treated like a babe in arms. All the things I wanted were brought to me, I was not even allowed to get myself water to drink. This excessive kindless gradually began to irritate me . . . It became a constant reminder that I didn't belong, that I was an invalid. It then became apparent that they would soon put the food into my mouth which they had already chewed for me, and push it down my throat. These thoughts of inadequacy drove me from home.

A new life opened for me. I got myself a wife, two bouncing boys and a property at Pampoenfontein, also a room at Sophiatown complete with piano. Within two years I had begged well over a few hundred pounds. The money had been used wisely. Only one problem confronts me now, I want enough money to provide for my old age . . . The two boys are also to be considered.

'For Christ's sake, Nathaniel,' Serurubele says, 'what's wrong with you. Why are you always so wrapped up in your thoughts . . . this is where I stay, remember?'

I say good-bye to him and go to my room. After having something to eat I settle down to some hard thinking. There are all sorts of insurances and societies, unions and what have you, which protect workers. Why not a beggars' union? I could rally all the beggars of the city into one union with some professional name like The United Beggars' Union, into whose funds every beggar would contribute ten shillings a week. In the city of Johannesburg alone, there are over a hundred beggars and if they could all be talked over, a capital of about two-thousand-four-hundred pounds could be realised in one year.

What a brilliant idea . . . an inspiration of genius. Sometimes

I feel depressed that the world has not had the vision to realise the potentialities of my genius . . . possibly it cannot accommodate Einstein and myself in the same generation. Anyway, so much for that.

I could promise to offer each a bonus of ten pounds a year. That would be smart . . . No beggar could resist such an offer. Maybe I should promise to buy each a propery somewhere cheap, say, buy one property a year for the needy ones like Serurubele, equip him with third-rate tools and interest him in turning out junk that nobody will care to give a second look at. The scheme would be costly, but at least it would go far in enlisting their confidence. Only one would get the property; the others would wait patiently until I get religion.

The following morning I'm at Room 14 bright and early. A white man with a bored expression on his face is sitting behind a big mahogany desk. I tell him my name. He takes some paper and writes on it. He tells me to go to the address written on the paper.

The faint showers that were falling outside have become heavier, and as I go out I say something nasty about the weather. A brilliant idea strikes me as a well-dressed lady is walking towards me. She looks like a mobile gold mine ready to be tapped . . . in fact, I can almost see the gold nuggets in her teeth. I put on a gloomy face, bend lower than usual and let my deformed carcass shiver. She stops and looks at me as if she's responsible for my deformity.

'Why, you poor boy, you're freezing to death,' she says, with melodrama. 'Here, go buy yourself something to eat.'

I feel the half-crown piece in my hand and give her the usual line of how the good Lord will bless her, and send her tons and tons of luck: but from the way she's dressed, she appears to have had more than her share of luck.

I play this trick all the way to the address I'm given, and by the time I get there, I count well over ten half-crowns. Not bad, I say to myself; at this rate I can become the richest and most famous beggar in the city. To think the department wants to pin me behind a desk! The idea is criminal, to say the least.

One of these days when I'm on my annual leave, I hope to write a book on begging, something like a treatise on the subject. It will be written with sensitivity and charm, brimful with sketches from life, and profusely illustrated with coloured photographs, with easy-to-follow rules on the noblest and oldest occupation in the world:

Begging! It will be a textbook for all aspiring beggars, young and old, who will reap a wealth of knowledge from my personal experience and genius. In fact, it will be the only one of its kind in world literature. Even millionaires will take up begging as a pastime to colour their humdrum existence.

It will naturally begin with a history of the art from its ancient crudity of maiming children as a preparation in their education, right up to the contemporary age of beggars who are driven to the city in the latest American cars . . . beggars with a bank balance big enough to impress the Receiver of Revenue. I can almost see it on the best-seller list for several months. This reverie almost causes me to lose my way.

I find the place and go in. My heart just misses a beat when I see the large number of people inside. Some, if not most, are deformed monstrosities like myself. What could be sweeter? I can see my plan taking shape.

The man in charge starts explaining the elementary principles of the typewriter. I pretend to be interested and ask many unnecessary questions, but intelligent enough to impress him. By five o'clock I'm running over the keyboard like a brilliant amateur.

On my way home I go via Serurubele's corner. He is still there and looking as miserable as ever. I suggest that we go home. I lure him to my room and when we get there I begin playing a certain tarantella like Rubeinstein, only my rendering is in A flat Major. Either my piano recital is good or my friend just loves bad sounds.

'You can have a house like this and everything that goes with it; it's yours for the taking. Why beg for other people when you can do it for yourself?'

'I've got to help with the rent and the food,' he says. 'How do you think I'm going to get a house like this? I can't just wish for it.'

'You don't have to, you must plan and work for it like I did. I have a plan that will give it to you in less than a year . . . Listen.'

I then start explaining to him about the society with particular emphasis on the good it will do to all beggars. I see his teeth sparkling behind thick lips. I put him in charge of organising them for our first meeting.

Last night I dreamt I was at the race course and I saw the winning double as plain as I see my twisted leg. I raid my savings in the room and make my way to Turfontein. When I get there I start scouting around for policemen. None are about and a soothing satisfaction comes with the realisation that I shall not bother myself with police badges. I put a pound win on two and seven, a double in the first leg. As I'm making my bet, a man with eyes as big and lethargic as an owl's is standing next to me and beaming like a blushing groom.

I'm too nervous to watch the race, so I decide to walk about and appreciate the scenery. Suddenly I feel as though someone is staring at me. I turn round and look straight at Miss Gallovidian, a welfare worker, who has the uncanny habit of showing up at the most unexpected places. I don't need a fortune-teller to tell me I'm in trouble. She has a notorious record of having safely deposited more than twelve beggars in the Refuge. My only chance is to get out of here before she can find a beefy policeman. I'm walking to the gate when I hear people talking about two and seven. I even forget the trouble Miss Gallovidian is going to bring me. I run as fast as a man with a twisted leg can to the Bookie. Only six tickets were sold, the loud speaker was saying, only I'm not interested.

As the Bookie is handing me the money Blushing Groom seems even happier than I am. His crooked teeth, which are dulled by tobacco, click every time the Bookie counts a hundred. His greasy lips are watering while a pair of bloodshot eyes are blinking with a dull brilliance. I hurts my eyes to look at him. I have hardly put the money in my pocket, when Gruesome pats me on the back says, nice and loud: 'We make it!'

I must have been a fool not to have been wise as to why Blushing Groom was acting the perfect chaperon.

'That's fine,' I say. 'What have *we* made?'

'Don't be bashful,' he says, 'we caught the richest double. Come, this calls for a celebration.' He extends a hand, and all the time he's smiling as if his wife has given birth to quadruplets.

'Look, pal,' I say. 'It's a good try. I couldn't have done better myself. This is the perfect set-up, isn't it? Well, I've got news for you: I caught that double alone, I don't know you and I don't care to. Go get yourself another piece of cheese . . . I'm not that easy.'

This ape suddenly stops smiling and looks at me like I had the plague. His broad, flat nose starts puffing out steam like an angry Spanish bull (only I'm not in the mood to make fancy passes like a toreador). All in all, he looks positively fierce, like the animal in the simile.

31

'Six hundred and seventy pounds is a lot of money,' he shouts. 'Nobody's going to cheat me out of my share. You being a cripple . . .'

'Shut up!' I yell. 'Never call me that again, you . . . You!' I swing a right cross to his face, but this ape is smart. He blocks it and lands a hard one on my chin. I rock back and land flat on my sitters, while jungle tomtoms beat out a solid conga in my head. After a while my heard clears and I get up, burning with rage. If I only had the strength, I would tear this ape apart.

Blushing Groom has put on quite a show; we have a good audience. Some white folk are threatening to beat his brains out . . . I sincerely hope they do.

Suddenly I see a police badge jostling its way through. This is no place for me! I dash and start zigzagging through the people. A junior confusion starts, with everybody trying to give way. I run a few minutes, stumble and fall on my face. The policeman bends down and grabs me firmly by the arm and whispers: 'Look, John, let's not have trouble. Come along quietly and everything will be just fine.'

Under these circumstances I have no choice but to submit. My mother always told me never to resist arrest, let alone striking a uniformed officer of the law. Me and my money part company after Blushing Groom had preferred charges. My submission causes me to spend a not-so-glorious week-end at the Bantu Refuge. My transfer there being arranged by the thoughtful sergeant in the charge office, who out of pure love could not have me thrown in with hardened criminals . . . what with the place filled with house-breakers, extortioners, professional pickpockets and a generous assortment of other unsavoury characters. Frankly, I hoped he would mind his own business. I might even have started a grap game and made me some money.

'I am almost certain that you will be back here in a few days,' the Magistrate had said. Somebody ought to tell him he has a great future . . . reading palms. He looks at me and a grin spreads over his pancake-like face. This place must be short of Magistrates; why has it got to be the same one all the time?

'Beggars who play the horses are a dangerous nuisance. They misuse kindness that is shown to them.'

Just my luck: now I have to listen to a lecture on morals. The Magistrate looks pleased with himself, and I don't like it. Miss

Gallovidian looks at me and smiles like a proud victress. She probably expects a promotion for this. I'm called on to the stand.

Some man with a thin face asks me to raise my right hand and swear to tell the truth. After saying my piece, the prosecutor starts questioning me as if he's promised thirty per cent of Blushing Groom's cut. After his session with me, he calls Blushing Groom to the stand.'

'Do you know this man?' the prosecutor says.

'No, sir.'

'How was it then you put up ten shillings to bet the horses with him?'

'I was losing all morning when I decided to try somebody's guesses. I met him, and we started talking.'

'Did anybody see you talking to him?'

'I don't know, but somebody must have.'

'Then what happened?'

'I asked him if he had a tip. He said he had one straight from the horse's mouth . . . A sure thing, he said. I then asked him if I could put up ten shillings. He agreed. I was afraid to make the bet, so I gave him the money and walked over to the Bookie's stand with him where he placed a pound win on two and seven.'

'Why were you afraid to make the bet?'

'I though he was luckier than I was . . . besides, I had been losing all morning.'

'Why did you strike him?'

'He was trying to cheat me out of my share, and tried to hit me when he couldn't.'

The Magistrate looks at me with something like contempt in his eyes. I won't have to put on a show for him this time. I might just as well kiss half my money good-bye. Blushing Groom's story is watertight.

'I'm thoroughly disappointed with you,' the Magistrate says. 'I didn't know you were a thief too. I don't believe you could have made that bet alone; beggars haven't got so much money. I believe his story, things like this do happen. The money will be shared equally between the two of you.'

'I don't believe you could have made that bet alone.' What a cheek! I'll have that hobo know I make more money in one week than he does in a month. I don't believe you . . . Good God!

I feel like committing mass murder as the court hands Blushing

Groom three hundred and thirty-five pounds of my money. This prehistoric beast has a swell racket. A few more jobs like this and he can retire and buy himself a villa on the Riviera.

Blushing Groom is magnificent, inspiring awe. He is completely uncompromising, thoroughly unscrupulous, without qualms or a conscience. He has wholly realised the separateness of good and evil and attained a purity in evil worthy of honest appraisal. He would not allow himself to be swayed from cheating me by my being a cripple. If I were allowed to choose a brother, he would be my only choice.

I take my share of the money and clear out before the Magistrate and Miss Gallovidian cook up another charge against me. On my way home I find it difficult to resist the temptation of stopping at some busy corner and doing my stuff. I might make up for some of the money, but I just happen to be wearing my best and have been a beggar long enough to know that people don't give money away to beggars who are dressed better than they. People who give alms to beggars do so to establish their superiority over the receiver, and like I said: I'm not an apprentice beggar.

When I get home I find a letter from my wife.

Our son, Tommy, is sick. Please come home . . .

I become afraid and anxious for my Tommy, and even the kind words of my outsize landlady fail to move me.

I had to wait for something like this to show me the folly of my ways. A man's place is next to his wife and family. I had hoped that some day I would be able to provide my boys with a decent education, to grow them like normal boys, not just sons of a helpless cripple . . . to find a place for them in the sun. I might be a big shot beggar but as a husband and father, I stink.

'If I should not see my friend Serurubele, will you . . .'

'Yes, I'll explain to him. I'll always have your room for you if you should ever want it again.'

Deep down I know that I will want it again. I have three hundred and thirty-five reasons why I should. Blushing Groom and the gullible public of Johannesburg will live in my mind for ever. . . I have to come back. I owe it to the profession.

The Park

JAMES MATTHEWS

He looked longingly at the children on the other side of the railings; the children sliding down the chute, landing with feet astride on the bouncy lawn; screaming as they almost touched the sky with each upward curve of their swings; their joyful demented shrieks at each dip of the merry-go-round. He looked at them and his body trembled and ached to share their joy; buttocks to fit board, and hands and feet to touch steel. Next to him, on the ground, was a bundle of clothing, washed and ironed, wrapped in a sheet.

Five small boys persued by two bigger ones, ran past, ignoring him. One of the bigger boys stopped. 'What are you looking at, you brown ape?' the boy said, stooping to pick up a lump of clay. He recognised him. The boy had been present the day he was put out of the park. The boy pitched the lump, shattering it on the rail above his head, and the fragments fell on his face.

He spat out the particles of clay clinging to the lining of his lips, eyes searching for an object to throw at the boys separated from him by the railing. More boys joined the one in front of him and he was frightened by their number.

Without a word he shook his bundle free of clay, raised it to his head and walked away.

As he walked he recalled his last visit to the park. Without hesitation he had gone through the gates and got onto the nearest swing. Even now he could feel that pleasurable thrill that travelled the length of his body as he rocketed himself higher, higher, until he felt that the swing would upend him when it reached its peak. Almost leisurely he had allowed it to come to a halt like a pendulum shortening its stroke and then ran towards the see-saw. A white boy, about his own age, was seated opposite him. Accordion-like their legs folded to send the see-saw jerking from the indentation it pounded in the grass. A hand pressed on his shoulder stopping a jerk. He turned around to look into the face of the attendant.

'Get off!'

The skin tightened between his eyes. Why must I get off? What have I done? He held on, hands clamped onto the iron attached to the wooden see-saw. The white boy jumped off from the other end and stood a detached spectator.

'You must get off!' The attendant spoke in a low voice so that it would not carry to the people who were gathering. 'The council say,' he continued, 'that us Blacks don't use the same swings as the whites. You must use the swings where you stay,' his voice apologising for the uniform he wore that gave him the right to watch that little white boys and girls were not hurt while playing.

'There no park where I stay.' He waved a hand in the direction of a block of flats. 'Park on the other side of town but I don't know where.' He walked past them. The mothers with their babies, pink and belching, cradled in their arms, the children lolling on the grass, his companion from the see-saw, the nurse girls — their uniforms their badge of indemnity—pushing prams. Beside him walked the attendant.

The attendant pointed an accusing finger at a notice board at the entrance. 'There. You can read for yourself.' Absolving him of all blame.

He struggled with the red letters on the white background. 'Blankes Alleen. Whites Only.' He walked through the gates and behind him the swings screeched, the see-saw rattled, and the merry-go-round rumbled.

He walked past the park each occasion he delivered the washing, eyes wistfully taking in the scene.

He shifted the bundle to a more comfortable position, easing the pain biting into his shoulder muscles. What harm would I be doing if I were to use the swings? Would it stop the swings from swinging? Would the chute collapse? The bundle pressed deeper and the pain became an even line across his shoulders and he had no answer to his reasoning.

The park itself, with its wide lawns and flower beds and rockeries and dwarf trees, meant nothing to him. It was the gaily painted red-and-green tubing, the silver chains and brown boards, transport to never-never land, which gripped him.

Only once, long ago, and then almost as if by mistake, had he been on something to beat it. He had been taken by his father, one of the rare times he was taken anywhere, to a fairground. He had stood captivated by the wooden horses with their gilded reins and scarlet saddles dipping in time to the music as they whirled by.

For a brief moment he was astride one, and he prayed it would last forever, but the moment lasted only the time it took him to whisper the prayer. Then he was standing clutching his father's trousers, watching the others astride the dipping horses.

Another shifting of the bundle and he was at the house where he delivered the clothing his mother had washed in a round tub filled with boiling water, the steam covered her face with a film of sweat. Her voice, when she spoke, was as soft and clinging as the steam enveloping her.

He pushed the gate open and walked around the back watching for the aged lap dog, which at his entry would rush out to wheeze asthmatically around his feet and nip with blunt teeth at his ankles.

A round-faced African girl, her blackness heightened by the white starched uniform she wore, opened the kitchen door to let him in. She cleared the table and he placed the bundle on it.

'I call madam,' she said, the words spaced and highly-pitched as if she had some difficulty in uttering the syllables in English. Her buttocks bounced beneath the tight uniform and the backs of her calves shone with fat.

'Are you sure you've brought everything?' was the greeting he received each time he brought the bundle, and each time she checked every item and as usual nothing was missing. He looked at her and lowered his voice as he said; 'Everything there, merrum.'

What followed had become a routine between the three of them.

'Have you had anything to eat?' she asked him.

He shook his head.

'Well, we can't let you go off like that.' Turning to the African woman in the white, starched uniform. 'What have we got?'

The maid swung open the refrigerator door and took out a place of food. She placed it on the table and set a glass of milk next to it.

The white woman left the kitchen when he was seated and he was alone with the maid.

His nervousness left him and he could concentrate on what was on the plate.

A handful of peas, a dab of mashed potatoes, a tomato sliced into bleeding circles, a sprinkling of grated carrot, and no rice.

White people are funny, he told himself. How can anyone fill himself with this? It doesn't form a lump like the food my mama makes.

He washed it down with milk.

'Thank you, Annie,' he said as he pushed the glass aside.

Her teeth gleamed porcelain white as she smiled.

He sat fidgeting, impatient to be outside away from the kitchen with its glossy, tiled floor and steel cupboards ducoued a clinical white to match the food-stacked refrigerator.

'I see you've finished.' The voice startled him. She held out an envelope containing the rand note—payment for his mother's weekly struggle over the wash tub. 'This is for you.' A five cent piece was dropped into his hand, a long fingernail raking his palm.

'Thank you, merrum.' His voice hardly audible.

'Tell your mother I'm going away on holiday for about a month and I'll let her know when I'm back.'

Then he was dismissed and her high heels tapped out of the kitchen.

He nodded his head at the African maid who took an apple from a bowl bursting with fruit and handed it to him.

He grinned his thanks and her responding smile bathed her face in light.

He walked down the path finishing the apple with big bites.

The dog was after him before he reached the gate, its hot breath warming his heels. He turned and poked his toes on its face. It barked hoarsely in protest, a look of outrage on its face.

He laughed delightedly at the expression which changed the dog's features into those of an old man.

'See you do that again.' He waved his feet in front of the pug's nose. The nose retreated and made an about-turn, waddling away with its dignity deflated by his affront.

As he walked, he mentally spent his sixpence.

I'll buy a penny drops, the sour ones that taste like limes, a penny bull's eyes, a packet of sherbet with the licorice tube at the end of the packet, and a penny star toffees, red ones that turn your spit into blood.

His glands were titilated and his mouth filled with saliva. He stopped at the first shop and walked in.

Trays were filled with expensive chocolates and sweets of a type never seen in the jars on the shelves of the Indian shop on the corner where he stayed. He walked out not buying a thing.

His footsteps lagged as he reached the park.

The nurse girls with their babies and prams were gone, their places occupied by old men, who, with their hands holding up their stomachs, were casting disapproving eyes over the confusion and clatter confronting them.

A ball was kicked perilously close to an old man, and the boy who ran after it stopped short as the old man raised his stick, daring him to come closer.

The rest of them called to the boy to get the ball. He edged closer and made a grab at it as the old man swung his cane. The cane missed the boy by more than a foot and he swaggered back, the ball held under his arm. The game was resumed.

He watched them from the otherside of the railings — the boys kicking the ball, the children cavorting on the grass, even the old men, senile on the seats; but most of all, the children enjoying themselves with what was denied him, and his whole body yearned to be part of them.

'Shit it!' He looked over his shoulder to see if anyone had heard him. 'Shit it!' he said louder. 'Shit on them! Their park, the grass, the swings, the see-saw, everything! Shit it! Shit it!'

His small hands impotently shook the tall railings towering above his head.

It struck him that he would not be seeing the park for a whole month, that there would be no reason for him to pass it.

Despair filled him. He had to do something to ease his anger.

A bag filled with fruit peelings was on top of the rubbish stacked in a waste basket fitted to a pole. He reached for it and frantically threw it over the railings. He ran without waiting to see the result.

Out of breath three streets further, he slowed down pain stabbing beneath his heart. The act had brought no relief, only intensified the longing.

He was oblivious of the people passing, the hoots of the vehicles whose paths he crossed without thinking. And once, when he was roughly pushed aside, he did not even bother to look and see who had done it.

The familiar shrieks and smells told him that he was home.

The Indian shop could not draw him out of melancholy mood and he walked past it, his five cent piece unspent in his pocket.

A group of boys were playing with tyres on the pavement.

Some of them called him but he ignored them and turned into a short side street.

He mounted the flat stoep of a two storey-house with a facade that must once have been painted but had now turned a nondescript grey with the red brick underneath showing.

Beyond the threshold the room was dim. He walked past the scattered furniture with a familiarity that did not need guidance.

His mother was in the kitchen hovering over a pot perched on a pressure stove.

He placed the envelope on the table. She put aside the spoon and stuck a finger under the flap of the envelope, tearing it into half. She placed the rand note in a spoutless teapot on the shelf.

'You hungry?'

He nodded his head.

She poured him a cup of soup and added a thick slice of brown bread.

Between bites of bread and sips of soup which scalded his throat, he told his mother that there would not be any washing coming during the week.

'Why?' What the matter? What I do?'

'Nothing. Merrum say she go away for month. She let mama know she back.'

'What I do now?' Her voice took on a whine and her eyes strayed to the teapot containing the money. The whine hardened to reproach as she continued. 'Why don't she let me know she going away then I look for another merrum?' she paused. 'I slave away and the pain never leave my back but it too much for her to let me know she go away. The money I get from her keep us nice and steady. How I go cover the hole?'

He wondered how the rand notes he had brought helped to keep them nicely steady. There was no change in their meals. It was, as usual, not enough, and the only time they received new clothes was at Christmas.

'I must pay the burial, and I was going to tell Mr. Lemonsky to bring lino for the front room. I'm sick looking at the lino full of holes but I can forget now. With no money you got as much hope as getting wine on Sunday.'

He hurried his eating to get away from the words wafted towards him, before it could soak into him, trapping him in the chair to witness his mother's miseries.

Outside, they were still playing with their tyres. He joined them half-heartedly. As he rolled the tyre his spirit was still in the park on the swings. There was no barrier to his coming and he could do as he pleased. He was away from the narrow streets and squawking children and speeding cars. He was in a place of green grass and red tubing and silver steel. The tyre rolled past him. He made no effort to grab it.

'Get the tyre.' 'You sleep?' 'Don't you want to play anymore?' He walked away ignoring their cries.

Rage boiled up inside him. Rage against the houses with its streaked walls and smashed panes filled by too many people; against the overflowing garbage pails outside doors; the alleys and streets; and against a law he could not understand—a law that shut him out of the park.

He burst into tears. He swept his arms across his cheeks to check his weeping.

He lowered his hands to peer at the boy confronting him.

'I think you cry!'

'Who say I cry? Something in my eye and I rub it.'

He pushed past and continued towards the shop; 'Cry baby!' the boy's taunt rang after him.

The shop's sole iron-barred window was crowded. Oranges were mixed with writing paper and dried figs were strewn on school slates. Clothing and crockery gathered dust. Across the window a cockroach made its leisurely way, antennae on the alert.

Inside the shop was as crowded as the window. Bags covered the floor leaving a narrow path to the counter.

The shopkeeper, an ancient Indian with a face tanned like cracked leather leaned across the counter. 'Yes, boy?' He showed teeth scarlet with betel. 'Come'n, boy. What you want? No stand here all day.' His jaws worked at the betel nut held captive by his stained teeth.

He ordered penny portions of his selection.

He transferred the sweets to his pockets and threw the torn containers on the floor and walked out. Behind him the Indian murmured grimly, jaws working faster.

One side of the street was in shadow. He sat with his back against the wall, savouring the last of the sun.

Bull's-eye, peppermint, a piece of licorice — all lumped together in his cheek. For a moment the part was forgotten.

He watched without interest the girl advancing.

'Mama say you must come'n eat.' She stared at his bulging cheek. One hand rubbing the side of her nose. 'Gimme.' He gave her a bull's eye which she dropped into her mouth between dabs at her nose.

41

'Wipe your snot!' he ordered her, showing his superiority. He walked past. She followed sucking and sniffing.

Their father was already seated at the table when they entered the kitchen.

'Must I always send somebody after you?' his mother asked.

He slipped into his seat and then hurriedly got up to wash his hands before his mother could find fault with yet another point.

Supper was a silent affair except for the scrapping of spoon across a plate and an occasional sniff from his sister.

A thought came into his mind almost at the end of the meal. He sat spoon poised in the air shaken by its magnitude. Why not go to the park after dark? After it had closed its gates on the old men, the children, and nurses with their prams! There would be no one to stop him.

He could think no further. He was lightheaded with the thought of it. His mother's voice, as she related her day to his father, was not the steam that stung, but a soft breeze wafting past him, leaving him undisturbed. Then qualms troubled him. He had never been in that part of town at night. A band of fear tightened across his chest, contracting his insides, making it hard for him to swallow his food. He gripped his spoon tightly, stretching his skin across his knuckles.

I'll do it! I'll go to the park as soon as we're finished eating. He controlled himself with difficulty. He swallowed what was left on his place and furtively watched to see how the others were faring. Hurry up! Hurry up!

He hastily cleared the table when his father pushed the last plate aside and began washing up.

Each piece of crockery washed was passed to his sister whose sniffing kept pace with their combined operation.

The dishes done, he swept the kitchen and carried out the garbage bin.

'Can I go play, mama?'

'Don't let me have to send for you again.'

His father remained silent buried behind the newspaper.

'Before you go,' his mother stopped him—'light the lamp and hang it in the passage.'

He filled the lamp with paraffin, turned up the wick and lit it. The light glimmered weakly through the streaked glass.

The moon, to him, was a fluorescent ball; light without

warmth—and the stars, fragments chipped of it. Beneath street lights card games were in session. He sniffed the nostril-prickling smell of dagga as he walked past. Dim doorways could not conceal couples clutching each other.

Once clear of the district, he broke into a trot. He did not slacken his pace as he passed through the downtown area with its wonderland shop windows. His elation seeped out as he neared the park and his footsteps dragged.

In front of him was the park with its gate and iron railings. Behind the railings, impaled, the notice board. he could see the swings beyond. The sight strengthened him.

He walked over, his breath coming faster. There was no one in sight. A car turned a corner and came towards him and he started at the sound of its engine. the car swept past, the tyres softly licking the asphalt.

The railings were icy-cold to his touch and the shock sent him into action. He extended his arms and with monkey-like movements pulled himself up to perch on top of the railings then dropped onto the newly-turned earth.

The grass was damp with dew and he swept his feet across it. Then he ran and the wet grass bowed beneath his bare feet.

He ran towards the swings, the merry-go-round, see-saw to chute, hands covering the metal.

Up the steps to the top of the chute. He stood outlined against the sky. He was a bird, an eagle. He flung himself down on his stomach, sliding swiftly. Wheeeeeee! He rolled over when he slammed onto the grass. He looked at the moon for an instant then propelled himself to his feet and ran for the steps of the chute to recapture that feeling of flight. Each time he swept down the chute, he wanted the trip never to end, to go on sliding, sliding, sliding.

He walked reluctantly past the see-saw, consoling himself with pushing at one end to send it whacking on the grass.

'Shit it!' he grunted as he strained to set the merry-go-round into action. Thigh tensed, leg stretched, he pushed. The merry-go-round moved. He increased his exertions and jumped on, one leg trailing at the ready to shove if it should slow down. The merry-go-round dipped and swayed. To keep it moving, he had to push more than he rode. Not wanting to spoil his pleasure, he jumped off and raced for the swings.

Feet astride, hands clutching silver chains, he jerked his body to gain momentum. He crouched like a runner then violently straightened. The swing widened its arc. It swept higher, higher, higher. It reached the sky. He could touch the moon. He plucked a star to pin to his breast. The earth was far below. No bird could fly as high as he. Upwards and onwards he went.

A light switched on in the hut at the far side of the park. It was a small patch of yellow on a dark square. The door opened and he saw a figure in the doorway. Then the door was shut and the figure strode towards him. He knew it was the attendant. A torch glinted brightly as it swung at his side.

He continued swinging.

The attendant came to a halt in front of him, out of reach of the swing's arc, and flashed his torch. The light caught him in mid-air.

God dammit!' the attendant swore. 'I told you before you can't get on the swings.'

The rattle of the chains when the boy shifted his feet was the only answer he received.

'Why you come back?'

'The swings, I come back for the swings.'

The attendant catalogued the things denied them because of their colour. Even his job depended on their goodwill.

'Blerry whites! They get everything!'

All his feelings urged him to leave the boy alone, to let him continue to enjoy himself but the fear that someone might see them hardened him.

'Get off! Go home!' he screamed, his voice harsh, his anger directed at the system that drove him against his own. 'If you don't get off, I go for the police. You know what they do to you.'

The swing raced back and forth.

The attendant turned and hurried towards the gate.

'Mama, Mama.' His lips trembled, wishing himself safe in his mother's kitchen, sitting next to the still-burning stove with a comic spread across his knees. 'Mama, Mama.' His voice mounted, wrenched from his throat, keeping pace with the soaring swing as it climbed the sky. Voice and swing. Swing and voice. Higher. Higher. Higher. Until they were one.

At the entrance of the park the notice board stood tall, its shadow elongated, pointing towards him.

The Urchin

CAN THEMBA

One sling of the braces would not keep up on the shoulder, just like one worm of pale-green mucus kept crawling down the chestnut lip and would suddenly dart back like a timid creature. But Macala wore his long pants (surely someone's—someone older's—castaway three-quarter jeans) with a defiant pride just ready to assault the rest of the known world. Other boys his ten-year age only had short pants.

He looked up and down from Mafuta's Chinaman store along Victoria Road, Sophiatown, and he thought of how his day ought to begin. Mafuta's was no good: he kept two too-ferocious dogs in his shop, and fairly-authenticated rumour had it that he also kept a gun that made a terrible noise. But the vistas up and down Victoria Road offered infinite possibilities for a man. To the left, there were queues on queues of half-frightened, half-foolish people who simply asked to be teased. Then Moosa's store with all those fruity, sweety things in the window; but they said Moosa trained at night with irons. Opposite, across Millar Street, there was a Chink butcher, but his counter was fenced off with wire, and Ooh! those cruel knives and hatchets. There must be a lot of money there for it to be protected so formidably. And, next to the butcher, the Bicycle Shop with its blaring juke-box: *Too roo roo roo tu! Too roo roo roo tu-tu!*, where a passer-by girl would suddenly break into a dance step, seductive beyond her years.

All like that, up to Chang's, and from there just the denuded places the demolition squad had left in Sophiatown.

To the right, Macala stared at Benghali House. The only double-storey building in the whole of Sophiatown. In front of it all sorts of pedlars met: sweet-potato sellers, maize sellers, and sweet-reed sellers, African pimpled squash sellers, shoe-lace sellers—all bedamned whether or not the shopkeeper alone held a licence to sell anything.

Macala's eyes glittered as he saw the Ma-Ndebele women squatting in their timeless patience behind their huge dishes of maize-cobs, dried *morogo* peanut cubes, wild fruits like *marula*, *mahlatswa*—things the urban African never sees on trees these days.

45

To Macala, these women with their quaint and beaded necks, and legs made to look like colourful pythons, were the fairest game.

He stepped off the veranda of Mafuta's shop, off the pavement, and sauntered swaggeringly towards those placid women in front of Benghali House. He was well aware that the street-corner loungers, enormous liars all of them, were watching him, thinking that the slightest move Macala made promised excitement and trouble.

He stopped in front of a Ndebele woman transfixed to her white dish, as if one with it, as if trade meant just being there at the strategic place and time: no bawling, no bartering, no bargaining. 'Dis—how much?' and that to Macala was English with a vengeance. She looked up at him with large baffled eyes, but before she spoke, Macala lifted his foot and trod on the edge of the dish, sending its contents churning out of it into the dust of Victoria Road's pavement. He shrieked with delight as he ran off.

What she hurled at him in virulent Ndebele may have been curses, prayers, lamentations, but to Macala it was reward enough; the kind of thing that proves the superiority of the townsman to these odd creatures from the country. And the passing generation's men and women shook their heads and muttered gloomily, 'the children of today, the children of today . . .'

His momentum took him to the vegetable vendor just opposite Mafuta's. In fluid career, he seized the handle of the cart and whirled it round and up for the devil of it. Potatoes, onions, pumpkins, cabbages went swirling into the air and plump tomatoes squashed on the macadam. The khaki-coated vendor stood aghast for a second before he broke into imprecations that shuddered even the sordid Sophiatown atmosphere. But Macala was off on his mischievous way.

He had passed the 'Fish and Chips' too fast for another tilt, and met his pals on the corner of Tucker and Victoria: Dipapang, Jungle and Boy-Boy. Together, they should have been 'Our Gang' but their organization was not tight enough for that.

Boy-Boy's was the brain that germinated most of the junior devilry of the team, but he did not quite have Macala's impetuous courage of execution. He looked like a social worker's explanation of 'conditions in the slums': thin to malnourished, delinquent, undisciplined, dedicated to a future gallows. Yet his father was an important man and his mother a teacher. Jungle qualified by the ease with which he could talk of using a knife, in real big-*tsotsi* fashion. Dipapang initiated nothing, thought nothing, was nothing, but was always so willing to join in, trying to finish anything the others cared to start.

'Heit, Macacix!' called Boy-Boy. 'It's how there?'

Macala suddenly felt in the mood for the jargon of the townships. The near-animal, amorphous, quick-shifting lingo that alarms farmboys and drives cops to all branches of suspicion. But it marks the city slicker who can cope with all its vagaries.

'It's couvert under the corzet,' Macala replied, bobbing his head this way and that to the rhythm.

'Hai, man, bigshot, you must be the reely-reely outlaw in this town,' Boy-Boy parried and lunged.

'Naw,' Macala feinted, 'dis town, Softtown's too small for me. I'll take Western and Corrie and Maclera and London, and smash them into a mashed potato.'

Boy-Boy fell for it, 'Whew!' he whistled, 'don't say you'll crowd me out!'

Macala took him by the throat and went in for the kill, 'Didn't I tell you, buster, to keep out of my country, or else . . .'

He proceeded to carry out the menacing 'or else' by choking Boy-Boy and slowly tripping him over a leg he had slipped behind him until they rolled over as Boy-Boy fell, and tumbled into the gutter.

Boy-Boy gasped, 'Ah give up, boss, da country's yours.'

The mock battle was over and everybody laughed . . . except Jungle. He was reputed to be 'serious' and that meant of the homicidal type. He sat there on the pavement drain with his mournful face, sharpening gratingly on the concrete his 3-Star jackknife which from some hazy movie memory he called his 'gurkha'. As the laughter trailed off, he suddenly drawled, 'Have you guys heard that Mpedi was arrested yesterday?'

They stared at him in genuine stupefaction. Then Boy-Boy said, 'Yerrrr! How'd it happen, Jungle?'

But Jungle was not one for elaborating a story. Very unsatisfactorily, he said, 'Waal, he was drinking at de English Lady's joint . . . and . . . and dey got him.'

'You mean he didn't shoot it out? You mean dey took him just like dat? But I bet ya dey couldn't put handcuffs on Mpedi!' But Macala was very unhappy about the tame way the idol of the township was arrested.

47

It was Boy-Boy who made a story of it. 'Yerrr! But *there* is an outee—a great outlaw!' He rose from the pavement and stood before the fascinated gaze of his pals. He stuck his thumbs into his belt and swayed his hips as he strutted up and down before them. Then he mimicked the bull-brained fearlessness of Mpedi, the mirror and form of almost all young Sophiatown, the clattering terror of men, and the perennial exasperation of the police station across the road.

'Ya! Da room was full—full to da door. Clevers, bigshots, boozers, bamboos, coat-hangers, hole-diggers, and bullets, blondes, figure 8's and capital I's, wash-planks and two-ton trucks. Da boys were in de stack and da dames were game . . .

'Then Bura Mpedi stepped in, his eyes blood-red. The house went dead-still. Ag, man, Bura Mpedi, man. He stood there and looked left . . . and looked right . . . His man was not there. He stepped in some more. The house was dead. He grabbed a beer from the nearest table and slugged it from the bottle. Who would talk?' Boy-Boy's upper lip curled up on one side in utter contempt, 'Heh, who would talk!'

Macala and his pals were caught in Boy-Boy's electric pause. Even Jungle was aroused by this dramatic display of township bullycraft.

Boy-Boy's histrionics continued, 'Yerrrre! A drunk girl came from under a table, and tried Mpedi for a drink. "Au, Bura Mpedi, give me a beer." Bura Mpedi put a boot on her shoulder and pushed her back under da table. Hai, man, hai, man, dat outee is coward-cool, man. And he hates cherry coat-hangers. But dat night his eyes were going all over looking for Mahlalela. Yeffies! If he'd caught Mahlalela dat night . . . !'

Lifted by the wide-eyed admiration of his pals, Boy-Boy went on to surpass himself. He flung out his right arm recklessly, and declared, 'Bat dat's nutting yet! You should have seen Bura Mpedi when dey sent four lean cops to come and take him. Payroll robbery, Booysens . . . one thousand pound! Assault with Grievous Bodily Harm, Newlands . . . three men down and out! Housebreakin' 'n *Thatha* . . . Lower Houghton!

'Dey came, man dey came. Four cops; two had guns, two had small inches. Dey surrounded da joint in Gibson Street, and dey called out to him to give up. Dey didn't know Mpedi with moonwash in his brains and a human intestine round his waist. He drew his point-three-five and his forty-five, and he came out shooting: Twah! Rwah! Rwah! Da two cops with the small inches ducked into a shebeen near by and ordered themselves a ha' nip brandy. One with da gun ran down Gibson Street for reinforces. Da last cop took a corner and decided to shoot it out with Mpedi. But da bullets came so fast he never got a chance to poke out a shot.

'Hee-e-e, I tell you Mpedi was da outee.' Then, still carried forward by the vibrance of his enthusiasm, Boy-Boy rounded off his dramatization by backing away slowly as he fired off imaginaary guns, and barked, 'Twah! Twah! Twah!'

But the elation that had swelled up in Macala was not shot through with envy. 'How come,' he grumbled, 'Da cops got him so easy now?' Yet what really worried him was that he knew how far he was beneath the fabulous Mpedi; that even in his own weight division, he could not make such an awe-inspiring impression. He was not even as good an actor as Boy-Boy to recount and represent the exploits of the almighties. He looked at Boy-Boy bitterly and told himself, 'I'll beat his brains out if he gets smart with me.'

It was Jungle who wrenched him out of his sour reverie. 'Boys, I think we should go finish off da Berliners,' Jungle said, prosaic-ally.

A flash of fear leapt into Boy-Boy's eyes, for he knew this meant war. Macala was himself a bit scared, but seeing the fear in Boy-Boy, he screwed his heart through a hole too small for it.

And Jungle's 'gurkha' went on scraping the pavement concrete, *screech-screech! screech-screech!*

'Come-ahn, let's go,' Macala suddenly decided.

They swaggered along Victoria Road, filling it from pavement to pavement as if they were a posse. Silent. Full of purpose. Deliberately grim. Boys and girls scampered for cover. Grown-ups stepped discreetly out of their way. Only the bigger tsotsis watched them with pride, and shouted encouragements like '*Da men who rule da town! Tomorrow's outeees!*'

On the corner of Meyer Street, they broke up a ring of young dicers and forced them to join up. Along the way they collected non-schoolgoing loafers who lounged against shop walls; blue-jeaned youngsters who twisted the arms of school-girls in rough love; odd-job boys who ran errands for shopkeepers; truants, pickpockets, little thugs, within their age-limit—the lot.

By the time they turned into Edith Street, they were a miniature army of hell-bent ruffians. Macala led them and felt the strange thrill of the force behind him. He chose Edith Street because it rose into a rocky hill with plenty of stones for ammunition, and dropped suddenly into that part of Sophiatown they called *Berlin*, where the walls were smeared with crude swastikas.

Macala split his men into two groups. Those with thick, bronze buckle belts were to go under Jungle through a cut in the row of houses precariously perched on huge boulders.

The excitement chopped Macala's breath into collops as he gave out his instructions. 'You boys get dem from de back. You start de war. When dey come running up Edward Road, dey'll meet us. Use dat butcher of yours Uncle Jungle.'

Jungle gave one of his rare smiles, and his men took position.

Macala and his group, first placing a sentinel on the hill-top, slowly clambered down the rocks and waited for Jungle to get around.

Though going into the den of the enemy, Jungle did not find it difficult to rout them. There was a biggish group of them playing dice in the usual ring, and when he swooped upon them, they instinctively thought it was the police and dashed up Edward Road, sticks and buckle belts raining on their heads.

Jungle himself had chosen a heftily-built fellow and was stabbing at him as he ran. Boy-Boy was later to describe it graphically, 'Yerre! Dat guy just wouldn't fall. Jungle had him—zip! But he ran on. Jungle caught him again in the neck—zip! He stumbled and trotted on his hands and feet. Jungle got him in the buttock—zip! But, yerrr! He just wouldn't fall!'

Before the Berliners could rally and make a stand, they had run into Macala's stone-throwing division. Though very one-sided the fight became fierce. The Berliners were now fighting, and because they were trapped and because they had to fight with their bare hands most of the time, they became young devils from the playgrounds of Hell.

Stones and all sorts of other missiles were hurled in all directions. Knives were brandished and plunged, big-buckled belts were swung in whistling arcs, arms were flailed in the centre of the imbroglio with desperate savagery. Women screamed, shops closed, traffic diverted itself. Now and then, a blood-bespattered boy would stagger off the street to a side wall just to sit down and watch, too done in to flee.

Then suddenly came the shrill warning cry, '*Arrara! Arrarayii!*'

The action stopped almost as abruptly as those ancient films which froze in mid-motion and transfixed the movement into a photograph. And just as suddenly after, they scattered all pell-mell. When the police van came round the corner, it was impossible to decide which flee-ers to pursue. For, now, everybody was running up and down and off the streets. The scores of small boys, ordinary pedestrians who had just alighted upon the scene, Fah-fee runners with full-blown cheeks a-chumping the incriminating tickets of their illicit lottery; everybody was running. In Sophiatown, you do not stop to explain to the police that you had nothing to do with it, or that you knew some of the culprits and could help the police.

The mobile squad were satisfied with merely clearing the street.

Breathless and bruised, Macala found himself at the open commonage called Maccauvlei, adjacent to Waterval Hospital, which served as the waste dumps to the city, and 'golf course' to those Africans who went in for the sport of leisure. Macala knew that most of his gang would sooner or later find their way there. He sat on a mound of ash, gasping heavily.

By the time Boy-Boy had arrived, he had regained his breath, and was pitching chalky, burnt-out pebbles rather pointlessly. Jungle came, for once, apparently, in his seventh heaven. Dipa-pang, too, grinned happily though his shirt had been torn down and hung like a hula. A few other stragglers from the Black Caps joined them, and then came the News. News that oddly took the shape of 'They say'.

'Dey say,' announced one urchin, 'dat one of de Berliners is dead.'

Stultifying fright seized them all. Some small boy simply broke out crying. Macala had trouble with a choking clod in his throat.

'Dey say,' came in another boy, 'de Berliners are going to call in de Big Berliners.'

'Agh,' grunted Macala in contempt, 'we'll go'n tell Bura Shark.'

'Dey say de cops're going to round us all up tonight.'

Despite all their bravado, all their big-shot stances and their blistering contempt for cops and the law, there is one thing that this knighthood really fears, and it was expressed by a crackling of interjections from each according to his own lights.

'Six lashes and reformatory!'

'De cane and off to a farm!'

'Cuts with a light cane and no fine!'

51

Someone elaborated the procedure by filling in the gory details:
'Dey say, two huge cops hold you down over a big bench an' you
got nothin' on. You can't move. Now, maybe de magistrate he said
"Six cuts". Dat's nothin'. If you cry, for every one you get two.
An' dose cops who give de lashes, dey train for you, dey pick up
weightlifting for you, dey grip a grip all day for you. Den when
de other cops got you on de bench, an' you can't move, an' you
don't want to cry, de lashing cop he takes de cane, he swishes it
over his head, one-two-three, whish! De tattoo jumps up on your
buttocks.

'Dey say, he den goes to sit down, lights a sigareete, and talks
with de other cops. Den he comes again. One of de cops holding
you turns your head so you can see de lashing cop coming. He
swishes de cane, one-two-three, whish!' Nother tattoo comes up,
dis time with blood. Red blood from your buttocks. He goes for
'nother puff at his cigarette, or maybe he looks for his tea dis time.

'He comes again. Dis time he sneezes his nose on your buttocks,
and makes jokes how black buttocks is tough. He swishes the cane,
one-two-three, whish! If you don't cry, maybe you get your six
lashes straight. But if you cry, only just *Maye Babo*—oh-ho-ho! . . .

'An' dey say, sometimes after you get lashes, six days, two weeks,
you can't sit in de bus, you give your seat to de aunties. Hai, dat
cane dey keep in de salt water when nobody get lashes!'

By that time the horror of the prospect had seeped through every
delinquent soul. It was Macala who spoke first.

He said determinedly, 'Me, I'm not going home tonight.'

But Boy-Boy did not like the idea. He knew that his mother would
not rest until she had found out where he was. Worse still, she might
even go ask the police to help her find him. 'Naw, Macacix, I'm
going home. I don't like cops catching me when my ma is not there.
I'm going home.'

As he walked away, the whole little gang suddenly broke up and
walked home their different ways. As they scattered, Macala went
frantic with panic. With consternation twisted in his face and his
arms floating like a blind man's in front of him, he looked half-
comic as he stood on that mount of ash.

'Hey, hey, you guys won't leave me alone. We're de boys . . .'

He heard a sound of impatience behind him, 'Aargh! Let them
go, Macala.' He turned round and reeled unsteadily a little as he
saw Jungle standing there, not looking frightened at all.

'Wh-what you going to do, Jungle?'

Jungle took out his 'gurkha' and scraped it across his palm from left to right, right to left. Then he said, 'I'm going home, Macala,' and that mournful expression crept across his countenance. 'And when de cops come to get me tonight . . .' He made an ugly motion with his knife under his chin. He walked away with the slow lanky movement of that gawky body of his.

By the time Macala decided to leave Maccauvlei, it was getting dark. But he knew where he was going. Rather unnecessarily, he skulked along the fences of the street, looking this way and that. Now and then, he would petrify at the zoom of a passing car or duck into an alley when headlights bore goldenly through the dark of the street. But ultimately he reached the open space where Gerty, Bertha, and Toby Streets used to be. He saw the dark building for which he was headed. He ran forward and stopped in front of it, but this side of the street. Slowly now. Somewhere here there was a night-watchman, a Zulu with a thick black beard and barbel moustache, black uniform and black face that rubbed him out of sight in the dark, and a gnarled knobkerrie known to have split skulls.

But Macala knew where the corrugated-iron fence had snarled out a lip of entrance for him. He went on his hands and knees, and crawled away from the immense double gate towards this entrance. He found it and coiled himself inside. He knew there were stacks of corrugated iron in this timber yard, and if he touched them, the racket would alert the night-watchman. So he did not go far, just nestled himself near his exit.

A little breeze was playing outside, hasting a piece of paper down the street, and now and then a bus or lorry would thunder by. But Macala slept, occasionally twitching in the hidden mechanics of sleep. Far from where he could hear, a woman's voice was calling stridently, 'Mac-a-a-ala! Mac-a-a-a-la! Hai, that child will one day bring me trouble.'

Mita

CASEY MOTSISI

It was Saturday morning. The sun peeped out slowly from the Easterly womb. Slowly, almost furtively as though it wanted to take Sophiatown by surprise. But Sophiatown cannot be taken by surprise. Sophiatown might go to sleep late in the night, drunk, violent and rowdy. But in the small hours of the morning she wakes up, yawns away her hangover and prepares herself for another uncertain day.

It is a habit. A habit forced upon her by the machinations of the law—the early morning beer raids, pass raids, permit raids. Raids, raids, raids. And yet a habit also nurtured by the very way of life typical in all other locations. A young man knocks at your door. You open it and recognise him as one of your relations. He has news—sometimes good, often bad. 'Father said I must come to let you know that Boikie is dead. The Tsotsis stabbed him last night.' . . . 'Uncle, Ma says I must come and find out if sister spent the night here.' Less often: 'Father says I must come and tell you that mother has given birth to twins. She wants auntie to come and spend the day with her.' It is a habit for Sophiatown to wake up early.

Mita was an early riser. About four o'clock she would have the home fires burning and she would stand with her back to the small stove humming her favourite tune: 'Stormy Weather'. That was at her parents' home in Western township, just a throw south of Sophiatown. But now she was staying in Sophiatown.

Mita's father, Mr Rabotho, who ran a small business at the Western Township Municipal Beer Hall, had told her some months back never to set foot in his house until she brought the father of her unborn child.

So Mita went to stay with the young man. Of course, the young man did not take it lying down. He argued. He wrangled. 'How can you be sure it's my child?' But Mita's insistent cry, 'It's yours, it's yours. I know!' finally triumphed.

But for the first time as far as she could remember, the morning Sophiatown sun had caught her napping. It was eight o'clock when she finally woke up. It was the pain. Lord, how can the human

54

body sustain such a torture! She tossed around in bed, her eyes tightly closed, her face meshed with pain. She knew her time had come, but doubt still played around with her mind.

'How can it be, it's hardly eight months,' she kept asking herself. 'But why the pain, the painful pain,' she wondered again. 'Is it because the baby is . . .'

But before her lips could form the word, 'illegitimate', her mind grabbed it and flung it against the cobweb-clustered ceiling.

'Tho-o-mas!' It was an unearthly scream that filtered through Mita's clenched teeth. The scream hesitated at the door, the window, at every little aperture then burst out into the open as though afraid to linger another second in the small dingy room.

But Thomas was not there. At that very moment he was cycling through the maze that is Johannesburg delivering parcels and letters for his firm . . .

'Ma Tladi, one of the yard's shebeen queens, burst through the door. She was just in time to grab Mita and stop her from falling off the bed. The two women grappled like street brawlers on the bed. 'Ma Tladi began screaming too when she felt Mita's teeth slithering into the pudgy wrist, but she fought on gallantly. Her usual weekend clashes with her husband were standing her in good stead. Two other women darted into the room, saw what was happening and automatically gave a hand.

In a few moments it was all over. The fighting, biting, wrestling. All over. The three fleshy women were smiling—an almost holy radiance in their faces. Once more a miracle had come to pass. It was a baby boy!

Mita was crying. But these were extremely beautiful tears, a sight to behold. Tears that are the language of every human soul passing through a moment of boundless ecstasy. Later a doctor was summoned. 'Ma Tladi paid the bill.

It was in the night when Mita heard the door open. A candle was burning in a saucer on the table. Thomas closed the door and stood looking at the bed. He knew that there were two lives in it. 'Ma Tladi had told him when he stopped there to buy a nip of brandy.

'You drunkard of a pig,' she had shouted at him. 'You come here saying "nip, auntie". You rubbish, You had better save that five shillings and go and buy your child clothes and napkins. Get out of here and stop saying "nip, nip, auntie", before I pour boiling water on your face, you drunkard!'

'Leave the boy alone, you dog.' 'Ma Tladi's husband had countered. 'Buy the nip and let's drink, my boy.'

'You keep that bablaas bek of yours shut before I bash it in with this pot,' 'Ma Tladi had fumed at her husband and pushed Thomas out of the house. As he tried to talk without a stagger to his room he could hear a commotion behind the locked door.

'Ma Tladi and her husband were clawing at each other's necks again.

Two lives in the bed. 'Ma Tladi had said to buy the baby clothes, but she hadn't said what the baby was. Thomas just stood there, staring, trying hard to appear as one who hadn't touched a drop. But Mita knew that he had been drinking, but she wasn't going to take him to task for it just this once. This was an occasion not to be marred by quarrels.

'It's a boy, Thomas.' Her voice was almost inaudible but Thomas heard her as clearly as if she had shouted the message through a megaphone. Thomas did not say a word. He just moved silently towards the bed and tried to flip the blanket to take a look at the baby. Mita stayed his hand gently and smiled into his face.

'No Thomas, you can't look at the child now. You'll have to wait for ten days before you can see it.' Thomas cursed at that old and stupid African custom. Mita saw the deep hurt in his eyes. She flipped the blanket over. 'But—you may take a little look. I'll close my eyes and pretend I'm asleep.'

Thomas did not take a 'little look'. He looked for a long time at the pinkish piece of life. A smile played upon his lips. 'Why won't he open his eyes and look at me, huh, honey? Boy, it looks just like you. I didn't know you were as pretty bas all this until now. Tootsie-tootsie-tootsi-e-e.' But the baby would not be 'tootsied' into opening its eyes.

Thomas talked for a long while. He told Mita all his plans for the baby. He was going to do everything for it—for Mita too. He was going to buy his son a tricycle. Nothing would be too good for him.

Yawning and wondering what a small child like that would do with a tricycle, Mita reminded Thomas that it was late and he should go to sleep.

That night Thomas slept on the saggy sofa. It wasn't very comfortable but he would have to get used to it. He didn't fall asleep immediately. For some time he lay awake thinking of a certain Friday night. It was a party at a friend's place in Toby Street.

He remembered drinking anything that he was offered. He also remembered forcing a young girl whose name he didn't know then to drink too, reassuring her that a 'little drink never did anybody no harm,' whenever the young girl showed signs of refusing.

After that he didn't remember much. But he did remember that the following morning he woke up feeling sick, his tongue thick and gummy. And there was a young girl snoring next to him in the same bed. He had taken a long look at the girl and he faintly remembered seeing her at the party. How he had reached home he could not remember. He remembered shaking her until she was awake.

On waking up the girl had looked around the room as if in a daze and asked where she was. 'In my room,' he told her. 'And how the blazes did you get here?' It had been an awkward situation and both tried to conceal their embarrassment by talking harshly to each other. She had later dressed up and left. He had never thought at that time that things would have turned out like this.

Here he was with the same young girl he had met at the party. The young girl who had mothered that pinkish piece of life.

When Thomas finally fell asleep, he slept like a log. The baby fretted and cried most of the night but Thomas did not hear a sound. In the morning he woke up with a vague feeling that he had dreamed he came home last night to learn that he was the father of a baby which was premature by about two months. A quick look at the bed reassured him that it was no dream.

He woke up and lit the pressure stove. There was a knock at the door and he said, 'Come in!' out of sheer habit. Then he remembered. He rushed to the door to see who it was. It was 'Ma Tladi. Thomas stood aside for her to enter. She greeted Mita and went about filling a kettle with water and placed it on the pressure stove. He sat down on the saggy sofa he had been sleeping on and watched as 'Ma Tladi went about her work. He wondered at this woman. He knew her as a heartless, money-loving woman who never let a chance to fight or swear slip past her if she could help it.

How could a woman like her assume such a motherly-role—and so expertly too? Thomas just sat down thinking of something he could do in order to be of help, but he knew that there was nothing he could do.

It was a relief for him when 'Ma Tladi gave him a sixpence and told him to go and buy some more paraffin at the Chinaman's shop. In a minute he was back with the paraffin. But he wanted an excuse to go out again and he said he forget to buy himself cigarettes.

Outside he met two of his friends. One of them asked him to buy them a little drink. He was just about to tell them that he had no money when he remembered that he had not given Mita his paypacket the previous night when he came home. He put his hand in his hip pocket and fingered the money. After a while he said yes, he would buy them a drink. He was a father and that called for a celebration . . .

They went to a shebeen in Tucker Street and he ordered a bottle of brandy. They drank in silence for a while. When the bottle was half-way through they all began talking with nobody paying attention to anyone.

Fanyana, one of the boys who had asked Thomas to buy them a drink, took out a pound and ordered four bottles of beer. After one bottle had been finished, the three boys talked more, chain-smoked and did very little drinking. They were down to two bottles when two girls walked into the room. Selina and Sponono. They were both about 28 years old, which made them five years Thomas' senior. Thomas had been trying to avoid Sponono ever since he realised he was in love with Mita.

'Ja, Thomas, you tickeyline,' Sponono said. Thomas looked up at his old flame, nodded his head and said, 'Hiya, Spo.' He could not account for the cold feeling that crawled through his stomach at the sight of Sponono.

Sponono sat down next to him on the bench. 'Why don't you buy us some gin, Thomas, or does that little bitch of yours take all your money?' Thomas did not answer. He stood up and said he was leaving. 'If you're going, I'm going too,' said Sponono. She stood up and the two walked out. Selina remained sitting with the other two boys.

Outside, Sponono thrust her hand into Thomas' pocket. It happened too fast for Thomas. Sponono's hand came out clutching at two one pound notes and a ten shilling note, which quickly disappeared between her bodice.

'Give me back my money,' Thomas yelled and took a swing at Sponono's face. It was a wild swing which did not land. Sponono held him close against her body, her eyes two balls of ice.

58

'Listen here, sonnyboy,' Sponono said. 'I'll give you back your stinking money, but first you're taking me home. Nobody ever gave me the brush-off and you're not going to be the first.' Thomas tried to resist but he knew it was hopeless. Sponono was as big as an ox and just about as strong.

As he walked home during the night, Thomas had lost all sense of time. He knew it was just before midnight from the stream of people chattering and walking briskly along the street. They were people from the bioscope. He decided to take a short cut home. He lurched through the muddy backyards, ducking under a fence here, jumping over a small wall there.

Then suddenly he felt the pain . . . a sharp pain in his head. Three boys were surrounding him, flaying madly at him with fists, kicking at his shins with their shoes. He tried to fight back but it was no use. He was overpowered.

He saw the glimmer of the knife's blade and he tried to ward it off with his hands. The blade sank into his spine and he pitched forward with a deep groan. He felt the hands going deftly through his pockets. In a moment they left him lying there and disappeared into the dark.

Thomas tried to raise his head but it felt as though it had been nailed to the ground. A coldness spread over him, the blood oozed out of him.

Somewhere in the distance, in a small dingy room, a new-born baby cried endlessly. The mother tried to soothe it. 'Daddy's coming home soon, my love, don't cry.'

But the baby continued to cry . . .

Tattoo Marks and Nails

ALEX LA GUMA

The heat in the cell was solid. It was usually hot in the cells, what with over one hundred prisoners packed in, lying on the concrete floor like sardines in a can or tangled like macaroni. But it was the middle of summer, and a week-end when prisoners are locked up early in the day until the following morning, there being only a skeleton staff of guards on duty; it was doubly, perhaps trebly hotter than usual.

The heat was solid. As Ahmed the Turk remarked, you could reach out before your face, grab a handful of heat, fling it at the wall, and it would stick.

The barred windows of the caserne were high up the walls, against the ceiling, and covered by thick wire mesh, its tiny holes themselves clogged and plugged with generations of grime.

We were all awaiting trial. The fact that all such prisoners were deprived of their clothes every time they were locked up in the cells did not make much difference. Naked bodies, or half-naked, only allowed the stench of sweat from close-packed bodies to circulate more freely.

'I know of only one place hotter than this,' said Ahmed the Turk, alleged housebreaker, assaulter and stabber. He smiled, flashing his teeth the colour of ripe corn in his dark handsome face. 'And I don't mean Hell,' he added.

Around us were packed a human salad of accused petty-thieves, gangsters, murderers, rapists, burglars, thugs, drinks, brawlers, dope-peddlars: most of them by no means strangers to the cells, many of them still young, others already depraved, and several old and abandoned, sucking at the disintegrating, bitter cigarette-end of life.

Now and then pandamonium would reign: different men bawling different songs, others howling or talking at the top of their voices, just for the sake of creating an uproar, others quarrelling violently and often fighting. Here and there parties crouched over games of tattered packs of hand-made or smuggled cards, draughts played with scraps of paper or chips of coal as counters on boards scraped on the floor.

Pandemonium would abdicate for a while when the guard reached the cell door on his rounds around the section and shouted through the peephole in the iron-bound door.

I wiped sweat from my face with a forearm and said: 'You were saying something about a place hotter than this.'

'Ja,' replied Ahmed the Turk. 'Wallahi. Truly.'

'And where would that be?' I asked. 'On top of a primus stove?'

'No man,' Ahmed replied. 'In the Italian prisoner-of-war camp by Wadi Huseni in Libya. I was mos there during the War.'

At the other end of the caserne, The Creature, so named after some fantastic and impossible monster of the films, and his gang were persecuting some poor wretch who had arrived that morning. The man, not as smart as others, not able to catch the wire, know the ropes, had been locked up with not even an undershirt on his body. He cringed, stark naked, before The Creature and his henchmen.

The gang-leader, and incidentally cell-head by virtue of his brutality and the backing of equally vicious hangers-on, was pointing at the poor joker's bare chest on which something colourfully gaudy had been tattooed, and snarling above the other noises in the cell: 'Listen, you jubas, there's only one tattoo like that in the whole blerry land, I bet you . . .'

'What's that basket up to?' I asked.

Ahmed the Turk stuck a crippled cigarette-end between his lips and struck a split match expertly on the wall. 'Going to hold a court, I reckon,' he said, blowing smoke. 'Never liked these—prison courts.'

A common occurrence in prisons was the 'trial', by the most brutalized inmates, of some unfortunate who might have raised their ire by bootlicking a guard, or rightly or wrongly accused of giving evidence against, squealing on, his fellow prisoners, or having annoyed them in some other way. Mock courts, much more dangerous than real ones, were held in the cells and 'sentence' meted out.

There had been the 'case' of a prisoner who had given offence to a cell-boss and his gang. It had been said that he had complained of them to a guard, an unforgivable offence. The gangsters 'tried' him, found him guilty and sentenced him to . . . he wasn't told. That, as some sadistic refinement, they kept secret among themselves.

The terrified man died a hundred times before, finally, unable to hold back weariness, he was forced to lie down to sleep. As he lay shivering in some unknown nightmare, a blanket was pressed over his head and face, and a half-dozen knives driven through the one in which he slept.

The next morning the guards found a dead man wrapped in a bloody blanket. No trace of blood on any of the rest of the packed humanity in the cell. There was no sign of a knife. Nobody had a knife, despite searches. The prison inquiry revealed nothing.

'Dammit,' I said, taking what was left of the butt from Ahmed. 'Hell, that rooker just come in. They got nothing on him.'

'Maybe he done something to them outside,' the Turk reckoned. He added, 'There was a court at Wadi Huseni, too.

'Forget them,' he advised, but he was listening to what The Creature was yelling at his gang and the grovelling victim. Then he smiled at me again.

'I was telling you about the P.O.W. camp by Wadi Huseni. Pally, there it was hot. Yellow sand and yellow sky. Man, just sand and sky and some thorn bushes, maybe. And the sun.

'I was in the Coloured Corps, mos, during the War. Lorry driver. Well, some blerry Eyeties supporting the Germans captured us at the time of the Rommel business. So they take us to this camp. A square of barb-wire fence with guards walking round and round it all the time. It was full of men, Aussies, English and others. And the sun, chommy. Burning, boiling, baking, frying, cooking, roasting.

'The Eyeties lived in tents near the prisoners' camp. We, we had no shelter, nothing man. They fixed up a shelter with sailcloth for the sick and wounded. The rest had to do what they could. Understand?'

Ahmed the Turk grinned. 'You call this hot, chommy? Pally, we used to cut slices off the heat, put them on our biscuits and make toast.'

I laughed, and wiped some more moisture from my nose. Ahmed the Turk smiled again and scratched himself under his once-gaudy, now grimy and sweat-stained shirt which he had managed to hang onto since he'd come in. He never got out of that shirt.

The Creature was yelling, '. . . Don't lie you basket . . . We know . . . Hear me. I said somebody chopped my brother, Nails, in the back with a knife . . . In the back, don't I say? . . . Over some blerry goose. Nails' goose, right? . . . The whore . . .'

'The Creature's saying up big likely,' Ahmed the Turk said. 'His brother, Nails. Just a big mouth like The Creature is, he was. But he had a nice girl, anyway.'

'. . . Couldn't say his name before he died . . . But that he had a dragon picked out on his chest, pally . . . a dragon, right? . . . Maybe like the one *you* got.'

'It wasn't me,' the naked prisoner babbled.

'Did you know his brother, Nails?' I asked.

'Yes, man,' Ahmed the Turk replied. 'Seen him around. Nails, tattoos, courts.' He laughed. 'Listen, chommy, it reminds me of that court in Wadi Huseni that time.

'Like I was saying, man, it was hot, hot, hot. Water reshun, one tin cup a day. Hot. Hot. Hot.

'After some time, the water supply runs down and the Eyeties are only handing out half-a-cuppy a day. Man, half-a-cuppy. Food they could keep. Biscuits and sardines. But water, man. Water.'

Ahmed the Turk sighed and flicked a rivulet from his brow. The water bucket in the cell itself had just been emptied of the last mouthful and the crowd around it was growling and snapping like mongrels.

The Creature was laughing. It was he who had collared the last of the water, and he was laughing merrily at the others. Then he turned back to his 'prisoner'.

'. . . Right in the back, hey? . . . Nails said we'd know you by that dragon on your chest . . . Well, we's got you now, pally . . .' He laughed again, the sound coming from his throat like the screeching of a hundred rusty hinges.

'I don't know nothing from it,' the man whispered. 'True as God, ou pal.'

The Creature went on laughing.

'I was telling about the water shortage,' Ahmed resumed. 'Yes, man. Half-a-cuppy a day in the middle of that seven kinds of Hell.'

I said, 'You reckoned the tattoo stuff reminded you of something.'

'I'm coming to that, man,' he said. 'Listen. After a while it got so everybody was getting pretty desperate for water, hey.

'Then some joker comes up with a scheme. He got a pack of cards, old, dirty, cracked, but still a full deck. 'Let's play for the water reshun,' this joker say. 'Half-a-cup of water is the limit, and winner takes the lot. Anybody want to play?'

Ahmed the Turk smiled. 'There was helluva lot of jubas in that camp wasn't going to take any chances with their water in a card game. Understand? No, pally. They stuck to what they had. But there was some other desperate johns willing to take a chance.

'Further, later on there's quite a clump in the game when the Eyeties have handed out the water. Well, somebody's got to win a card game, don't I say? And one of the boys has a merry old time with nearly two pints of water that he wins.

'Next day the joker with the deck is ready for a game again, quick as the water was handed out. Another rooker wins this time.

'Well, pally, for a couple of days different johns are winning water, and a lot of birds lose their rations. But they are still willing to play.

'Then all of sudden, the luck of the joker who owns the deck changes, and he starts to win the whole pot every day, day after day. Oh, he has a time awright. And with all the losers looking on, likely.

'Dammit, he had water so he could use some of it just to pour over his head like a shower bath, mos. And never parted with a drop of water to the other burgs. There are jokers going crazy for an extra drop in that camp. But our friend just has himself a grand time winning water from a lot of squashies.

'Until the other johns start to think about it.'

Ahmed the Turk laughed again and scratched under his shirt. He went on: 'Maybe they start reckoning it's funny for this joker to keep on winning all the time. Further, these johns are getting more and more desperate, having no water.

'So, it happens, after the joker had won another game and is pouring his winnings into a big tin he'd got for the purpose, one of the gang, a big Aussie, say: 'Look, cobber. Let's take a look at the deck, hey?'

'The joker looks up at the Aussie, while he is pouring cups of water into his tin, and reckons: "What deck, hey? What about the deck? What for you want to see the deck? The deck's okay, man."

' "Let's see the deck, cobber," the Aussie says. A big boy, like most of those Aussies are. And everybody else is quiet now, looking at the joker, some of them grinning through their beards and their dusty and broken lips.

'Well, "The hell with you," the joker reckons and starts to get up. The next thing, the Aussie lets go with a fist as big and hard as a brick.'

Ahmed the Turk grinned, showing his teeth, and rubbed his jaw, brushing sweat from it and wiping the moist hand on the front of his shirt. At the other end of the caserne, The Creature and his gang were still worrying the naked man, like a pack of dogs with a rat.

'What about the tattoo marks?' I asked. I was beginning to eye him with suspicion now.

'I'm coming to that, man,' he replied, scowling across to where The Creature and his inquisition were in session. 'That pig . . . Anyway, pally, so this Aussie lets blow with his fist.

'Further, when this joker wakes up, he is flat on his back on the sand with his shirt off, and what's more, he is being held down like that by some of the boys. And looking up, he can see this big Aussie standing over him, smiling and fanning out the deck of cards in his big hands. The joker can't make a move with the men holding him down.

'Then further, the Aussie says: "Cobber, playing with marked decks, hey? Cheating your pals out of water, hey? Well, cobber, we sort of held a court martial right here, in your—er—absence. Well, cobber, the court has found you guilty, and we're about to carry out the sentence, cobber." And the Aussie laughs, likely, and everybody else laughs. Except the card joker, naturally. So they carry out the sentence.'

'What was it?' I asked.

Ahmed the Turk scowled. 'Why, this Aussie has got a kind of a knife made from a six-inch flattened nail. And he uses this to well —not actually to do some tattooing on the joker's chest—but really some carving.

'Ja, man. They write it on his chest with that long nail, deep into the flesh so it would never go away, while he's struggling and screaming: PRIVATE SO-AND-SO, A CHEAT AND A COWARD. And the joker got to carry those words in scars around with him long as he lives.'

I gazed at Ahmed the Turk. Then, 'Jesus,' I said. 'What happened to the joker afterwards?'

Ahmed shrugged. 'He escaped. He couldn't stand it, living among thsoe other P.O.W.'s after that, I reckon. Maybe the basket was collecting that water to get away across the desert, in any case.

'Anyway, soon afterwards, he's gone. Got through the wire

somehow, and gone he is.' Ahmed the Turk paused. 'That's why I said this court of The Creature, and Nails, and tattooing reminded me also of Wadi Huseni.'

'Ahmed,' I asked him. 'What was the joker's name?'

'I forget now.'

He was gazing across the muttering, heaving, writhing tangle of perspiring prisoners to where the gang was holding their 'court'.

'Turk,' I said again to him, quietly. 'I never did, and nobody here ever did see you with your shirt off, have they?' I was looking at his sweat-stained shirt.

He looked back at me and grinned. 'Hell, man. Why should I take it off? Might get pinched. Besides, it isn't as hot here as it was in that Wadi Huseni camp, mos.' He looked again across at the court. 'Never did like these prison trials,' he muttered. Then shouted: 'Creature, you pig! Why don't you leave the poor basket alone? Can't you see he's . . . scared?'

The Creature looked across at us, his mob flanking him, the poor naked john grovelling and crying. Then he laughed and turning away from his victim, began picking a path among the packed prisoners, towards where we squatted. The gang trailed after him, ignoring the naked man. He couldn't get away, could he? The noise in the cell had dropped to an apprehensive mutter.

The Creature made his way across, kicking bodies and legs out of his path, swearing at the impeding jumble of humanity.

He was half naked, wearing a pair of filthy pajama pants, and over it a pair of khaki shorts confiscated from another unfortunate. A ludicruous sight, yet dangerous as a rabid dog. His face was disfigured and reminded one of a tangled knot of rope, with some of the crevices filled in, topped by a blue, badly shaven skull. He came up, sneering with rotten teeth.

Then he stopped, looking at Ahmed the Turk, and laughed.

He said, 'Turk, I been sizing you up a long time, mos, Turk. Ou Turk, you reckon mos you a hardcase.'

Ahmed the Turk laughed at him. The Creature breathed hard into his big chest, and laughed again in return, so that the rope-knot face squirmed and quivered like some hideous jelly.

'Turk,' he went on. 'Turk, somebody chopped my brother, Nails, in the back. Don't I say? Only thing poor ou Nails knew about the juga he had something picked out, tattooed on his chest, man. A dragon, poor ou Nails said.

'Well, Turk, me I been looking for this pig. Don't I say? When I get him, me and my men going to hold court, inside or outside, 'cording to where we get him.'

Ahmed the Turk grinned. 'What the hell it's got to do with me?' There was a lot of sweat on his face, and he wiped it away, leaving a dirty smear.

The Creature eyed him. 'Turk, you been saying up a lot since you come in here . . . Okay, youse a big-shot, mos . . . But I been hearing things around, ou Turk. I been hearing things like you was messing around ou Nails' goose, also. Don't I say? Okay. Awright. Maybe it's just talk, hey?'

He laughed again, and then went on. 'Okay, Turk, youse a big-shot, mos, outside.' Then he repeated more or less, my own recent request of Ahmed the Turk. 'Come to think about it, Turk. Nobody seen you here with that shirt off, hey? Why don't you take off your shirt, Turk? It's mos hot here, man. Don't I say? Or maybe you heard outside there was word around I was looking for a juba with stuff tattooed on his chest. A dragon, maybe, Turk? Why don't we see you with that shirt off, Turk?'

Ahmed the Turk licked moisture from his lips. He said, 'The hell with you.'

'Turk,' The Creature said. 'Turk, my boys can hold you while we pull off the shirt. Just as you like, ou Turk.'

The gang edged nearer, surrounding us. Ahmed the Turk looked at The Creature and then looked at me. His face was moist.

Then he laughed, and pulled himself up from his cramped position.

'Awright, all you baskets,' he sneered, and unbuttoned his shirt.

The Prisoner Who
Wore Glasses

BESSIE HEAD

Scarcely a breath of wind disturbed the stillness of the day and the long rows of cabbages were bright green in the sunlight. Large white clouds drifted slowly across the deep blue sky. Now and then they obscured the sun and caused a chill on the backs of the prisoners who had to work all day long in the cabbage field. This trick the clouds were playing with the sun eventually caused one of the prisoners who wore glasses to stop work, straighten up and peer short-sightedly at them. He was a thin little fellow with a hollowed-out chest and comic knobbly knees. He also had a lot of fanciful ideas because he smiled at the clouds.

'Perhaps they want me to send a message to the children,' he thought, tenderly, noting that the clouds were drifting in the direction of his home some hundred miles away. But before he could frame the message, the warder in charge of his work span shouted: 'Hey, what you tink you're doing, Brille?'

The prisoner swung round, blinking rapidly, yet at the same time sizing up the enemy. He was a new warder, named Jacobus Stephanus Hannetjie. His eyes were the colour of the sky but they were frightening. A simple, primitive, brutal soul gazed out of them. The prisoner bent down quickly and a message was quietly passed down the line: 'We're in for trouble this time, comrades.'

'Why?' rippled back up the line.

'Because he's not human,' the reply rippled down and yet only the crunching of the spades as they turned over the earth disturbed the stillness.

This particular work span was kown as Span One. It was composed of ten men and they were all political prisoners. They were grouped together for convenience as it was one of the prison regulations that no black warder should be in charge of a political prisoner lest this prisoner convert him to the views. It never seemed to occur to the authorities that this very reasoning was the strength of Span One and a clue to the strange terror they aroused in the warders. As political prisoners they were unlike the other prisoners in the sense that they felt no guilt nor were they outcasts of society. All guilty men instinctively cower, which was why it was the kind of prison where men got knocked out cold with a blow at the back of the head from an iron bar. Up until the arrival of Warder Hannetjie, no warder had dared beat any member of Span One and no warder had lasted more than a week with them. The battle was entirely psychological. Span One was assertive and it was beyond the scope of white warders to handle assertive black men. Thus, Span One had got out of control. They were the best thieves and liars in the camp. They lived all day on raw cabbages. They chatted and smoked tobacco. And since they moved, thought and acted as one, they had perfected every technique of group concealment.

Trouble began that very day between Span One and Warder Hannetjie. It was because of the shortsightedness of Brille. That was the nickname he was given in prison and is the Afrikaans word for someone who wears glasses. Brille could never judge the approach of the prison gates and on several previous occasions he had munched on cabbages and dropped them almost at the feet of the warder and all previous warders has overlooked this. Not so Warder Hannetjie.

'Who dropped that cabbage?' he thundered.

Brille stepped out of line.

'I did,' he said meekly.

'All right,' said Hannetjie. 'The whole Span goes three meals off.'

'But I told you I did it,' Brille protested.

The blood rushed to Warder Hannetjie's face.

'Look 'ere,' he said. 'I don't take orders from a kaffir. I don't know what kind of kaffir you tink you are. Why don't you say Baas. I'm your Baas. Why don't you say Baas, hey?'

Brille blinked his eyes rapidly but by contrast his voice was strangely calm.

'I'm twenty years older than you,' he said. It was the first thing that came to mind but the comrades seemed to think it a huge joke. A titter swept up the line. The next thing Warder Hannetjie whipped out a knobkerrie and gave Brille several blows about the head. What surprised his comrades was the speed with which Brille had removed his glasses or else they would have been smashed to pieces on the ground.

That evening in the cell Brille was very apologetic.

'I'm sorry, comrades,' he said. 'I've put you into a hell of a mess.'

'Never mind, brother,' they said. 'What happens to one of us, happens to all.'

'I'll try to make up for it, comrades,' he said. I'll steal something so that you don't go hungry.'

Privately, Brille was very philosophical about his head wounds. It was the first time an act of violence had been perpetrated against him but he had long been a witness of extreme, almost unbelievable human brutality. He had twelve children and his mind travelled back that evening through the sixteen years of bedlam in which he had lived. It had all happened in a small drab little three-bedroomed house in a small drab little street in the Eastern Cape and the children kept coming year after year because neither he nor Martha ever managed the contraceptives the right way and a teacher's salary never allowed moving to a bigger house and he was always taking exams to improve his salary only to have it all eaten up by hungry mouths. Everything was pretty horrible, especially the way the children fought. They'd get hold of each other's heads and give them a good bashing against the wall. Martha gave up something along the line so they worked out a thing between them. The bashings, biting and blood were to operate in full swing until he came home. He was to be the bogey-man and when it worked he never failed to have a sense of godhead at the way in which his presence could change savages into fairly reasonable human beings.

Yet somehow it was this chaos and mismanagement at the centre of his life that drove him into politics. It was really an ordered beautiful world with just a few basic slogans to learn along with the rights of mankind. At one stage, before things became very bad, there were conferences to attend, all very far away from home.

'Let's face it,' he thought ruefully. 'I'm only learning right now what it means to be a politician. All this while I've been running away from Martha and the kids.'

And the pain in his head brought a hard lump to his throat. That was what the children did to each other daily and Martha wasn't managing and if Werder Hannetjie had not interrupted him that morning he would have sent the following message: 'Be good comrades, my children. Co-operate, then life will run smoothly.'

The next day Warder Hannetjie caught this old man of twelve children stealing grapes from the farm shed. They were an enormous quantity of grapes in a ten gallon tin and for this misdeed the old man spent a week in the isolation cell. In fact, Span One as a whole was in constant trouble. Warder Hannetjie seemed to have eyes at the back of his head. He uncovered the trick about the cabbages, how they were split in two with the spade and immediately covered with earth and then unearthed again and eaten with split-second timing. He found out how tobacco smoke was beaten into the ground and he found out how conversations were whispered down the wind.

For about two weeks Span One lived in acute misery. The cabbages, tobacco and conversations had been the pivot of jail life to them. Then one evening they noticed that their good old comrade who wore the glasses was looking rather pleased with himself. He pulled out a four ounce packet of tobacco by way of explanation and the comrades fell upon it with great greed. Brille merely smiled. After all, he was the father of many children. But when the last shred had disappeared, it occurred to the comrades that they ought to be puzzled. Someone said: 'I say, brother. We're watched like hawks these days. Where did you get the tobacco?'

'Hannetjie gave it to me,' said Brille.

There was a long silence. Into it dropped a quiet bombshell.

'I saw Hannetjie in the shed today,' and the failing eyesight blinked rapidly. 'I caught him in the act of stealing five bags of fertilizer and he bribed me to keep my mouth shut.'

There was another long silence.

'Prison is an evil life,' Brille continued, apparently discussing some irrelevant matter. 'It makes a man contemplate all kinds of evil deeds.'

He held out his hand and closed it.

'You know, comrades,' he said. 'I've got Hannetjie. I'll betray him tomorrow.'

Everyone began talking at once.

'Forget it, brother. You'll get shot.'

Brille laughed.

'I won't, he said. 'That is what I mean about evil. I am a father of children and I saw today that Hannetjie is just a child and stupidly truthful. I'm going to punish him severely because we need a good warder.'

The following day, with Brille as witness, Hannetjie confessed to the theft of the fertilizer and was fined a large sum of money. From then on Span One did very much as they pleased while

Warden Hannetjie stood by and said nothing. But it was Brille who carried this to extremes. One day, at the close of work Warder Hannetjie said: 'Brille, pick up my jacket and carry it back to the camp.'

'But nothing in the regulations says I'm your servant, Hannetjie,' Brille replied coolly.

'I've told you not to call me Hannetjie. You must say Baas,' but Warder Hannetjie's voice lacked conviction. In turn, Brille squinted up at him.

'I'll tell you something about this Baas business, Hannetjie,' he said. 'One of these days we are going to run the country. You are going to clean my car. Now, I have a fifteen year old son and I'd die of shame if you had to tell him that I ever called you Baas.'

Warder Hannetjie went red in the face and picked up his coat.

On another occasion Brille was seen to be walking about the prison yard, openly smoking tobacco. On being taken before the prison commander he claimed to have received the tobacco from Warder Hannetjie. All throughout the tirade from his chief, Warder Hannetjie failed to defend himself but his nerve broke completely. He called Brille to one side.

'Brille,' he said. 'This thing between you and me must end. You may not know it but I have a wife and children and you're driving me to suicide.'

'Why don't you like your own medicine, Hannetjie?' Brille asked quietly.

'I can give you anything you want, Warder Hannetjie said in desperation.

'It's not only me but the whole of Span One,' said Brille, cunningly 'The whole of Span One wants something from you.'

Warder Hannetjie brightened with relief.

'I think I can manage if it's tobacco you want,' he said.

Brille looked at him, for the first time struck with pity, and guilt. He wondered if he had carried the whole business too far. The man was really a child.

'It's not tobacco we want, but you,' he said. 'We want you on our side. We want a good warder because without a good warder we won't be able to manage the long stretch ahead.'

Warder Hannetjie interpreted this request in his own fashion and his interpretation of what was good and human often left the prisoners of Span One speechless with surprise. He had a way of slipping off his revolver and picking up a spade and digging along-side Span One. He had a way of producing unheard of luxuries likd boiled eggs from his farm nearby and things like cigarettes, and Span One responded nobly and got the reputation of being the best work span in the camp. And it wasn't only take from their side. They were awfully good at stealing certain commodities like fertilizer which were needed on the farm of Warder Hannetjie.

Riva

RICHARD RIVE

A cold, misty July afternoon about twenty years ago. I first met Riva Lipschitz under the most unusual circumstances. At that time I was a first year student majoring in English at University, one of the rare Coloured students then enrolled at Cape Town. When I first saw her Riva's age seemed indefinable. Late thirties? Forty perhaps? Certainly more than twenty years older than I was. The place we met in was as unusual as her appearance. The Rangers' hut at the top of Table Mountain near the Hely Hutchinson Reservoir, three thousand feet above Cape Town.

George, Leonard and I had been climbing all day. George was talkative, an extrovert, given to clowning. Leonard was his exact opposite, shy and introspective. We had gone through High School together but after matriculating they had gone to work while I had won a scholarship which enabled me to proceed to University. We had been climbing without rest all afternoon, scrambling over rugged rocks damp with bracken and heavy with mist. Twice we were lost on the path from India Ravine through Echo Valley. Now soaking wet and tired we were finally in the vicinity of the Rangers' hut where we knew we would find shelter and warmth. Some ranger or other would be off duty and keep the fire warm and going. Someone with a sense of humour had called the hut *At Last*. It couldn't be the rangers for they never spoke English. On the way we passed the hut belonging to the white Mountain Club, and slightly below that was another hut reserved for members of the Coloured Club. I made some remark about the White club house and the fact that prejudice had permeated even to the top of Table Mountain.

'For that matter we would not even be allowed into the Coloured Mountain Club hut,' George remarked, serious for once.

'And why not?'

'Because, dear brother Paul, to get in you can't only be Coloured, but you must also be not too Coloured. You must have the right complexion, the right sort of hair, the right address and speak the right sort of Walmer Estate English.'

'You mean I might not make it?'

74

'I mean exactly that.'

I made rapid mental calculations. I was rather dark, had short, curly hair, came from Caledon Street in District Six, but spoke English reasonably well. After all I was majoring in it at a White University. What more could one want?

'I'm sure that at a pinch I could make it,' I teased George. 'I speak English beautifully and am educated well beyond my intelligence.'

'My dear Paul, it won't help. You are far too Coloured, University of Cape Town and all. You are far, far too brown. And in addition you have a lousy address.'

I collapsed in mock horror. 'You can't hold all that against me.'

Leonard grinned. He was not one for saying much.

We trudged on, instinctively skirting both club huts as widely as possible, until we reached *At Last*, which was ten minutes slogging away, just over the next ridge. A large main room with a very welcome fire going int the cast-iron stove. How the hell did they get that stove up there when our haversacks felt like lead? Running off the main room were two tiny bedrooms belonging to each of the rangers. We removed damp haversacks and sleeping bags then took off damp boots and stockings. Both rangers were off duty and made room for us at the fire. They were small, wiry Plattelanders; a hard breed of men with wide-eyed, yellow faces, short hair and high cheekbones. They spoke a pleasant, soft, gutteral Afrikaans with a distinct Malmesbury brogue, and broke into easy laughter especially when they tried to speak English. The smell of warming bodies filled the room and steam rose from our wet shirts and shorts. It became uncomfortably hot and I felt sleepy, so decided to retire to one of the bedrooms, crawl into my bag and read myself to sleep. I lit a lantern and quietly left the group. George was teasing the rangers and insisting that they speak English. I was reading a novel about the massacre in the ravines of Babi Yar, gripping and revolting; a bit out of place in the unnatural calm at the top of a cold, wet mountain. I was beginning to doze off comfortably when the main door of the hut burst open and a blast of cold air swept through the entire place, almost extinguishing the lantern. Before I could shout anything there were loud protests from the main room. The door slammed shut again and then followed what sounded like a muffled apology. A long pause, then I made out George saying something. There was a short snort which was followed by peals of loud, uncontrolled laughter. I felt it was uncanny. The snort, then the rumbling laughter growing in intensity, then stopping abruptly.

By now I was wide away and curious to know to whom the laugh belonged, though far too self-conscious to join the group immediately. I strained to hear scraps of conversation. Now and then I could make out George's voice and the low, soft Afrikaans of the rangers. There was also another voice which sounded feminine, but nevertheless harsh and screechy. My curiosity was getting the better of me. I climbed out of the sleeping bag and as unobtrusively as possible joined the group around the fire. The newcomer was a gaunt, angular White woman, extremely unattractive, looking incongruous in heavy, ill-fitting mountaineering clothes. She was the centre of the discussion and enjoying it. She was in the middle of making a point when she spotted me. Her finger remained poised in midair.

'And who may I ask is that?' She stared at me. I looked back into her hard, expressionless grey eyes.

'Will someone answer me?'

'Who?' George asked grinning at my obvious discomfit.

'Him. That's who.'

'Oh him?' George laughed. 'He's Paul. He's the greatest literary genius the Coloured people have produced this decade. He's written a poem.'

'How exciting,' she dismissed me. The others laughed. They were obviously under her spell. 'Let me introduce you. This is Professor Paul. First year B.A., University of Cape Town.'

'Cut it out,' I said very annoyed at him. George ignored my remark.

'And you are? I have already forgotten.'

She made a mock, ludicrous bow. 'Riva Lipschitz. Madame Riva Lipschitz. The greatest Jewish watch-repairer and mountaineer in Cape Town. Display shop, 352 Long Street.'

'Alright, you've made your point. Professor Paul — Madame Riva Lipschitz.'

I mumbled a greeting, keeping well in the background. I was determined not to participate in any conversation. I found George's flattering her loathsome. The bantering continued to the amusement of the two rangers. Leonard smiled sympathetically at me. I remained poker-faced waiting for an opportunity when I could slip away. George made some amusing remark (I was not listening) and Riva snorted and started to laugh. So that was where it came from. She saw the look of surprise on my face and stopped abruptly.

'What's wrong, Professor? Don't you like the way I laugh?'

'I'm sorry, I wasn't even thinking of it.'

'It makes no difference whether you were or not. Nevertheless I hate being ignored. If the others can treat me with the respect due to me, why can't you? I'm like a queen am I not George?'

I wasn't sure whether she was serious or not.

'You certainly are like a queen.'

'Everyone loves me except the Professor. Maybe he thinks too much..'

'Maybe he thinks too much of himself,' George added.

She snorted and started to laugh at his witticism. George glowed with pride. I took in her ridiculous figure and dress. She was wearing a little knitted skullcap, far too small for her, from which wisps of mousey hair were sticking. A thin face, hard around the mouth and grey eyes, with a large nose I had seen in caricatures of Jews. She seemed flat-chested under her thick jersey which ran down to incredible stick-thin legs stuck into heavy woolen stockings and heavily studded climbing boots.

'Come on, Paul, be nice to Riva,' George encouraged.

'Madame Riva Lipschitz, thank you. Don't you think I look like a queen, Professor?'

I maintained my frigid silence.

'Your Professor obviously does not seem over-friendly. Don't you like Whites, Professor? I like everyone. I came over specially to be friendly with you people..'

'Whom are you referring to as *you people*?' I was getting angry. She seemed temporarily thrown off her guard at my reaction but immediately controlled herslef and broke into a snort.

'The professor is extremely sensitive. You should have warned me. He doesn't like me but we shall remain friends all the same; won't we, Professor?'

She shot out her hand for me to kiss. I ignored it. She turned back to George and the rest of her stay pretented I was not present. When everyone was busy talking I slipped out quietly and returned to the bedroom.

Although falling asleep, I could pick up scraps of conversation. George seemed to be explaining away my reaction, playing the clown to her queen. Then they forgot all about me. I must have dozed off for I awoke suddenly to find someone shaking my shoulder. It was Leonard.

'Would you like to come with us?.'

'Where to?.'

'Riva's Mountain Club hut. She's invited us over for coffee, and to meet Simon, whoever he is.'

'No, I don't think I'll go..'

'You mustn't take her too seriously.'

'I don't. Only I don't like her type and the way George is playing up to her. Who the hell does she think she is, after all? What does she want with us?.'

'I really don't know. You heard she said she was a watch-repairer somewhere in Long Street. Be reasonable, Paul. She's just trying to be friendly.'

'While playing the bloody queen? Whom does she think she is because she's White.'

'Don't be like that. Come along with us. She's just another person.'

George appeared grinning widely. He attempted an immitation of Riva's snort.

'You coming or not?' he asked laughing. For that moment I diskliked him intensely.

'I'm certainly not.' I rolled over in my bag to sleep.

'Allright, if that's how you feel.'

I heard Riva calling for him, then after a time she shouted 'Goodbye, Professor, see you again some time.' Then she snorted and they went laughing out at the door. The rangers were speaking softly and I joined them around the fire then fell asleep there. I dreamt of Riva striding with heavy, impatient boots and thin-stick legs over mountains of dead bodies in the ravines of Babi Yar. She was snorting and laughing while pushing bodies aside, climbing ever upwards over dead arms and legs.

It must have been much later when I awoke to the door's opening and a stream of cold air rushing into the room. The fire had died down and the rangers were sleeping in their rooms. George and Leonard were stomping and beating the cold out of their bodies.

'You awake, Paul?' George shouted. Leonard shook me gently.

'What scared you?' George asked, 'Why didn't you come and have coffee with the queen of Table Mountain?'

'I can't stand her type. I wonder how you can.'

'Come off it, Paul. She's great fun.' George attempted a snort and then collapsed with laughter.

'Shut up, you fool. You'll wake up the rangers. What the hell did she want here?'

George sat up, tears running down his cheeks. He spluttered and it produced more laughter. 'She was just being friendly, dear brother Paul, just being friendly. Fraternal greetings from her Mountain club.'

'Her White Mountain club?'

'Well yes, if you put it that way, her White Mountain club. She could hardly join the Coloured one, now, could she? Wrong hair, wrong address, wrong laugh.'

'I don't care where she goes as long you keep her away from me. I have no need to play up to Jews and Whites.'

'Now really, Paul,' George seemed hurt. 'Are you anti-Semitic as well as being anti-White?' My remark must have hit home.

'No, I'm only anti-Riva Lipschitz.'

'Well anyhow, I like the way she laughs.' He attempted another imitation, but when he started to snort he choked and collapsed to the floor coughing and spluttering. I rolled over in my bag to sleep.

Three months later I was in the vicinity of Upper Long Street. George worked there as clerk at a furniture store in Bree Street. I had been busy with an assignment in the Hiddingh Hall library and had finished earlier than expected. I had not seen him since we had last gone mountaineering, so strolled across to the place where he worked. I wanted to ask about himself, what he had been doing since last we met, about Riva. A senior clerk told me that he had not come in that day. I wandered around aimlessly, at a loss what to do next. I peered into second-hand shops without any real interest. It was late afternoon on a dull, overcast day and it was rapidly getting darker with the promise of rain in the air. Upper Long Street and its surrounding lanes seemed more depressing, more beaten up than the rest of the city. Even more so than District Six. Victorian double-storied buildings containing mean shops on the ground floors spilled over into mean-side streets and lanes. To catch a bus home meant walking all the way down to the bottom of Adderley Street. I might as well walk all the way back. Caledon

Street, the noise, dirty and squalor. My mood was as depressing as my immediate surroundings. I did not wish to stay where I was and at the same time did not wish to go home immediately. What was the number she had said? 352 or 325? I peered through the windows of second-hand bookshops without any wish to go inside and browse. 352, yes that was it. Or 325? In any case I had no money to buy books even if I had the inclination to do so. Had George been at work he might have been able to shake me out of this mood, raise my spirits.

I was now past the swimming baths. A dirty fly-spotted delicatessen store. There was no number on the door, but the name was boldly displayed. *Madeira Fruiters*. Must be owned by some homesick Portuguese. Next to it what seemed like a dark and dingy watchmaker's. *Lipschitz — Master Jewellers*. This must be it. I decided to enter. A shabby, squat, balding man adjusted an eye-piece he was wearing and looked up from a work-bench cluttered with assorted, broken watches.

'Excuse me, are you Mr. Lipschitz?' I wondered whether I should add 'Master-Jeweller'.

'What exactly do you want?' He had not answered my question. 'What can I do for you?' His accent was gutteral and foreign. I thought of Babi Yar. I was about to apologise and say that I had made some mistake when from the far side of the shop came an unmistakable snort.

'My goodness, if it isn't the Professor?' and then the familiar laugh. Riva came from behind a counter. My eyes had become accustomed to the gloomy interior. The squat man was working form the light filtering in thrugh a dirty window. Rickety showcases and counters cluttered with watches and cheap trinkets. A cat-bin, still wet and smelling pungently stood against the far counter.

'What brings the Professor here? Coming to visit me?' She nodded to the squat man indicating that all was in order. He had already shoved back his eye piece and was immersed in his work.

'Come to visit the queen?'

This was absurd. I could not imagine anything less regal, more incongruous. Riva, a queen. As gaunt as she had looked in the Ranger's hut. Now wearing an unattractive blouse and old-fashioned skirt. Her face as narrow, strained and unattractive as ever. I had to say something, explain my presence.

'I was just passing.'

'That's what they all say. George said so last time.'

What the hell did that mean? I started to feel uncomfortable. She looked at me almost coyly. Then she turned to the squat man.

'Simon. I think I'll pack up now. I have a visitor.' He showed no sign that he had heard her. She took a shabby coat from a hook.

'Will you be late tonight?' she asked him. Simon grumbled some unintelligible reply. Was this Simon whom George and Leonard had met? Simon the mountaineer? He looked most unlike a mountaineer. Who the hell was he then? Her boss? Husband? Lover? Lipschitz — the Master Jeweller? Or was she Lipschitz, the Master Jeweller? That seemed most likely. Riva nodded to me to follow. I did so as there was no alternative. Outside it was dark already.

'I live two blocks down. Come along and have some tea.' She did not wait for a reply but began walking briskly, taking long strides. I followed as best I could a pace behind.

'Walk next to me,' she almost commanded. I did so. Why was I going with her? The last thing I wanted was tea.

'Nasty weather,' she said. 'Bad for climbing. 'Table Mountain was wrapped in a dark mist. It was obviously ridiculous for anyone to climb at five o'clock on a weekday afternoon in heavy weather like this. Nobody would be crazy enough. Except George perhaps.

'George,' she said as if reading my thoughts. 'George. What was the other one's name?'

'Leonard..'

'Oh yes, Leonard, I haven't seen him since the mountain. How is he getting on?' I was panting to keep up with her. 'I don't see much of them except when we go climbing together. Leonard works in Epping and George is in Bree Street.'

'I know about George.' How the hell did she?

'I've come from his work. I wanted to see him but he hasn't come in today.'

'Yes, I knew he wouldn't be in . So you came to see me instead? I somehow knew that one day you would put in an appearance.'

How the hell did she know? Was she in contact with George? I remained quiet, out of breath with the effort of keeping up with her. What on earth made me go into the shop of Lipschitz — Master Jeweller? Who the hell was Lipschitz — Master Jeweller?

The conversation had stopped. She continued the brisk pace, taking her fast, incongruous strides. Like stepping from rock to rock up Blinkwater Ravine, or Babi Yar.

'Here we are.' She stopped abruptly in front of an old triple-storied Victorian building with brown paint peeling off its walls. On the upper floors were wide balconies ringed with wrought-iron gates. The main entrance was cluttered with spilling refuse bins.

'I'm on the first floor.'

We mounted a rickety staircase, then a landing and long, dark passage lit at intervals by a solitary electric bulb. All the doors, where these could be made out, looked alike. Riva stopped before one and rummaged in her bag for a key. Next to the door was a cat litter smelling sharply. The same cat?

'Here we are.' She unlocked the door, entered and switching on alight. I was hesitant about following her inside.

'It's quite safe, I won't rape you,' she snorted. This was a coarse remark. I waited for her to laugh but she did not. I entered, blinking my eyes. Large, high-ceilinged, cavernous bed-sitter with a kitchen and toilet running off it. The room was gloomy and dusty. A double-bed, round table, two uncomfortable-looking chairs and a dressing table covered with bric-a-brac. There was a heavy smell of mildew permeating everything. The whole building smelt of mildew. Why a double-bed? For her alone or Simon and herself?

'You live here?' It was a silly question and I knew it. I wanted to ask 'You live here alone or does Simon live here also?' Why should I bother about Simon?

'Yes, I live here. Have a seat. The bed's more comfortable to sit on.' I chose one of the chairs. It creaked as I settled into it. All the furniture must have been bought from second-hand junk shops. Or maybe it came with the room. Nothing was modern. Jewish, Victorian, or what I imagined Jewish Victorian to be. Dickensian in a sort of decaying nineteenth century way. Riva took off her coat. She was all bustle.

'Let's have some tea. I'll put on the water.' Before I could refuse she disappeared into the kitchen. I must leave now. The surroundings were far too depressing. Riva was far too depressing. I remained as if glued to my seat. She reappeared. Now to make my apologies. I spoke as delicately as I could, but it came out all wrongly.

'I'm very sorry, but I won't be able to stay for tea. You see, I really can't stay. I must get home. I have lot of work to do. An exam tomorrow. Social Anthropology.'

'The trouble with you, Professor, is that you are far too clever,

82

but not clever enough.' She sounded annoyed. 'Maybe you work too hard, far too hard. Have some tea before you go.' There was a twinkle in her eye again. 'Or are you afraid of me?'

I held my breath, expecting her to laugh but she did not. A long pause.

'No', I said at last, 'No, I'm not afraid of you. I really do have an exam tomorrow. You must believe me. I was on my way home. I was hoping to see George.'

'Yes, I know, and he wasn't at work. You've said so before.'

'I really must leave now.'

'Without first having tea? That would be anti-social. An intellectual like you should know that.'

'But I don't want any tea, thanks.' The conversation was going around in meaningless circles. Why the hell could I not go if I wished to?

'You really are afraid of me. I can see that.'

'I must go.'

'And not have tea with the queen? Is it because I'm White? Or Jewish? Or because I live in a room like this?'

I wanted to say 'It's because you're you. Why can't you leave me alone?' I got up determined to leave.

'Why did you come with me in the first place?'

This was an unfair question. I had not asked to come along. There was a hiss from the kitchen where the water was boiling over onto the plate.

'I don't know why I came. Maybe it was because you asked me.'

'You could have refused.'

'I tried to.'

'Look, I'm going now. I have overstayed my time.'

'Just a second.' She disappeared into the kitchen. I could hear her switching off the stove then the clinking of cups. I stood at the door waiting for her to appear before leaving.

She entered with a tray containing the tea things and a plate with some assorted biscuits.

'No thank you,' I said determined that nothing would keep me, 'I said I was leaving and I am.'

She put the tray on the table. 'All-right then, Professor. If you must then you must. Don't let me keep you any longer.' She looked almost pathetic that moment, staring dejectedly at the tray. This was not the Riva I knew. She was straining to control herself. I felt dirty, sordid, sorry for her.

'Goodbye,' I said hastily and hurried out into the passage. I bumped into someone. Simon looked up surprised, then mumbled some excuse. He looked at me puzzled and then entered the room.

As I swiftly ran down the stairs I heard her snorting. Short pause and then peals of uncontrollable laughter. I stumbled out into Long Street.

Hungry Flames

J. ARTHUR MAIMANE

The sun was hot. The air was still in the mid-day torpor that hangs over Johannesburg on a December day. There was a dull rumbling from beyond the rusted corrugated iron wall, punctuated by strident car hooters and the wailing of tortured tyres as motorists weaved their way through the mass of jay-walkers hurrying to the beerhall across the street.

He shifted his weight: the iron wall he was leaning against burnt through a new part of his worn-out sleeve; a bit hotter where there was a hole in the sleeve.

'Come on, Sonny! Gimme a piece of your meat.'

The eyes had given up pleading years ago. But not the voice—at least, not completely.

'Naw. Go get your own.' A voice that should still be innocent grunted round a mouthful of fried meat. 'Have I got to do your stealing for you, now?'

Two other boys of the same age, who sat a little apart—one chewing a cob of yellow mealies, and another at a big, bluish sweet potato—snickered.

Boy looked over their small, unwashed heads, towards the dusty, toasting football pitch. His eyes came back to Sonny.

The hollow hurt in his stomach grew the longer he looked at the rhythmic movement of Sonny's jaws. He hadn't eaten since the night before. And today something had gone wrong. He had failed with all the pedlars who sold flyblown meat, peeling corn-cobs and all other kinds of foods, to the beerhall patrons across the street.

Maybe it was because he was hungrier than usual. Anyway, he had failed—his timing had been bad. And now his pals—some of whom had managed to get their lunch by making use of the diversion he created in his unsuccessful attempts to steal—wouldn't give him a bite.

'Please, Sonny?'

'Naw!'

'But you always give me?'

'Not today.'

'I'm really hungry.'

'Me too.'

The eyes that couldn't plead anymore were moistening.

'I'm your pal, Sonny?'

'Not when I'm really hungry.'

Boy—they called him Boy because nobody had ever bothered to ask him his real name, and he had almost forgotten it—fingered the bottle in his pocket.

Benzine. He could sprinkle some on his dirty shirt sleeve and take a few whiffs. He'd forget his misery then.

The thought made his empty stomach turn, with revulsion. He was too hungry for that. Maybe after he had eaten . . .

The pain in his stomach was getting so bad he couldn't stand up straight anymore—even with the support of the corrugated iron wall. He was getting dizzy, and there was a thin screeching in his ears.

The film over his eyes was blurring his vision.

'Damn them! Damn my mother—and my father too. And damn my mother's man—and my father's woman, too!'

His friends looked up politely.

The 13-year old voice cursed on, heaping all the curses it had ever heard on its parents and anybody else connected with them, including the parents who bore them.

It had taken almost five years to bring him to this.

It had started with his mother's fist gallon of Hops—that is, the first she drank. It was one of the many concoctions brewed in Johannesburg townships and hidden in a hole to keep it safe from the police and make it ferment faster—that's the amount she had to drink, then, to get drunk. She still had resistance.

The amount had shrunk with every week-end, all night 'party'. And she had wanted to get drunk more often with every beating his father had given her when she staggered into the smoky shelter they called a home below the Orlando railway lines.

And her stubbornness had increased. To the point where she fought back when his father beat her. A drunk woman and a drunk man fighting: breaking the few sticks of furniture in the room, wrenching the drunken door further off its hinges and then plunging into the ever-present mud puddle at the door-step.

Hitting, swearing, scratching and tearing. Neighbours looking on. Passers-by stepping over the muddy, struggling, half naked bodies. Till somebody separated them. Or they were too tired to fight on. Or even get up.

Then night would close in and the maudling reconciliations would begin, punctuated by the hoarse squeaking of the rusty bed springs. Developing to grunts, moans and heavy breathing.

Then quiet. And sleep. A dark void.

His mind had adjusted itself. He had long stopped whimpering in a corner when they fought. And no longer listened with wonder to the groans, moans, and heavy breathing.

Then his father had started staying out nights. There were curse-laden quarrels and more fights, when he returned.

And then the men had started drifting in. They would come in late. When she was sure his father wouldn't come back that night.

Then he had started staying away for weeks. And the men had come in earlier.

There was the man with the ragged beard and scarred face, who had been so impatient. First the liquor then the pawing. At first she had refused. 'Wait', she would say, 'Let the boy sleep first.' But the Hops had been too strong for her, and she had surrendered before her son's puzzled eyes.

And the moans and heavy breathing had followed—right in front of him, with enough light from the flickering candle for him to see it all.

He had cried himself to sleep the first night. That was the last time he allowed himself to cry.

There was the day his father had come back after two weeks. There had been a regular man in the house for the last ten days, and his father had found him lying on the bed.

That had been a fight! All three were sober.

His father, with puffed lips and a swelling eye, had blindly packed his clothes and left.

He would never live with a loose woman, his father had sworn to the neighbours.

And she would never live with a man who had other women away from home, she had screamed at him.

The next morning his mother had told him to call the 'regular' father.

He refused. He was beaten.

It was the first of many beatings. But he refused to cry. That angered his mother more.

The beatings had gone on until he had decided in desperation to run away and search for his father. He had heard—when the women living in the same lane shouted their gossip at the communal tap—that his father was in George Goch. Living with another woman.

Where is George Goch? he had asked the older boys.

You take the train to the city. Then you take another one. You get off at George Goch—the other side of the city.

He had done it. Sonnyboy, who lived in the next shanty and sold sweets on the trains, had guided him.

His friends left him at the little station called George Goch with many trains rumbling around him. Where is George Goch—the location? Over the bridge, boy, and across the street—but look out for the cars. You will walk down the road. You will see it. Go in through the gate.

He got there.

Where is my father? Who is your father? Johannes. What is his surname? I don't know. Where you come from? Orlando Shelters. Poor boy.

He wandered up and down the narrow streets, flanked by match-box houses that had similar grim expressions on their identical dirty faces. They seemed to cringe behind the many fruit trees crowded in the stamp-sized yards.

You could get lost here. The houses, the streets—and even the trees—look the same.

Can you give me a piece of bread, Mother?

Go away!

Can you please give me a piece of bread, Mother?

Whose child are you?

Can you please, please give me a piece of bread, Mother?

Here—and go away!

Can you please, please give me a piece of meat, Mother?

You'll have to work for it, boy.

I will, Mother—very hard.

Come in.

Big, evil-smelling drums. Wash them all, boy. And fast. They must be ready in the evening for the brewing.

I wonder if she brews hops?

When the sun set, he was standing inside the gate to the fenced-in location. The only entrance, he had been told. Hundreds of men and women streamed in. He didn't see his father.

Back to the huge dirty woman with bigger and dirtier drums.

If I work some more for you Mother, can I get more food and a place to sleep?

Yes.

Saturday and Sunday—when he managed to get away from the drums as enough had been brewed—he looked into every face, searching in every noisy yard. He had given up asking.

He saw him the next Saturday night. He could have seen him earlier, if it wasn't so dark in the backyard where the men were drinking, laughing and shouting at each other.

He had to tug him hard by the sleeve before he was noticed.

Dull, vacant eyes turned on him.

'Whatchu want, boy?'

'You know me, Father?'

A long, red-eyed look; a belch from a stomach-full of foul-smelling beer.

'You my son?'

'Yes, Father.' He giggled. 'I have been looking for you—for . . . many days now!'

'Good boy!' An arm around his neck, squeezing his breath out of him. 'You see this little boy, Kumalo? My son! Not seen him long time. Come all the way from Orlando to look for his father. Good boy. Knows his mother is a no-good bitch who puts any man who can buy her drink in my bed.'

He belched again, and the boy surreptitiously put his hand over his mouth and nose.

'Your father will take you home—my home! Don't you worry. Take you to your new mother. Nice woman—see your little sister.'

New Mother. Last time it was a new Father. Trepidation grabbed his stomach with a hard, icy hand—and twisted.

Maybe she won't want me to call her mother. Maybe I'll like her and call her mother.

He helped his father down the streets; shadows long before them as they walked out of the circle of a street light, shortening to a round blob as they entered the circle of the next. Then long shadows again; in front now. Then shorter. And then the blobs.

They turned into a gate. Round to the back. A tin shanty near the back fence. Heavy knock on the low door.

'Who's there?'

'Me!' A pause.

Rattle of a turning key; squeak of the opening door; a shaft of light.

Tiny room. Crowded with a double bed, elevated on bricks; wardrobe with a broken full-length mirror; big oval table and six chairs; sofa and stove. Hot and stuffy. A crying child, perched on a woman's tilted hip.

'You're drunk again. Who is the dirty little boy?'

'Boy . . . dirty? Oh! Yes. My son. Come all the way from Orlando to be with his father.'

'You mean . . . he's coming to stay here?'

'Of course! He's my son, isn't he?'

He stayed there three months. Then he left. Nobody had asked him to call the woman 'mother'. But he had done it.

'You happy, my boy? Like your father's new home, eh? And your new mother. Fine woman. Not like that bitch in Orlando. She . . .'

'She's my mother. Don't say such things about her!'

'Ha! You talk back like that to your father?'

'You talk like that about my mother?'

'Ha!'

Nobody talked much to him. He got his food two times a day, the sofa to sleep on, and nothing else. He wanted more; he wanted a home, not a house to sleep and eat in.

'Carry your bag, missus?'

'Boy. Don't beg here! Don't you know this is not allowed here?'

'Not begging. Want to earn money for bread.'

'You talk back? I arrest . . .'

He was gone, dodging through the thick Saturday morning market crowds.

The small of freshly fried meat hung in the still, hot air, keeping aloof from the many other smells. It made him hungry and faint.

The heavy, moist smell of fermented beer from beyond the red-painted corrugated iron wall tried to push him away. But the sharp, salty smell of frying meat on the coal braziers and on the row of tables below the iron wall backoned at him.

How long have I been standing here? Won't somebody give me just a tiny bit of meat to take away the dryness in the mouth? And choke the hurt in my stomach.

'Come here!'

He looked around. The little boy was thin. Hungry, like me. His head seemed too big for his scrawny neck. The eyes were deep and bright, with a furtive question behind them.

'What is it?'

'Hungry?'

'Yes.'

'Come.'

Over the street, and along the railway line, skirting a rusted, flaking corrugated iron wall. A group of boys squatting in the sun. Smoking.

'Where you come from?'

'Orlando and George Goch.'

'Hungry? Want to join us and steal food?'

'Yes. Food.'

'He's afraid! Sissy.'

'You afraid?'

'Yes . . . no!'

'Take this, give you pluck.'

Dirty little balled up rag; smelling of benzine.

'Put it in your mouth—and pull!'

The fumes seared his dry throat, twisted his guts, and made him cough.

He fell on his knees and tried to vomit. Only a lonely, ragged ribbon of foamy saliva hung from his lower lip, waving in the breeze like a tired banner.

'Ha-ha-ha-ha-ha! Sissy!'

'Naw; he's too hungry. Time to get lunch anyway. You stick here, boy. Back soon—with food.'

He lay there on the knotty tufts of turf that seemed to press right through his empty stomach to his spine. His mouth hung open. Trying to vomit again. Nothing. He had to blow three times before the banner of saliva fell down. He spat. Nothing.

Shouts and curses from the direction of the food-laden tables outside the beerhall. Scurrying feet and hoarse snickers.

They were squatting round him.

'Here, eat.'

'Where you get it?'

'Stole it.'

'Won't they catch us here?'

'Naw. They can't leave those tables alone for a minute!'

They stole everywhere: shops, food-peddlers, cafes, at the market. Anywhere where there was food. Sometimes when their ragged pants began to trip them and encumber their running, they stole clothes.

Where's your mother father, Sonny?

'Donno. Pa was arrested—sent to the farms.'

'Mother?'

'I donno.'

'One year . . . two years . . . how long?'

'Donno.'

He looked down. Sonny had finished his meat and was stretched out in the ragged sliver of shade from the rusted, perforated iron wall.

He looked across the shimmering football ground. Bantu Sports Ground. Bantu Hungry Childrens' Ground.

There was shouting and laughter from the street behind him. Must be near two o'clock. They're going back to work now. Stomachs full of beer. Half drunk.

Sonny was snoring: a smile on his dirty little face. Dirty, distended little stomach going up and down, peeping through the torn, dirty rag that was once a shirt, and receding again.

The other two were also asleep. Rather, unconscious. A few whiffs of benzine had helped pull the loose corners of the blanket of sleep tightly round their young worldly-wise brains.

The painful lump in the pit of his stomach made a violent turn. He gasped and sat down quickly on the thick turf. He had never been this weak before from hunger.

He stretched out and closed his eyes. Maybe if I can sleep I'll feel better when I wake up.

He lay on his back. But his empty stomach pressed down nauseatingly on his spine.

He turned on to his stomach. But the turf seemed to press through his stomach to his spine.

He lay on his side. His stomach hung down to one side and was uncomfortable.

He tried a few variations on these positions, but none was satisfactory. At last he sat, leaning weakly against the hot wall, his legs stretched out before him. His head was light and the buzzing in his ears was deafening.

I must do something! he told himself, his watery eyes wandering listlessly over his sleeping friends. The greedy, selfish pigs! Leaving me to starve to death while they sleep so soundly. They deserve to burn in hell.

Why not? He suddenly went cold, then numb, at the thought that flashed through his head.

Why shouldn't they burn? Especially Sonny: He deserves it more—he was supposed to be my friend!

I'll fry him some nice meat!

He feverishly fumbled for the bottle of benzine in his pocket, afraid the mad thought would leave him before he had carried it out.

His fingers were too weak to pull out the cork, and he had to use his teeth.

This will frighten Sonny—he always said he didn't want to go to hell. He leaned over, and carefully sprinkled the benzine over Sonny's clothing, making sure none was wasted on the bare flesh that showed through the tears.

Not too much, he cautioned himself: Just enough to teach him a lesson!

He brought out a dirty match stick from his shirt pocket and part of a match box. With a few dirty papers gathered into a heap, he carefully struck a light, shielding the flame with his palms, and lit the papers.

Then he scooped the burning papers in his hands and hastily dumped them on his friend's stomach.

For a moment nothing happened.

Then long orange flames shot up. Sonny jumped up screaming and cursing—followed by the screams of the other two urchins, who had been awakened by the sudden searing heat.

Before he was properly on his feet, Sonny was running towards the street, screaming all the way.

And he followed dumbly behind.

In the crowded street a surprised man grabbed Sonny and another hung on to Boy when he cannoned into him.

The room was cool and quiet. It had a high, beautiful ceiling. Everybody walked on tip-toe and talked in whispers. Many white faces and only a few black ones.

A white woman stood up.

'Your Honour, the welfare officers have investigated this boy's background,' she said. 'It's rather sketchy. We went to the place in Orlando where his mother lived; she has moved, and nobody seemed to know where to. Same for his father.'

'This is disgraceful! How can this kind of thing be allowed to happen in a civilised country?'

'It does, Your Honour. I have several more cases on my dockets. It's shameful!' She bit her lower lip and visibly stopped herself from giving this new Juvenile Court magistrate a lecture on what does happen in a civilised country.

'What do you suggest?'

'Send him to Wierda Hostel, Your Honour.'

The harsh, dry scribbling of pen on paper.

Then, turning to the interpreter:

'Tell this boy that we are sending him to a house of correction. Tell him if he was older he would have gone to prison for almost killing the other boy. Tell him that at Wierda they will teach him to read and write, and he will learn a trade. When he is big, he can come out into the world and be a responsible citizen.'

The interpreter turned towards the frightened, puzzled and clean-scrubbed boy. He looked vacantly above the boy's head and recited, in the vernacular what he had told scores of such boys: a little of what the magistrate had said, and more of his own personal advice.

'You have no father, you have no mother, my boy. You have nothing but yourself. Nobody owes you a living. At "Six Mile" you will learn two things: how to make an honest and dull living; and how to make a dishonest and easy one. The choice is yours . . . and may God help you, for it is hard to choose!' The interpreter ended, already facing the bench with a vacant face.

A uniformed policeman led the boy into a room where a few boys were already gathered.

'Another client for the Tsotsi Factory,' he said casually to the man in charge and walked back to the court-room.

The Music of the Violin

NJABULO S. NDEBELE

Vukani was doing homework in his bedroom when voices in the living room slowly filtered into his mind. He lifted his head to look up as if to focus his ears. No. He could not recognize the voices. Now and again the hum of conversation was punctuated with laughter. Then he grew apprehensive, the continuing conversation suddenly filling him with dread. He tried to concentrate on his work: 'Answer the following questions: How did the coming of the whites lead to the establishment of prosperity and peace among the various Bantu tribes? . . .' But the peace had gone from his mind. The questions had become a meaningless task. Instinctively, he turned round to look at his music stand at the foot of his bed. Yesterday he had practiced some Mozart. Then he saw the violin leaning against the wall next to the stand. Would they come to interrupt him? He felt certain they would. He stood up, thinking of a way to escape.

There was another peal of laughter from the living room, and Vukani wondered again who the visitors were. As he opened the door slowly, he was met by another thunderous roar. Escape would be impossible. He had to go through the living room and would certainly be called by his mother to be introduced to the visitors, and then the usual agony would follow. A delicate clink of cups and saucers told Vukani the visitors had been served tea. Perhaps it was coffee. Most probably tea. Visitors generally liked tea more. Another roar. His father and the male visitor were laughing. He knew now that the visitors were a man and a woman, but he did not know them. Becoming curious, he opened the door another inch or so, and saw the woman visitor, who sat close to where the passage to the bedrooms began. Vukani's mother, still in her white nursing uniform, sat close to the woman visitor in another heavily cushioned chair. They were separated by a coffee table.

'I couldn't make it at all to the meeting last Saturday,' said Vukani's mother.

'Which meeting, dearie?' asked the woman.

The men laughed again.

'Don't you laugh so loudly,' Vukani's mother shouted.

'You see,' Vukani's father was saying, 'I had caught the fellow by surprise, as I usually do to all of them.'

'That's the only way to ensure that the work gets done,' said the other man.

'Indeed,' agreed Vukani's father.

'So?' asked the other man.

'So I said: "Show me the students' garden plots." I saw a twitch of anguish cross his face. But he was a clever fellow, you see. He quickly recovered and said: "Of course Sir, of course, come along." So we went. There was a wilderness around the school. These bush schools! I wouldn't have been surprised if a python had stopped us in our tracks. So, after about two hundred yards of walking and all the wilderness around us, I began to wonder. So I say to this teacher: "Mr Mabaso" that was the fellow's name, "these plots, they are quite far, aren't they?" "We're just about there, Sir," he said.'

'Man alive!' exclaimed the other man. 'This story is getting hot. Let me sip one more time.' There was some silence while the man sipped his tea. Vukani's mother also lifted her cup to her lips. The women were now listening too.

'So,' continued Vukani's father, 'we walked another two hundred yards and I turned to look at the man. "We're just about there, Sir." I only needed to look at him and he would say: "We're just about there, Sir." ' Everybody laughed. 'You see, the fellow was now sweating like a horse.'

'So?' asked the woman visitor while laughing. She was wiping her eyes with Kleenex.

'Then this fellow, Mabaso, shows me a hill about a mile away and says: "We're going there to that hill, Sir, the plots are behind it. You see, Sir, I figured that since the wind normally hits the hill on the side we are looking at now, I should have the plots on the leeward side to protect the plants." What bosh!' There was more laughter and the male visitor said, in the middle of laughter: 'Beatrice, give me some Kleenex, please.' His wife stood up and disappeared from Vukani's view. She returned soon. Vukani heard a nose blowing.

'Please don't laugh, fellow Africans,' said Vukani's father. 'The man is a genius. What's this poem by the English poet? The man blushes unseen in the wilderness. He knew I would not go any further. So I really have no proof that there were no garden plots.'

'Of course there weren't any,' asserted Vukani's mother.

'Of course there weren't,' everybody agreed.

'You school inspectors,' said the male visitor, 'have real problems with these bush schools.'

'You don't know, you!' agreed Vukani's father. 'We just can't get it into these teachers' heads that we have to uplift the Black nation. And we cannot do that through cheating and laziness. We will not develop self-reliance that way. That fellow was just not teaching the students gardening, and that is dead against government policy.' Vukani shut the door. In spite of himself, he had been amused by the story. He went back to the desk and tried to continue with the homework. He could not. What about going out through the window? No. That would be taking things too far. He wondered where Teboho, his sister, was. Probably in her bedroom. Teboho and their mother were having too many heated exchanges these days. Their mother tended to make too many demands on them. Vukani wished he could go and talk to Teboho. They had grown very close together. Then he suddenly became frantic again and went back to the door. He had to escape. When he opened the door, as slightly as before, it was the woman visitor who was talking.

'You just don't know what you missed, you,' she was saying. The men laughed again.

'Please, you men!' appealed Vukani's mother. But they laughed once again.

'Do you want us to leave you and go to the bedroom?' threatened Vukani's mother. 'And you know if we go in there we won't come out.'

'Peace! Peace!' said Vukani's father. 'Peace, women of Africa!' Then he lowered his voice as he continued to talk to the other man.

'Now, come on, what have I missed?' asked Vukani's mother, eagerly.

'Well, you just don't know what you missed,' said Mrs Beatrice pulling the bait away from the fish.

'Please don't play with my anxiety.'

'I want to do just that,' said Mrs Beatrice, clapping hands once and sitting forward in her chair, her legs thrust underneath. She kept on pulling down her tight fitting skirt over her big knees. But after each effort, the skirt slipped back, revealing the knees again.

'You women are on again about the Housewives' League?' remarked Vukani's father, interrupting the women.

'Day in and day out,' said the other man, supporting Vukani's father.

'Of-course yes!' said Mrs Beatrice with emphatic pride.

'Forget about these men,' pleaded Vukani's mother, 'and give me a pinch of the story.'

'Mother-of-Teboho, you really missed,' Mrs Beatrice started. 'A white woman came all the way from Emmerentia, high class, exclusive suburb mind you, to address the meeting on Jewish recipes. Came all the way to Soweto for that. It was wonderful.'

'Was it not Mrs Kaplinsky?'

'As if you know!'

'Ha, woman! please, give me! give me! begged Vukani's mother with great excitement, clapping her hands repeatedly. 'I'm fetching my pen, I'm fetching my pen. Give me those recipes.' But she did not leave to go and fetch her pen.

'I'm selling them, dearie. Business first, friendship after.' They laughed.

'Ei! women and food,' exclaimed the other man.

'What! We cook for you,' retorted his wife.

'Exactly,' concurred Vukani's mother. 'More tea?'

'No thanks, dearie.'

'Hey you men, more tea?' But the men were already back to their conversation, and burst out laughing. But Vukani's father answered while laughing, suddenly coming into Vukani's view as he brought his empty cup to the coffee table between the women. 'No thanks' he was saying, 'no thanks . . . he he he heheheee . . . that was a good one . . . no thanks . . . what a good one.' Then he took out a handkerchief from the pocket of his trousers, wiped the eyes, wiped the whole face, and then wiped the lips. 'A jolly good evening, tonight,' he remarked. Then he went back to his chair, disappearing from Vukani's view.

'Thanks for the tea,' said the other man, blowing his nose.

'Teboho!' called Vukani's mother. 'Please come and clear up here!' Teboho appeared carrying a tray. She had on denim jeans and a loose blouse.

'That was a nice cup of tea, Teboho,' said the other man. Teboho replied with a shy smile.

'When are you going back to varsity?' he asked.

'We have six more weeks,' replied Teboho.

'You are lucky to have children who are educating themselves

98

dearie,' said Mrs Beatrice.

'Oh, well,' said Vukani's mother shrugging her shoulders, as Teboho disappeared into the kitchen. There was some silence.

'Sometimes these South African Jews sicken me,' said the other man reflectively.

'Why?' The two women asked.

'Well, they're hypocrites! I mean look, they say they were killed left and right by the Germans, but here they are, here, helping the Boers to sit on us.'

'How can you say such a thing?' asked his wife. 'People like Mrs Kaplinsky are very good friends of ours. Some of her best friends are Africans.'

'Because she gives you recipes?'

'Food, my dear husband, belongs to mankind, not just to one race.'

'Yes, exactly,' agreed Vukani's mother. 'Like art, literature and things. Completely universal.'

'Well! . . .' said the man, but he did not pursue the matter further.

'In fact this reminds me,' said Vukani's mother with sudden enthusiasm, her eyes glittering, 'instead of sitting here talking politics, we should be listening to some music. Have you heard my son play? He plays the violin. A most wonderful instrument!'

'Yes,' said Vukani's father, 'you know . . .'

Vukani swiftly shut the door, shutting out the living room conversation with an abruptness that brought him sharply to himself as he moved to the center of the room. He began to feel very lonely and noticed he was trembling. It was coming now. He looked at the history homework on the desk; then looked at the reading lamp with its circular light, which seemed to be baking the open pages of the books on the desk with its intensity, such that the books looked as if they were waiting for that delicate moment when they would burst into flame.

Then he thought of Doksi, his friend. He wondered where he was and what he was doing at that moment. Friday evening? Probably watching his father cutting the late evening customers' hair and trimming it carefully while he murmured a song, as always. Doksi had said to Vukani one day that when he was a grownup, he would like to be a barber like his father. And Doksi did love hair. Vukani remembered his favourite game: a weekly ritual of hair burning. Every Saturday afternoon Doksi would make a fire out in the yard and when it was burning steadily, toss knots of hair into it. The hair would catch fire with a crackling brilliance that always sent him into raptures of delight. He never seemed to mind the smell of the burning hair. One Saturday after burning hair Doksi had said, while making the sign of the cross over the smoking fire: 'When God had finished burning hair, he thought that it was good.' Vukani had playfully accused him of sacrilege. But Doksi had continued suddenly looking serious: 'Dead things catch fire,' he said. Vukani was suddenly caught by a wishful fascination to see the books on the desk aflame. Perhaps he should lower the lamp: bring it closer to the books. It was a silly idea, yet he lowered the lamp all the same. But the papers shone defiantly with a sheen. It was futile. Then he saw his violin again, and felt the sensation of fear deep in his breast.

He looked at the violin with dread; as something that could bring both pain and pleasure all at once. It was like the red dress which Miss Yende their class teacher in standard four, occasionally wore. She had once said to the class: 'When I wear this red dress, know children that I will not stomach any nonsense that day. Know that I will expect sharp minds; I will expect quick responses to my questions, and I will expect absolute seriousness. And I shall use the stick with the vengeance of the God of the Old Testament.' That. dress! It was a deep velvety red that gave the impression the dress had a flowery fragrance. Yet, because it also signalled the possibility of pain, it also had a dreadful repulsiveness.

Vukani tried to brace himself for the coming of the visitors. It was always like that. Every visitor was brought to his room, where he was required to be doing his school work or practicing on the violin. Then he had to entertain these visitors with violin music. It was always an agonizing nuisance to be an unwilling entertainer. What would happen if he should refuse to play that night? He knew what his mother would say. It was the same thing all the time. His eyes swept round the room. He was well provided for. There was the beautiful desk on which he did his work; bookshelves full of books, including a set of *Encyclopedia Brittanica*; a reading lamp on the desk; two comfortable easy chairs; a wardrobe full of clothes; his own portable transistor radio; a violin and music stand; a chest full of games: Monopoly, chess and many others. His mother never tired of telling him how lucky he was: 'There is not a single boy in the whole of Soweto, including Dube, where we live, who has a room like yours. Can you count them for me? Never! This room is as good as any white boy's. Isn't it exactly like Ronnie Simpson's? You yourself, you ungrateful boy, had seen that room when we visited the Simpson's in Parktown North. Kaffir children! That's what. Always ungrateful!'

What did all this really mean to him when it brought so much pain? Vukani remembered what teacher Maseko had said at assembly one morning: 'Children, I would rather be a hungry dog that runs freely in the streets, than a fat, chained dog burdened with itself and the weight of the chain. Whenever the whiteman tells you he has made you much better off than Africans elsewhere in this continent, tell him he is lying before God!' There were cheers that morning at assembly, and the children had sung the hymn with a feeling of energetic release:

> I will make you fishers of men
> Fishers of men
> Fishers of men
> I will make you fishers of men
> If you follow me.

Three weeks later, teacher Maseko was fired. The Principal made the announcement at morning assembly. He spoke in Afrikaans, always. Concluding the announcement, he said: 'Children, a wandering dog, that upsets garbage bins, ejects its dung all over the place, is a very dangerous animal. It is a carrier of disease and pestilence, and when you see it, pelt it with stones. What should you do to it?'

'Pelt it with stones!' was the sombre response of the assembled children that morning. Vukani wondered whether teacher Maseko was that dog. But how could anybody pelt teacher Maseko with stones?

Vukani heard another roar of laughter from the living room. But why did his mother have to show off at his expense in this manner? That Friday, as on all Mondays, Wednesdays and Fridays, he had carried his violin to school. The other children at school just never got used to it. It was a constant source of wonder and ridicule. 'Here's a fellow with a strange guitar!' some would say. Others would ask him to play the current township hits. It was so, every day. Then one day his violin had disappeared from class while he had gone out to the boys' toilet. He was met with stony faces when he pleaded for its return after school. Everybody simply went home and there was no sign of the violin. What would he say to his music teacher in town? What would he says to his mother. When he went out of the classroom, he found Doksi waiting for him. They always went home together, except on the days when Vukani had to go to town for his music lessons after school.

'Doksi,' he said, 'I can't find my violin. Somebody took it.'

'These boys of shit!' Doksi cursed sympathetically. He had not waited for details. He knew his friend's problem. 'Do you suspect anybody?'

'I can't say,' replied Vukani, 'the whole class seems to have ganged up on me. There are somethings that always bring them together.'

'Even Gwendoline?' asked Doksi with a mischievous smirk across his face.

Gwendoline was the frail, brilliant, beautiful girl who vied with Vukani for first position in class. Vukani had always told Doksi that he would like to marry that girl one day. And Doksi would always say: 'With you it's talk talk all the time. Why don't you just go to this girl and tell her you love her? Just look at how she looks at you. She is suffering, man!'

'Look,' said Vukani, 'this is no time for jokes. My violin is lost.'

'The trouble with you Vukani is that you are too soft. I would never stand this nonsense. I'd just face the whole class and say: "Whoever took my violin is a coward. Why doesn't he come out and fight?" I'm sure it was taken by one of those big boys whom everybody fears. Big bodies without minds! They ought to be working in town. Just at school to avoid paying tax. But me, they know me. They know what my brothers would do. My whole family would come here looking for the bastards.'

'Let's go and tell the principal,' suggested Vukani. The principal was one of those Vukani had entertained one day in his bedroom. 'But maybe we shouldn't,' said Vukani changing his mind.

'Let's go and find out from the girls sweeping your classroom,' suggested Doksi. They went back.

Most of the children had gone now. Only those whose turn it was to clean the classrooms remained. The girls were singing loudly and the room was full of dust.

'Leave it to me,' said Doksi.

102

There were four girls in there. Gwendoline and Manana were as old as Doksi and Vukani. The other two girls, Topsana and Sarah were older. Much older.

'Hey you, girls,' shouted Doksi squaring his shoulders and looking like a cowboy about to draw. 'Where is the bloody violin?' The bigger girls simply laughed.

'And who are you, toughie?' said Sarah, pushing a desk out of the way for Topsana to sweep.

'Hey you, Vukani,' called Topsana, 'I want to soothe your heart. I've long been waiting for this moment. Come and kiss me.' The smaller girls giggled, and Vukani regretted that they had come back. 'I mean it,' said Topsana. 'I know who took your violin. It's safe. You'll find it at home. I made them promise to take it there. There now, I want my kiss. I want to kiss the inspector's son.'

Meanwhile, Doksi turned to the younger girls; 'Hey you, what is the joke? What's there to laugh at.'

'Hha!' protested Manana, sweeping rather purposefully, 'laughing is laughing.'

'I can show you a thing or two,' Doksi said. 'Punch you up or something.'

'Doksi,' appealed Vukani, 'please let's go.' Doksi clearly felt the need for retreat, but it had to be done with dignity. He addressed all the girls with a sweep of his hand: 'You are all useless. One of these days I'll get you. Come on, Vukani, let's go.'

The walk home for Vukani had been a long one. Better not to tell the parents. If Topsana had been telling the truth, then he should wait. Nobody asked about the violin that night. But he would never forget the morning following that day, when his mother stormed into his bedroom, black with anger. She simply came in and pulled the blankets off him. Then she glared at him holding the violin in one of her hands. Vukani had felt so exposed, as if his mother would hit him with the violin. It was very early in the morning. His mother was already dressed up in her uniform, ready to go to work. If she was on day duty, she had to leave very early for the hospital.

'Vukani!' she shouted, 'what desecration is this? What ultimate act of ungratefulness is this? Is this to spite me? Is this an insult? Tell me before I finish you off.'

'What's happening Dorcas?' Vukani saw his father entering the bedroom.

'Can you believe this? I found this violin on the doorstep outside, as I was leaving for work. Can you believe this?'

'Vukani,' said his father, 'what on earth should have made you do such a thing?'

'I didn't put it there, Baba,' Vukani replied.

'Nonsense,' shouted his mother, 'you don't have to lie. Ungrateful boy, you have the nerve to tell your parents a lie.'

'Wait a minute, dear, maybe we should hear what he has to say.' Vukani had nothing to say. The deep feeling of having been wronged could only find expression in tears. He heard the violin land next to him and he recoiled from its coldness. He also heard his mother leave saying that he was crying because of his sins. She never knew what happened.

But that was last year. Today he had been humiliated again in public, and there were people in that living room who wanted to humiliate him again. Right inside his home. It was all because of this violin. The homework had made him forget the latest ordeal for a while. The homework was like a jigsaw puzzle; you simply looked for pieces which fitted. All the answers were there in the chapter. You just moved your finger up and down the page until you spotted the correct answer. There was no thinking involved. But now it was all gone. It was not South African History, the story of the coming of the whiteman he was looking at; he was now faced with the reality of the violin.

There was that gang of boys who always stood under the shop veranda at Maponya's shopping complex. They shouted, 'Hey, music man,' whenever he went past their 'headquarters' on his way home to Dube. That very Friday they had done more than shout at him from a distance. They had stopped him and humiliated him before all those workers who were returning from work in town.

'Hey, music man,' had called the one who seemed to be their leader. Vukani, as a rule, never asnwered them. He just walked on as if he had not heard anything. But that afternoon, as he was coming up from the Phefeni station, and was turning round the corner to go down towards the A.M.E. church, it was as if the gang had been waiting for him.

'Hey, music man!' this time it was a chorus. A rowdy chorus. Through the corner of his eye, Vukani saw two boys detach themselves from the gang. He dare not turn to look. He had to act unconcerned. He tried to quicken his step as imperceptibly as possible.

'Music man! Don't you know your name?' They were behind him now. Crossing the street had been no problem for them. They simply walked onto the street and cars came to a screeching halt. They were the kings of the township. They just parted the traffic as Moses must have parted the waves of the sea. Vukani wanted to run, but he was not going to give himself away. If he ran and they caught up with him, they could do a lot of harm to him. He had had that feeling once: the feeling of wanting to take advantage of something weaker than him when he found a stray dog trying to topple a garbage bin. If the dog stood its ground and growled, Vukani would become afraid. But if the dog took to its heels with tail tucked between the legs, Vukani would suddenly be filled with the urge to run after the dog, catch it, and beat it to death. A fleeing impala must excite the worst destructive urge in a lion. Vukani had once seen a fim in which a lion charted at a frightened impala. There had been a confidence in the purposeful strides of the lion, as if it felt this was just a game that would surely end with the bringing down of the prey.

'Dogs of the street! Don't talk like that to your mother. Whose child are you?'

'I'm your child,' said Bhuka with a certain flourish. This time more of the crowd laughed.

'He's the child of his mother!' said the boy behind Vukani. None laughed to that one. He was in the shadow of his leader.

'You are laughing,' said the woman, bravely addressing the crowd. 'You are laughing at this boy being harassed, and you are laughing at me being insulted by these street urchins. I could be your mother, and this could be your son. *Sies!* You rogues, just let decent people be.' The woman then left, taking Vukani's hopes with her. But she had not left Bhuka unsettled. He had to move his prey to safer ground. Too many lesser animals could be a disturbance. He tightened his grip around Vukani's tie pulling him across the street towards the 'headquarters'. Vukani looked at the fist below his chin, and saw that it had a little sixth finger. There were two shining copper bangles round the wrist.

Part of the crowd left, but another part wanted to see the game to its end. They followed the trio to the shop. The gang then had Vukani completely encircled.

'Do you have a sister?' Bhuka snapped. Vukani had trouble breathing now. Bhuka realized this and loosened the grip. Vukani

105

thought of Teboho at home. If she came here she would fight for him. 'I asked you a question. Do you have a sister?' Vukani nodded. 'Hey man, talk! Is your voice precious. His master's voice!'

'Yes,' answered Vukani in a whisper.

'I want to fuck her. Do you hear? I want to eat her up thoroughly. Do you hear? Tell her that.' Bhuka then paused and jerked Vukani to and fro so that Vukani's head bobbed. He then stopped and glowered at Vukani. 'And what song will you play when I am on top of her?' There was a festive laugh from the crowd. Bhuka looked round with acknowledgement. 'Tell me now, can you play *Thoko Ujola Nobani*?' It was a current hit.

Vukani felt tears in his eyes. He winked many times to keep them in. Why couldn't they just leave him alone? That day would be final, he would simply tell his parents that he did not want to play the violin again. If they still insisted, he would run away from home.

'Please leave me alone,' he heard himself say.

'I asked you. Can you play *Thoko Ujola Nobani*?' Vukani shook his head.

'Why, music man?'

'I'd have to learn how to play it first. I can't just play it like that.'

'Next time you pass here you must be knowing that song. And come with your sister.' Then he gave Vukani a shove at the chest, and Vukani reeled backwards and fell on his back. But he still held on to the violin.

'Next time we greet you nice nice, you must greet nice nice.' Vukani got up timidly and hurried away, glancing backwards occasionally. Somehow he felt relieved. It could have been worse. The stories he had heard about the violence of this gang were simply unbelievable. He felt deep inside him the laughter that followed him as he slunk away. Just after passing A.M.E. church, he saw the rubbish heap people had created at the corner and wished he were brave enough to throw the violin there.

'My son,' his mother had said one day when Vukani complained about the harrassment he suffered as a result of the violin, 'You should never yield to ignorance.'

'But maybe you should buy me a piano,' Vukani had said. 'I can't carry that in the street.'

'If Yehudi Menuhin had listened to fools, he wouldn't be the greatest living violinist. A violin you have, and a violin you will play.' That's how it had ended. But his agony continued three times a week.

Then the door opened. 'Here he is!' said Vukani's mother as she led the visitors in. His father took the rear. Vukani blankly looked at the homework: Question three: Who introduced the European type of education among the Bantu? . . . But Vukani felt only the solid presence of four people behind him.

'Vuka,' said his mother, 'I did not hear you practise today.' It was not clear from her voice whether she was finding fault with her son or was just trying to have something to say by way of introduction. Vukani turned round and smiled sheepishly. They all looked at him as if they expected him to defend himself, their eyes occasionally going to the table as if to see what he was doing.

'Are you doing your homework son?' asked the male visitor.

'E!'

'Good, hard working boy!' he said patting Vukani on the shoulders. Vukani felt in that hand the heaviness of condescension.

'He's a very serious-minded boy,' added his mother with obvious pride.

'You are very happy, dearie, to have a child who loves school,' observed Mrs Beatrice.

'And here is my Mozart's violin,' said Vukani's father, pointing at the violin against the wall. He took the case, opened it and took out the violin.

'Vuka!'

'Ma!'

'These visitors are the mother and father of Lauretta. Do you know her?'

'No, I don't think I do,' said Vukani shaking his head.

'But you are at the same school together! Surely you know Lauretta the daughter of Doctor Zwane. Stand up to greet them.' Vukani then remembered the girl who was well known at school for her brilliance. She was two classes ahead of Vukani. But Vukani wondered if she could beat Gwendoline. Vukani greeted the visitors and went back to his seat.

'Vuka, you will play the visitors something, won't you? What will you play us?' asked the mother. Vukani looked at the violin in his father's hands. He was explaining to Dr Zwane the various kinds of violins.

'This type,' he was saying, 'is very rare. You do not find it easily these days. Not at all.'

'It must have been very expensive,' observed Dr Zwane appreciatively, 'one can judge from its looks.'

'Five hundred and fifty rand down,' jutted Vukani's mother.

'Made to specifications. You just tell them how you want it and they make it. This is special.'

'One has to pay to produce a Mozart,' said Vukani's father with finality.

'We had Lauretta started on ballet recently,' said Mrs Zwane, as if suggesting that they were also doing their duty. 'I'm happy to note that she seems to be doing well. All these things have to be taught at our schools. You school inspectors have a duty to ensure that it happens.'

'Indeed,' agreed Vukani's father. 'But do you think the Boers would agree? Never. Remember they say Western Civilization is spoiling us, and so we have to cultivate the indigenous way of life.' The conservation was stopped by Vukani's mother.

'Okay now,' she clapped her hands, 'What will you play us?'

Vukani's father brought the violin to Vukani, who took it with his visibly shaking hands. He saw the red, glowering eyes of Bhuka that afternoon. He heard the laughter of people in the streets. He remembered being violently shaken awake by his angry mother one morning. He remembered one of his dreams which came very frequently. He was naked in the streets and people were laughing. He did not know how he became naked. It always occurred that way. He would be naked in the streets and people would be laughing. Suddenly he would reach home and his mother would scold him for bringing shame to the family. But the dream would always end with his leaving home and flying out into the sky with his hands as wings.

Vukani found he had instinctively put the violin on his left shoulder. And when he realized that, he felt its irksome weight on him. What did people want of him? He did not want to play. He did not want to play. And for the second time that day, he felt tears coming to his eyes, and again he winked repeatedly to keep them from flowing. This was the time.

'Mama!'

'Yes, son.' But Vukani did not go on. His mother continued. 'Why don't you play some selections from Brahms? You know some excerpts from his *only* violin concerto? Perhaps Mozart? Yes Mozart. I know that sometimes one is in the mood for a particular composer.

What about Liszt? Where are your music books? There is something on the music stand; what is it? Ahh! It's the glorious, beautiful Dvorak! Tum tee tum! Tum tee tum!' She shook her head, conducting an imaginary orchestra. 'Come up and play some of this Dvorak.' Vukani wanted to shout, but his throat felt completely dry. He wanted to sink into the ground. He tried to swallow. It was only dryness he swallowed, and it hurt against the throat. Standing up would be agonizing. His strength and resistance were all gathered up in his sitting position. All the strength would be dissipated if he stood up. And he would feel exposed, lonely and vulnerable. The visitors and his parents soon noticed there was something amiss.

'What is it Vuka?' asked his mother. 'Is there something wrong?'

'Nothing wrong, ma,' said Vukani, shaking his head. He had missed his opportunity. Why was he afraid? Why did he not act decisively for his own good? Then he felt anger building up in him, but he was not sure whether he was angry with himself, or with his parents together with the visitors, whose visit was now forcing him to come to terms with his hitherto unexpressed determination to stop doing what brought him suffering.

At that moment there was a dull explosion seemingly coming from the kitchen, of something massive suddenly disintegrating into pieces. There was a moment's silence, then Vukani's mother muttered: 'The bloody street girl has done it again,' and she stormed out of the bedroom. Her voice could be heard clearly in the kitchen: 'Awu, lord of the heavens! my . . . my expensive . . . my precious . . . my expensive . . . this girl has done it again.'

And then she mimicked Teboho's voice: ' "That's how its planned. That we be given a little of everything, and so prize the little we have that we forget about freedom." Fancy. Forgive me; but I had to remind this show-off girl that I was her parent.'

There was a moment's silence of embarrassment. The adults all exchanged glances. A wave of sadness crossed Vukani's mother's face. But it did not last.

'One can never know with children, dearie,' observed Mrs Zwane, breaking the silence.

'Indeed!' said her husband. There was another silence.

'Well, Vuka,' said Vukani's father at last. 'Can you heal our broken spirits?'

'Yes!' agreed his mother, 'we have been waiting for too long.'

Vukani thought of his sister. He wanted to go to her. They were very lonely. Their parents disapproved of many of their friends. Even Doksi. His mother had said he should have friends of his own station in life. What would a barber's son bring him? All this had brought Vukani and Teboho very close. He decided then that he would not let his sister down. But could he? He thought of dashing the violin against the wall, and then rushing out of the house. But where would he go? Who did he know nearby? The relatives he knew lived very far. He did not know them all that well, anyhow. He remembered how envious he would be whenever he heard other children saying they were going to spend their holidays with their relatives. Perhaps with a grandmother or an uncle. He remembered once asking his mother when were they ever going to visit his uncle. His mother had not answered him. But then there was that conversation between his parents.

'By the way,' asked Vukani's mother. 'when did you say your sister would be coming?'

'Next month.' There was a brief silence and his father continued. 'Why do you ask? I have been telling you practically everyday.'

'I was just asking for interest's sake.'

'Well,' said the father, putting down the *Daily Mail* and picking up the *Star*, 'I just feel there is more to the question than meets the eye.'

'You think so?'

'Yes, I think so.' There was some silence.

'Relatives,' the mother came out, 'can be a real nuisance. Once you have opened the door, they come trooping in like ants. We cannot afford it these days. Not with the cost of living. These are different times. Whites saw this problem a long time ago. That is why they have very little time for relatives. Nuclear family! That's what matters. I believe in it. I've always maintained that. If relatives want to visit, they must help with the groceries. There I'm clear, my dear. Very clear.' Vukani's father had said something about 'Whites are whites; Africans are Africans.' But Vukani's aunt never came. Nobody ever said anything about her. Yet, Doksi liked to say: 'Its nice to have many relatives. Then when you are in trouble at home, you can always hide with one of them. And your father will go from relative to relative looking for you. When he finds you, he will be all smiles trying to please the relatives.''

'Vukani!' called his mother, 'we are still waiting, will you start playing now?'

Vukani stood up slowly, feeling every movement of his body, and walked round to the music stand. Then he faced his mother, and something yielded in him.

'Ma, I don't want to play the violin anymore.' There was a stunned silence. Vukani's mother looked at her husband, a puzzled expression on her face. But she quickly recovered.

'What?' she shouted.

'I don't want to play the violin anymore.' Vukani was surprised at his steadiness.

'This is enough!' screamed his mother. 'Right now . . . right now. You are going to play that violin right now.'

'Now you just play that instrument. What's going on in this house?' His father's voice put in some fear into Vukani.

'Wait, dearie,' pleaded Mrs Zwane. 'Maybe the boy is not well.'

'Beatrice,' answered Vukani's mother, 'there is nothing like that. We are not going to be humiliated by such a little flea. Play, cheeky brute!'

'Today those those boys stopped me again.' Vukani attempted to justify his stand.

'Who?' shrieked his mother, 'those dogs of the street? Those low things?'

'What's bothering him?' asked Dr Zwane. Vukani's mother explained briefly. Then turning toward her husband she said: 'As I told you the other day, he keeps complaining that people laugh at him because he plays the violin.'

'Jealousy,' shouted Mrs Zwane. 'Plain jealousy. Jealousy number one. Nothing else. Township people do not want to see other Africans advance.'

'Dear,' answered Vukani's mother. 'You are showing them some respect they do not deserve. If you saw they are jealous, you make them people with feeling. No. They do not have that. They are not people: they are animals. Absolutely raw. They have no respect for what is better than they. Not these. They just trample over everything. Hey, you, play that instrument and stop telling us about savages.'

Vukani trembled. He felt his head going round now. He did not know what to do now to escape from his ordeal. The tears came back, but this time he did not stop them. He felt them going down his cheeks, and he gave in to the fury in him: 'I do not want to

111

play . . . I do not want to play . . . not any more! . . .' Then he choked and could not say anything more. But what he had said had carried everything he felt deep inside him. He felt free. There was a vast expanse of open space deep inside him. He was free. He could fly into the sky. Then he heard Dr Zwane say:

'How difficult it is to bring up a child properly in Soweto! To give them culture. African people just turn away from advancement.'

Those words seemed to build a fire in Vukani's mother. They sounded like a reflection on her. She let go at Vukani with the back of her hand. Vukani reeled back and fell on the bed, letting the violin drop to the floor. It made no noise on the thick carpet. Then she lifted him from the bed, and was about to strike him again when Teboho rushed into the bedroom, and pulled her mother away from her brother.

'Ma! What are you doing? What are you doing?' she screamed.

'Are you fighting me?' shrieked her mother, 'you laid a hand on your mother. Am I bewitched?'

'You never think of anybody else. Just yourself.'

'Teboho,' called her father, 'don't say that to your mother.'

'Please, dearie, please,' appealed Mrs Zwane. 'There is no need for all this. How can you do this to your children?'

'*Sies!* What disgraceful children! I am a nursing sister, your father is an inspector of schools. What are you going to be, listening to savages? You cannot please everybody. Either you please the street, in which case you are going to be a heap of rubbish, something to be swept away, or you please your home, which is going to give you something to be proud of for the rest of your useless life!'

'Dorcas! That's enough now,' said Vukani's father with calm, but firm finality. Vukani's mother looked at her husband with disbelief, a wave of shock crossing her face. She looked at the visitors, who stared at her. Then she turned for the door, went to her bedroom, banging the door violently. Soon, there was bitter sobbing in the main bedroom. Then it turned into a wail of the bereaved.

Call Me Not A Man

MTUTUZELI MATSHOBA

For neither am I a man in the eyes of the law,
Nor am I a man in the eyes of my fellow man.

By dodging, lying, resisting where it is possible, bolting when I'm already cornered, parting with invaluable money, sometimes calling my sisters into the game to get amorous with my captors, allowing myself to be slapped on my mouth in front of my womenfolk and getting sworn at with my mother's private parts, that component of me which is man has died a countless times in one lifetime. Only a shell of me remains to tell you of the other man's plight, which is in fact my own. For what is suffered by another man in view of my eyes is suffered also by me. The grief he knows is a grief that I know. Out of the same bitter cup do we drink. To the same chain-gang do we belong.

Friday has always been their chosen day to go plundering, although nowadays they come only occasionally, maybe once in a month. Perhaps they have found better pastures elsewhere, where their prey is more predictable than in Mzimhlope, the place which has seen the tragic demise of three of their accomplices who had taken the game a bit too far by entering the hostel on the northern side of our location and fleecing the people right in the midst of their disgusting labour camps. Immediately after this there was a notable abatement in the frequency of their visits to both the location and the adjacent hostel. However the lull was only short-lived, lasting only until the storm had died down, because the memory tarnishes quickly in the locations, especially the memory of death. We were beginning to emit sighs of relief and to mutter 'good riddance' when they suddenly reappeared and made their presence in our lives felt once again. June, Seventy-six had put them out of the picture for the next year, after which they were scarcely seen. Like a recurring pestilence they refuse to vanish absolutely from the scene.

A person who has spent some time in Soweto will doubtless have guessed by now that the characters I am referring to are none other than some of the so-called police reservists who roam our dirty streets at weekends, robbing every timid, un-suspecting person, while masquerading as peace officers to maintain law and order in the community. There are no greater thieves than these men of the law, men of justice, peace officers and volunteer public protectors in the whole of the slum complex because, unlike others in the same trade of living off the sweat of their victims, they steal out in the open, in front of everybody's eyes. Of course nothing could be done about it because they go out on their pillaging exploits under the banners of the law, and to rise in protest against them is analogous to defiance of the powers that be.

So, on this Friday too we were standing on top of the station bridge at Mzimhlope. It was about five in the afternoon and the sun hung over the western horizon of spectacularly identical coalsmoke-puffing roof-tops like a gigantic, glowing red ball which dyed the foamy clouds with the crimson sheet of its rays. The commuter trains coming in from the city paused below us every two or three minutes to regurgitate their infinite human cargo, the greater part of whom were hostel-dwellers, who hurried up Mohale Street to cook their meagre suppers on primus stoves. The last train we had seen would now be leaving Phefeni, the third station from Mzimhlope. The next train had just emerged from the bridge this side of New Canada, junction to East and West Soweto. The last group of the hostel people from the train now leaving Phefeni had just turned the bend at Mohale Street where it intersects with Elliot. The two hundred metre stretch to Elliot was therefore relatively empty, and people coming towards the station could be clearly made out.

As the wheels of the train from New Canada squealed on the iron tracks and it came to a jerking stop, four men, two in overalls and the others in duster-coats, materialised around the Mohale Street bend. There was no doubt who they were, from the way they filled the whole width of the street and walked as if they owned everything and everybody in their sight. When they came to the grannies selling vegetables, fruit and fried mealies along the ragged, unpaved sides of the street, they grabbed what they fancied and munched gluttonously the rest of the way towards us. Again nothing could be done about it, because the poverty-stricken vendors were not licensed to scrape together some crumbs to ease the gnawing stomachs of their fatherless grandchildren at home, which left them wide open for plunder by the indifferent 'reserves'.

114

'Awu'! The Hellions,' remarked Mandla next to me. 'Let's get away from here, my friend.'

He was right. They reminded one of the old western film; but I was not moving from where I was simply because the reservists were coming down the street like a bunch of villains. One other thing I knew was that the railway constable who was on guard duty that Friday at the station did not allow the persecution of the people on his premises. I wanted to have my laugh when they were chased off the station.

'Don't worry about them. Just wait and see how they're going to be chased away by this copper. He won't allow them on the station,' I answered.

They split into twos when they arrived below us. Two of them, a tall chap with a face corroded by skin-lightening cream and wearing a yellow golf cap on his shaven head, and another stubby, shabbily dressed, middle aged man with a bald frontal lobe and a drunk face, chewing at a cooked sheep's foot that he had taken from one of the grannies, climbed the stairs on our right hand side. The younger man took the flight in fours. The other two chose to waylay their unsuspecting victims on the street corner at the base of the left hand staircase. The first wave of the people who had alighted from the train was in the middle of the bridge when the second man reached the top of the stairs.

Maybe they knew the two reservists by sight, maybe they just smelt cop in the smoggy air, or it being a Friday, they were alert for such possibilities. Three to four of the approaching human wall turned suddenly in their tracks and ran for their dear freedom into the mass behind them. The others were caught unawares by this unexpected movement and they staggered in all directions trying to regain balance. In a split second there was commotion on the station, as if a wild cat had found its way into the fowlrun. Two of those who had not been quick enough were grabbed by their sleeves, and their passes demanded. While they were producing their books the wolves went over their pockets, supposedly feeling for dangerous weapons, dagga and other illegal possessions that might be concealed in the clothes, but really to ascertain whether they had caught the right people for their iniquitous purposes. They were paging through the booklets when the Railway policeman appeared.

'Wha-? Don't you fools know that you're not supposed to do that shit here? Get off! Get off and do that away from Railway property. Fuck off!' He screamed at the two reservists so furiously that the veins threatened to burst in his neck.

'Arrest the dogs, baba! Give them a chance also to taste jail!' Mandla shouted.

'Ja,' I said to Mandla, 'You bet, they've never been where they are so prepared to send others.'

The other people joined in and we jeered the cowards off the station. They descended the stairs with their tails tucked between their legs and joined their companions below the station. Some of the commuters who had been alerted by the uproar returned to the platform to wait there until the reservists had gone before they would dare venture out of the station.

We retained where we had been and watched the persecution from above. I doubted if they ever read the passes (if they could), or whether the victims knew if their books were right or out of order. Most likely the poor hunted men believed what they were told by the licensed thieves. The latter demanded the books, after first judging their prey to be weak propositions, flicked through the pages, put the passes into their own pockets, without which the owners could not continue on their way, and told the dumbfounded hostel men to stand aside while they accosted other victims. Within a very short while there was a group of confused men to one side of the street, screaming at their hostel mates to go to room so and so and tell so and so that they had been arrested at the station, and to bring money quickly to release them. Few of those who were being sent heard the messages since they were only too eager to leave the danger zone. Those who had money shook hands with their captors, received their books back and ran up Mohale Street. If they were unlucky they came upon another 'roadblock' three hundred metres up the street and the process would be repeated. Woe unto them who had paid their last money to the first extortionists, for this did not matter. The police station was their next stopover before the Bantu Commissioners, and thence their final destination, Modder Bee Prison, where they provided the farmers with ready cheap labour until they had served their terms for breaking the law. The terms vary from a few days to two years for 'loaferskap' (idleness); which is in fact mere unemployment, for which the unfortunate men were not to blame. The whole arrangement stinks of forced labour.

The large 'kwela-kwela' swayed down Mohale Street at a break-neck speed. The multitudes scattered out of its way and hung onto the sagging fences until it had passed. To be out of sight of the people on the station bridge, it skidded and swerved into the second side street from the station. More reservists poured out of it and went immediately to their dirty job with great zeal. The chain-gang which had been lined along the fence of the house nearest the station was kicked and shoved to the kwela-kwela, into which the victims were bundled under a rain of fists and boots, all of them scrambling to go in at the same time through the small door. The driver of the kwela-kwela, the only uniformed constable among the group, clanged the door shut and secured it with the locking lever. He went to stand authoritatively near one of the vendors, took a small avocado pear, peeled it and put it whole into a gargantuan mouth, spitting out the large stone later. He did not have to take the trouble of accosting anyone himself. His gangsters would all give him a lion's share of whatever they made, and moreover, buy him some beers and brandy. He kept adjusting his polished belt over his potbelly as the .38 police special in its leather holster kept it down. He probably preferred to wear his gun unconventionally, cowboy style.

A boy of about seventeen years of age was caught with a knife in his pocket, a dangerous weapon. They slapped him a few times and let him stand handcuffed against the concrete wall of the station. Ten minutes later his well-rounded sister alighted from the train to find her younger brother among the prisoners. As she was inquiring from him why he had been arrested and reprimanded him for carrying a knife, one of the younger reservists came to stand next to her and started pawing her. She let him carry on, and three minutes later her brother was free. The reservist was beaming all over the face, glad to have won himself a beautiful woman in the course of his duties and little knowing that he had been given the wrong address. Some of our black sisters are at times compelled to go all the way to save their menfolk, and as always, nothing can be done about it.

There was a man coming down Mohale Street, conspicuous amidst the crowd because of the bag and baggage that was loaded on his overall-clad frame. On his right shoulder was a large suitcase with a grey blanket strapped to it with flaxen strings. From his left hand hung a bulging cardboard box, only a few inches from the ground, and tilting him to that side. He walked with the bounce of someone used to walking in gumboots or on uneven ground. There was the urgency of someone who had a long way to travel in his gait. It was doubtless a 'goduka' (migrant labourer) on his way home to his family after many months of work in the city. It might even have been years since he visited the countryside.

He did not see the hidden kwela-kwela, which might have forewarned him of the danger that was lurking at the station. Only when he had stumbled into two reservists, who stepped into his way and ordered him to put down his baggage, did he perhaps remember that it was Friday and raid-day. A baffled expression sprang into his face as he realised what he had walked into. He frantically went through the pockets of his overalls. The worried countenance deepened on his dark face. He tried again to make sure, but he did not find what he was looking for. The men who had stopped him pulled him to one side, each holding him tightly with the sleeve of his overall. He obeyed meekly like a tame animal. They let him lift his arms while they searched him all over the body. Finding nothing hidden on him, they demanded the inevitable book, although they had seen that he did not have it. He gesticulated with his hands as he explained what had caused him not to be carrying his pass with him. From a few feet above them I could barely hear what was said.

''Strue, madoda,' he said imploringly, 'I made a mistake. I luggaged the pass with my trunk. It was in a jacket that I forgot to search before I packed it into the trunk.'

'How do we know that you're not lying?' asked one of the reservists in a querulous voice.

'I'm not lying, mfowethu. I swear by my mother, that's what happened,' explained the frightened man.

The second reservist had a more evil and uncompromising attitude. 'That was your own stupidity, mister. Because of it you're going to jail now; no more to your wife.'

'Oh, my brother. Put yourself in my shoes. I've not been home to my people for two years now. It's the first chance I have to go and see my twin daughters who were born while I've been here. Feel for another poor black man, please, my good brother. Forgive me only for this once.'

'What? Forgive you? And don't give us that slush about your

children. We've also got our own families, for whom we are at work right now, at this moment,' the obstinate one replied roughly.

'But, mfo. Wouldn't you make a mistake too?'

That was a question the cornered man should not have asked. The reply this time was a resounding slap on the face. 'You think I'm stupid like you, huh? Bind this man Mazibuko, put the bloody irons on the dog.'

'No, man. Let me talk to the poor bloke. Perhaps he can do something for us in exchange for the favour of letting him proceed on his way home,' the less volatile man suggested, and pulled the hostel man away from the rest of the arrested people.

'Ja. Speak to him yourself, Mazibuko. I can't bear talking to rural fools like him. I'll kill him with my bare hands if he thinks that I've come to play here in Johannesburg!' The anger in the man's voice was faked, the fury of a coward trying to instil fear in a person who happened to be at his mercy. I doubted if he could face up to a mouse. He accosted two boys and ran his hands over their sides, but he did not ask for their passes.

'You see, my friend, you're really in trouble. I'm the only one who can help you. This man who arrested you is not in his best mood today. How much have you got on you? Maybe if you give something he'll let you go. You know what wonders money can do for you. I'll plead for you; but only if I show him something he can understand.' The reservist explained the only way out of the predicament for the trapped man, in a smooth voice that sounded rotten through and through with corruption, the sole purpose for which he had joined the 'force'.

'I haven't got a cent in my pocket. I bought provisions, presents for the people at home and the ticket with all the money they gave me at work. Look, nkosi, I have only the ticket and the papers with which I'm going to draw my money when I arrive at home.' He took out his papers, pulled the overall off his shoulders and lowered it to his thighs so that the brown trousers he wore underneath were out in the open. He turned the dirty pockets inside out. 'There's nothing else in my pockets except these, mister, honestly.'

'Man!'

'Yessir?'

'You want to go home to your wife and children?'

'Yes, *please,* good man of my people. Give me a break.'

'Then why do you show me these damn papers? They will feed

your own children but not mine. When you get to your home you're going to draw your money and your kids will we scratching their tummies and dozing after a hectic meal, while I lose my job for letting you go and my own children join the dogs to scavenge the trashbins. You're mad, mos.' He turned to his mate. 'Hey, Baloyi. You man says he hasnt got anything, but he's going to his family which he hasn't seen for two years.'

'I told you to put the irons on him. He's probably carrying a little fortune in his underpants. Maybe he's shy to take it out in front of the people. It'll come out at the police station, either at the charge office or in the cells when the small boys shake him down.'

'Come on, you. Your hands, maan!'

The other man pulled his arms away from the manacles. His voice rose desperately, 'Awu my people. You mean you're really arresting me? Forgive me! I pray do.'

A struggle ensued between the two men.

'You're resisting arrest? You ——,' and a stream of foul vitriolic words concerning the anatomy of the hostel man's mother gushed out of the reservist's mouth.

'I'm not, I'm not! But, please listen!' The hostel man heaved and broke loose from the reservist's grip. The latter was only a limp of fat with nothing underneath. He staggered three steps back and flopped on his rump. When he bounced back to his feet, unexpectedly fast for his bulk, his eyes were blazing murder. His companions came running from their own posts and swarmed upon the defenceless man like a pack of hyenas upon a carcase. The other people who had been marooned on the bridge saw a chance to go past while the wolves were still preoccupied. They ran down the stairs and up Mohale like racehorses. Two other young men who were handcuffed together took advantage of the diversion and bolted down the first street in tandem, taking their bracelets with them. They ran awkwardly with their arms bound together, but both were young and fit and they did their best in the circumstances.

We could not stand the sickening beating that the other man was receiving any more.

'Hey! Hey. Sies maan. Stop beating the man like that. Arrest him if you want to arrest him. You're killing him, dogs!' we protested loudly from the station. An angry crowd was gathering.

120

'Stop it or we'll stop you from doing anything else forever!' someone shouted.

The psychopaths broke their rugger scrum and allowed us to see their gruesome handiwork. The man was groaning at the base of the fence, across the street where the dirt had gathered. He twisted painfully to a sitting position. His face was covered with dirt and blood from where the manacles that were slipped over the knuckles had found their marks, and his features were grotesquely distorted. In spite of that, the fat man was not satisfied. He bent and gathered the whimpering man's wrists with the intention of fastenig them to the fence with the handcuffs.

'Hey, hey, hey, Satan! Let him go. Can't you see that you've hurt that man enough?'

The tension was building up to explosion point and the uniformed policeman sensed it.

'Let him go boys. Forgive him. Let him go,' he said, shooting nervous glances in all directions.

Then the beaten-up man did the most unexpected and heartrending thing. He knelt before the one ordering his release and held his dust covered hands with the palms together in the prayer position and still kneeling he said, 'Thank you very much, my lord. God bless you. Now I can go and see my twins and my people at home.'

He would have done it. Only it never occurred in his mind at that moment of thanksgiving to kiss the red gleaming boots of the policeman.

The miserable man beat the dust off his clothes as best he could, gathered his two parcels and clambered on the stairs, trying to grin his 'thanks' to the crowd that had raised its voice of protest on his behalf. The policeman decided to call it a day. The other unfortunates were shepherded to the waiting kwela-kwela.

I tried to imagine how the man would explain his lumps to his wife. In the eye of my mind I saw him throwing his twins into the air and gathering them again and again as he played with them.

'There's still a long way to cover, my friend,' I heard Mandla saying into my ear.

'Before?' I asked.

'Before we reach hell. Ha, ha, ha! Maybe there we'll be men.'

'Ha, we've long been there. We've long been in hell.'

'Before we get out then.'

The Promise

GLADYS THOMAS

I, Maria Klaasen, came from the Swartland to this city. I remember when it all happened so suddenly on that beautiful farm-fresh morning. I was busy making the morning mieliepap for the children who were hungry and restless. Beta was lucky to be at school still, and so was little Mannetjie, my baby brother, the apple of my father's eye. Mama worked over at the big house as a housemaid.

When I think back I remember her often saying, 'You're not going to be no maid, Maria. You've got your Standard Six and you are a smart girl. You're going back to school as soon as Mannetjie is bigger.'

To return to school became my only wish! I often prayed to God to help me. Papa worked in the fields, leaving at four o'clock every morning. On that particular morning I was woken by the clanging sound of the labourers' spades.

I remember that the atmosphere was tense between Mama and Papa. I overheard her say, 'Where do we go from here? You know you cannot do any other work except work in the fields. Even if you had grown up in the big house and your mother had been their maid like me, our days here are numbered. It cuts no ice! Why must your mouth always run away with you when you're drunk?'

'But it's the truth.'

'I know it is the truth. But these people don't like it!'

It all happened the previous Saturday when the 'Oubaas' took the farmworkers on their monthly outing to the dorp. The children would run around and the wine flowed freely. The teenagers preferred the cinema and had to hike back at night to the farm. Wives would sit and breastfeed their babies unashamedly while the men had a good time in the small country bar. The young girls would do the shopping and be on the lookout for rummage sales. I remember the town square being packed on the outings with babies' bare bums and mothers with their exposed breasts; the rummage sales, purchased meat and groceries, and drunk men urinating in the side streets. Who cares, they seemed to think we were away from the farm for a holiday.

That morning Papa got drunk and started swearing at the passing whites. Said they're all a lot of slave drivers and told them to look at our women in their rags and at the near-naked babies. Someone shouted that he needed a soapbox and the people laughed at the suggestion.

One of the neighbouring farmers quietly went over to the Hotel and called out to the 'Oubaas' who came rushing out, red up to his ears. He took Papa by the scruff of the neck and threw him into the truck and shouted at him, 'Sit op jou gat totdat ons huistoe gaan, verdomde dônner.' Papa struck his head against the side of the truck and I was so upset at the punishment meted out to him that I stood crying near the truck until we moved off.

When we arrived back at the farm the 'Oubaas' asked the others to hold Papa, but they pretended to be too drunk and attempted to stumble off to their shacks. He called them back and told them to see what would happen to people who liked to make political speeches. He called his son, who had returned recently from army training, to help hold Papa. My mother pleaded with the 'Oubaas' but he was determined to use his whip.

'Hy praat nie op so 'n manier van die dusvolk nie!'

'Asseblief, Oubaas,' my mother pleaded.

'Wat gaan aan in jou gedagtes? Ek neem vir hulle dorp toe and hy wil politiek praat!'

The whip came cracking down over my father's back. After I don't know how many strokes, the children became hysterical. He stopped finally with the sweat streaming down his face, told us that it was his teatime and walked back to the big house. The other workers, by now sober, carried Papa inside and I washed his face.

Mama had to go back to the old house to serve tea to the 'Oubaas'. It was then that I made my decision to get the hell out of there and move to the city. I kept on patting the wet facecloth over the wrinkled face and tried to cheer him up.

'I'll read for you tonight, Papa.'

'I'll be alright, child,' he said softly.

My mother always brought reading matter from the big house; magazines, with beautiful fashions that I dreamt of wearing, and other books. At night I would lie between them and read in the candle light: love stories, fiction, articles, anything that happened to take Papa's fancy. He and Mama liked to listen to the stories that I read them and he often remarked that he never dreamt that one of his children would one day be able to read and write. He looked real proud during our reading sessions.

'Go sleep now, Papa, so that the swelling can go down.'

'What do you think of me, Maria?'

'I love you, Papa.' I closed the door and went to feed the chickens and look for Beta who had run away when she saw the whip.

The following morning the children ate their mieliepap and Beta left for school which was miles away from the farm. Mannetjie was having his afternoon nap and I was washing napkins. I looked down the road opposite our shack and saw a car approaching. That road, I was told, would take you all the way to Johannesburg. While hanging up the napkins I saw the big silver car stop near our shack. A man and a woman got out and walked towards me. She wore a flowing sari of floral chiffon and he a safari suit, just like those the friends of 'Oubaas' wore when they came to visit on Sundays.

She was smiling in a very friendly way and asked my name. I told her, and she asked if I would like to come to Cape Town to help her. She explained that they owned a large supermarket near the city and needed help. She asked if she could speak to Mama. I told her that Mama would be back soon and that Papa would be coming for his bread and coffee soon as it was almost lunch time. I took them inside and she sat down on the old wooden chair in our little kitchen while he stood arms folded, looking around. He said 'Look, we have no time to waste. Get done with your business quickly as we have a long journey back and you know what happens when I'm not at the shop.'

Finally I had to call Mama and tell her what the people wanted. At first she was adamant: 'Not on your life. You're not leaving here.' I begged and pleaded with her to let me go. Mama greeted them and they told her about the help they needed. She offered them tea but he refused. Papa came in from the fields and the man told him about their proposition for me. Papa didn't agree either, saying that the City was wicked and that I was only seventeen.

'I promise we will look after her and let her finish her schooling. That's a promise,' he said. Papa showed interest at this suggestion and enquired, 'But how can she go to school and work?'

'There are many schools in our area. She can go to night school. I promise we will treat her like one of the family.'

'I like her,' the woman said, 'Don't stand in her way. You won't regret it.'

Papa finally agreed and the man gave him twenty rands which he could not resist. God, how he must work a whole month for that

124

sort of money!

While Mama was weeping silently, Papa asked, 'Do you rather want her to spend her young life here on this fucking farm like me? Since my childhood I've worked for them. Come now, it's best for her.'

'She can come home once a month, that's a promise.'

'I'm only glad that she can go to school. Look after my girl!' Mama assented.

I got into the big silver car and after all the goodbyes we slid away from the farm which I haven't seen again. For a long while I could still hear Mannetjie crying for me. I really loved that child with his fat chubby cheeks. I sat back in the car and thought my whole life was going to change and silently thanked God. I prayed to Him to keep my family safe, and that there would be no more whippings. We drove on what seemed to be an endless road while the two in the front seats spoke about their friends, their new houses, and about new schemes to make more money.

We arrived at a large house with a shopping complex attached. I read the name 'Allie's Supermarket' written large across the front of the building. It looked grand with the good fresh fruit displayed on the pavement and the pretty dresses in the windows. I thought that I would get a smart dress like those that I had seen in the magazines back home. He came round to her side and opened the car door for her. She told me that this was their shop. I stood on the pavement not knowing what to do. 'You go round the back and I'll come to show you around soon. Go through that big gate.'

I carried my bag through the back gate and came face to face with a huge Alsatian dog. At first I wanted to scream with fright but I talked to him softly. 'Hello, boy. Hello, hello boy.' The dog wagged his tail and followed me to the back door. I sat on my case and waited and waited and became hungry. The dog remained sitting at my feet. The yard was wet and cold and the broken cement patches formed puddles of water. There were fruit boxes piled high. They smelled mouldy. I looked at my surroundings and felt like crying when I heard footsteps coming down the lane.

A man appeared with a heavy bag on his back. After he put the load down I saw this tall, black and handsome figure. He came towards me and said, 'Hello. You're coming to stay here?'

'Yes,' I whispered, the tears stinging my eyes. He saw this and became very sympathetic.

'Don't cry. What is your name?'

'Maria,' I answered and started weeping again. He took out a clean white handkerchief, as white as his strong teeth, and his lovely smile disarmed me. I wiped my tears shyly.

'Don't cry. I'll help you.' We heard footsteps approaching.

'Ben! Where the fucking hell are you?'

'Coming, baas. I was drinking water.'

'Now shake your arse, man,' the voice said angrily.

Ben wiped his face with the handkerchief which was now wet with my tears.

To pass the time I patted the dog and spoke to it. As Ben walked off he said, 'That's funny. That dog doesn't like strangers but he likes you.'

I sat in the wet yard for what seemed hours. Eventually she came out. 'My God, child! I was so busy behind the counter. Come, I'll show you your room. Here we are. This is not the farm so see that you keep it clean.' When she left I wanted to shout to her that I was hungry but she had disappeared.

It was a dull tiny room with a single iron bed, and a fruitbox with a vase on it. I hung my jacket on a wire hanger and it was obvious that someone had lived here recently. She returned and said that Ben would have to sleep in the fruitshed. 'Can't trust these kaffirs. Come to the kitchen and eat something. You must be starved. My mother runs the house and she'll give you supper. What standard did you pass at school?'

'Standard Six, Missis.' Immediately I thought, here comes the shop assistant job and the night school. I felt relieved and glad as I entered the kitchen for my first meal in the city.

In the large American kitchen on a small table in the corner stood a plate of curry and a mug of tea. The food was strong but I was hungry. I sat looking around the big tiled kitchen with cupboards all matched in colour, like in the books back home.

The two teenage girls of the family came into the kitchen. They were about my age. One was so fat that she even had droopy cheeks and I could not see her neck. They walked past me as if I didn't exist, and opened the fridge, taking two bottles of cool-drink and opening them next to the table where I was eating. What a luxury, I thought, for the only cool-drinks I knew of came from a packet of powder that makes ten glasses. We only had the drinks on Sundays and I remember Mannetjie gulping down one glass after another, hoping to fill his stomach to last till next Sunday, the little glutton!

The girls drank half of the bottles and dumped them on the main table. Their grandmother asked them to clear the dinner table but they walked out grumbling. 'That will be the day,' and 'We've got homework to do.' The fat one opened the fridge again and I peeped inside and was amazed by so much food and drink. Only the whites have fridges like this one back home on the farm. We used to keep our food in a gauze wire cupboard which hung on a tree outside.

'Come, girl. I haven't got all night.'

I said grace and thanked the old lady.

'Here's a dishcloth. You can dry the dishes for me,' the old lady said in a frustrated voice. 'I don't know why they did not bring two girls. Expect me, with my old body, to be busy all day.'

I went on with the dishes.

'You're going to work in the shop. There's a lot of shoplifting going on lately. But they could've brought another girl to help me.'

I remembered the twenty Rands which Papa could not resist. I bade her goodnight after I had finished the dishes and went through the wet yard to my room with the dog following me. Ben saw me passing and brought me a candle. I thanked him and asked him for something to read. He brought me the *Sunday Post*. The dog whined at the door until I let him in. I felt homesick when I read the depressing news of how people lived in Johannesburg. I dropped off to sleep with the newspaper in my hands.

The next morning I awoke to someone calling my name. 'Maria! Maria! Come, get up. Come clean the girls' shoes. You *must* wake up earlier. The girls must get to school on time.' The word school reminded me of her promise.

I sat at the back door cleaning their shoes which they took from me without even a thank you or a nod. My mind strayed to the previous night and to the cool drinks which they had wasted.

Ben passed me with brooms and buckets and called me over to him.

'I hear you must stand guard for the day.'

'What does that mean?' I enquired.

'While I pack all the goods outside you must stand there and watch if anyone steals. There are a lot of people passing by. This is a busy area what with all the schools and the bus terminus and station nearby.'

'You mean I must stand there all day and just watch if people steal?'

'They trust no one,' Ben replied knowlingly.

Every morning thereafter, after a mug of hot coffee and bread, I would wash off the pavement. Ben had his section and I had mine. Buckets of soapy water was splashed over the pavement and I then swept down the gutter. Then I was posted in front of the shop, begging people to come in to see the 'bargains' inside. I also had to look out for shoplifters. I hated every moment of this work. Some days the sun blazed down so fiercely that I felt faint. I watched with envy the girls from the different schools passing in the afternoons, wondering when I would be sent to school.

She fetched her daughters from school in the afternoon. They would get out of the big car and bang the doors shut. Running past me they would rush to the icecream counter inside the shop and come out licking large pink icecreams or suckers. Sometimes I felt hungry and tired but lunch often was just leftovers.

Sometimes Ben would pass me a sweet secretly and whisper, 'Don't let them see you eat.' He always came to talk to me or to give me something which he had taken in the shop without them noticing. I shall always remember him carrying the heavy sugar bags on his back.

One afternoon he came over and said, 'You look pale. Are you sick?'

'Yes,' I said, embarrassed.

'Don't let them see you cry like that. What is the matter?'

'My stomach is cramping so,' I replied.

He disappeared into the shop and after a while returned with a pack of sanitary towels. The blood had started to run down my legs. I was so grateful to him. I had to go inside the shop to ask permission to go to the toilet.

'Yes, and don't be long,' he said.

After I had cleaned myself up I walked back to the cursed job, watching people. If people stole they must be hungry, I reasoned. Standing in that busy street and watching everyone going somewhere. That night I felt so sick that I fell down on the bed into a deep sleep. I was sure that I was suffering from sunstroke. The dog slept in his usual place and I dreamt about Papa, Mama, Beta and Mannetjie. I was woken by a faint knocking at my door. I immediately knew it was Ben and I was glad of the opportunity to speak to someone again.'

'Come in, Ben,' I said softly.

'How're you feeling now?'

'Fine, thanks. What is the time? You're still up? I've slept already.'

'Eleven o'clock. I had to pack the shelves in the shop. During the day it is too full of people.

'They pay you well, Ben?'

'Not a damn. Here's a chocolate for you. Have it.'

'Thanks. You must be careful, Ben. I don't like these people. They'll send you to jail even for a chocolate bar.

'I know. I want you to have it. I'm going to look after you.'

'I'm not a child, Ben.'

'Who cried like a big baby today?' he laughed. 'Why did you come to this place?'

'I thought it better than the farm and she promised to send me to High School. I want to learn more, Ben. That's why I came.'

'My girl, you won't even reach a schoolgate. These people don't keep their promises.'

After that night he came every evening and I loved him when he kissed me. He was so big and strong. We spoke about how much we loved each other and he even said that I was as pure as a lily. He always brought me little things from the shop. One night he brought me lipstick and mascara and held the mirror for me to make up my face. I was as thrilled as he for that was the first time I had used make-up. I knew I looked attractive and was shy when he said, 'Hell, you are beautiful.' That night we made love for the first time and fell fast asleep, oblivious of the danger of being found together. Later he woke me and said that he must get the hell out of that place.

'We can't get away from them, Ben. Don't talk about my family. I will have to learn to forget about them. I've got no money even to go and visit them. Besides, she doesn't let me off, even on Sundays.'

One night after a long day in the sun, I washed and got to bed early. He came in and pulled open the blankets and looking at my body he said, 'I've never seen such curves.' We laughed and read the newspaper.

'I must wake up at four o'clock tomorrow. It's market day and that man mustn't find me here. He asked me today why we never catch anyone stealing.'

'Must I say people steal if they don't? Don't worry, I'll wake you, Ben.' Then we fell asleep but our happiness was short-lived. The next morning we were woken to loud banging at the door.

'Come out of there, kaffir. And you, farm-bitch. Get out this minute. You can both go back to where you come from.'

We jumped up and dressed in a hurry. Ben looked worried.

'Don't worry,' I said kissing him and peeped through the window. It was still dark and the stars were still glowing brighly. The yard lights were on when we came out of the room.

'Pack your things and go,' he commanded.

'Where can we go?' Ben asked.

'You had time to think of that before.'

When we left he searched our bundles and locked the yard gate behind us.

'You can collect your papers at the Bantu Administration,' he sneered through the gate. 'You know what that means!'

We walked out of that cold wet yard into the cold misty dawn like two thieves. The lights in the huge house were still not switched on. The dog followed us as we walked towards the station. We avoided the main road because of the patrolling vans. We had no papers and the bundles made it obvious that we were now vagrants. We sat cuddled up, shivering with cold in the waiting room, hoping that the Railway Police wouldn't find us.

When the first train came along I said, 'Ben, where do we go from here?' He replied that he had friends at the Epping vegetable market and that I must wait for him on Cape Town station. I said that I would miss the dog and wondered if he wouldn't be killed by a car before he reached home or whether that damp wet yard wouldn't eventually claim him. Ben reassured me, saying that he would get me a dog when we had a place to stay. I knew that those two fat girls would not feed the dog. Even in the train I was still worried about the dog. It was then that Ben realised that he had left his passbook in his white jacket, in the fruitshed.

'I don't want to see that man again. Let the book rot there! I hate that book!'

We reached Cape Town and Ben said I should wait for him until he returned from Epping. I sat till lunch time thinking, what if he doesn't come back? Where will I get money to go back to the farm? I watched the throngs of people coming and going. They all looked so serious; everyone seemed to know where they were going. I wished I was one of them.

Ben finally returned soon after lunch time. I saw from his worried face that his journey had been in vain. He bought a packet of fish and chips and we ate hungrily.

'I found nothing. The shanties were all numbered last week and the people are afraid of taking in others for fear of having their homes bulldozed.'

We roamed the streets of Cape Town day after day, sleeping in servants' rooms at night. Ben knew a lot of people, friends he had made when he used to come to Cape Town to the wholesalers for Allie's Supermarket. Days turned into months and we moved from place to place until we met his friend, Lucas. He pitied us as he felt we were so young. 'To live like this! I stay near the mountain. Come and live with me,' he told Ben.

We arrived at the mountain home which was just a large hole like a cave, with mattresses on the floor, but it was clean. 'This is better than the streets,' Ben said. That night Ben asked me if I'd rather go home to the farm or live there with him like this. Because I loved him I told him that I couldn't leave him. There were many others who lived like us. Outcasts of the city. Lucas had lost his wife a while back and I was accepted as the lady of the house.

One day while I was busy cleaning out our hole, making the beds and sweeping. Lucas came to tell me that they had arrested Ben. 'I expected something like this to happen,' he said.

'But why?' I asked unbelievingly.

'Pass! He's got no papers!' Lucas replied.

I wept for a long time but I am still waiting for him. I lay down on the mattress and sobbed my heart out. Rita, one of the friends I came to know, tried to comfort me. 'Alright, my girl. Don't cry. Come let's have a drink.' I followed her and got drunk for the first time.

I lay on the grass in a drunken stupor and hated the nauseous feeling of everything revolving around me. In my drunken dream I saw his outstretched arms reaching for me: 'Ben, Ben? You've come to take me away from here?' Instead the dull pain of a fist smashing into the side of my face confused and alarmed me. I opened my eyes but could not focus properly nor could I lift my arms, which seemed so heavy, to protect myself. Vaguely in the distance I was sure I heard Rita's high-pitched sensual laughter.

I shouted for assitance in the direction of the voice but received no answer.

Then I realised that the figure standing over me was not Ben's. He hit out at my face again. As I slipped into unconsciousness, I felt him tearing at my underwear and his heavy weight on me muffled my screams. No one heard or cared.

The Day of the Riots

MBULELO VIZIKHUNGO MZAMANE

'But can't you really let me put up here for the night?' Johannes Venter asked for the umpteenth time.

'Goodness gracious, no, Mr Venter,' Sipho answered. 'Can't you understand? If you're unable to leave tonight, under cover of darkness, you have no chance of coming out alive tomorrow, in broad daylight.'

'But things may have changed in the morning.'

'Yes, for the worse. Don't you realise, sir, that those children only let us go because they know me? They may very well start boasting in the streets. And when the older ones hear the story, there's no telling what will become of us all if they find you here.'

Sipho's children peered into the sitting-room where he and Johannes Venter were talking.

Hambani niyolala nina,' he said.

They darted back to the kitchen but did not go to bed as he had instructed.

'No, you just can't sleep here, Mr Venter,' Sipho said. 'We simply must think of a way of getting you out of the township with a minimum of delay. Oh! yes, I think I've got it. I'll go and report your presence to the police. They'll be able to escort you safely out of the township. I'll be back shortly. Just make yourself at home. My wife will keep you company till I return. Would you like something to eat?'

'No, I'm all right, thank you.'

'Okay, some tea then. Won't be long, sir.'

Sipho hurried into the kitchen. His wife, Daphne, and their children were huddled together around the coal stove like a brood of chickens.

It was blustering wintry weather. The wind howled and lashed violently against the windows. Gushes of cold air entered through the numerous cracks on the walls, especially where the walls met the roof. The ill-fitting door was stuffed with paper and cloths to keep out some of the cold air.

Daphne was listening to the children's accounts of the day's events when Sipho entered. He closed the door after him.

133

'Will you stay with him until I come back!' Sipho said. 'I'll go and call the police.'

'He can't sleep here,' Daphne said.

'I'm trying to see to it that he doesn't,' Sipho said.

'*Kodwa wena ubumusa kuphi lomuntu?*' Daphne asked.

Sipho thought what an unfair question it was. How could she conceivably ask why he'd brought Venter, as though he'd had any choice in the matter?

'Please, let's not go into that now,' he said.

'Where will you find the police,' she asked.

'Where else? At the police station, of course. That's what they should be doing, protecting people instead of mowing down our children.'

'*Baba*, they burnt down the police station this afternoon,' Sandile said. He was their eldest son and was ten years old.

Sipho looked at Daphne. She nodded.

There was a loud knock at the door.

Johannes Venter sprang to his feet and made for the kitchen. He stood trembling at the door.

'Excuse me, there's someone knocking,' he said. 'D'you think they've come for me?'

'*Nkulunkulu wam*'!' Daphne exclaimed. 'What did I say? There's only one thing we can do now,' she continued in Zulu. 'You've got to hide him outside, in the coal box.' She quickly sized up Johannes Venter from head to foot. 'He's not such a big man. He'll fit in all right. Quick, we've no time to lose. Get him out before whoever is knocking comes round to the back door.'

They were talking in whispers.

Johannes Venter was shaking uncontrollably. How did one live under such constant threats? He was made to feel even more forlorn by being left out of the conversation which went on in a language he didn't understand. Nor did he feel the least reasured by being ignored each time he asked to be told what they planned to do with him. Was he going to be surrendered to the mercy of those savage children they'd met running riot in the streets? Why hadn't he simply dumped Sipho at the entrance to the township and driven home to his wife and children? But how could he have known that he'd be trapped in this infernal place?

'Risky! But I can't, for the life of me, think of anything else, besides simply letting him out through the window,' Sipho said.

'My God! Do you want a white corpse in our yard in the morning?' Daphne asked.

'No, no, not that. I guess your plan will do. But don't open the door yet. While I get him out, you and the children create as much fracas as you can. Get them to sing something at the top of their voices. And start shouting to whoever is at that door that you're coming. Take your time opening that door.'

'What shall I ask them to sing?'

'Oh, anything. "Rock of ages" or something.'

'But they dont know that one.'

'Get them to sing something else they know then.'

'I know what we'll sing.' It was Nomsa, their five-year old daughter. 'Let's sing that new song Sandile and Siswe taught me today, the one I heard the Black Power (only she pronounced it "Powder") children singing when they came back from fighting the police. Sandile and Sizwe were there, *baba*. They were all shouting "Black Powder! Black Powder!" and "Amandla! Amandla!" Start it Sizwe.'

'I don't know which one you mean,' Sizwe said. 'There were many songs we sang today.'

Sizwe was two years older than Nomsa. He and Sandile went to school in the township. During the day they had been involved in a demonstration, together with children from other primary and secondary schools in the township. They marched through the streets, singing old liberation songs and others they had composed themselves, to protest against the enforcement of Afrikaans as a medium of instruction in certain subjects throughout African schools. The students planned to converge at the township's largest soccer stadium to voice their opposition to the scheme.

The police met them in the streets, before they could reach the stadium, and asked them through loudspeakers to disperse. They told the students that in terms of the Riotous Assemblies Act, which the children had never heard about, they were breaking the law by staging a protest march without obtaining permission from the police first.

'You are here. Give us your permission then,' someone in the crowd shouted. And the chant caught on, 'Give us your permission then.'

'Legalise *dagga*!' someone else shouted. There was loud laughter but no one took up the shout.

135

The police then used teargas to try and disperse the students. Far from scattering about in a disorganised fashion, the students soon developed a technique for containing the teargas. Armed with cloths and buckets of water requisitioned from nearby houses, they covered the canisters with wet cloths as soon as they hit the ground. In this way many of the canisters were prevented from exploding. Thus unable to break the march the police resorted to shooting. At first they aimed above the heads of the crowd, but as the students surged forward resolutely they fired at their front ranks. Some students retaliated by throwing stones at the police. In the ensuing scuffle a few people were injured, including some police and onlookers, and several children were shot dead.

Incensed by the police action the students ran riot.

'Amandla! Power!' they shouted, with clenched fists raised in the air.

'We'll burn down all their buildings . . . Away with the abominable System!'

Working in groups which struck their targets almost simultaneously, the students acted too fast for the police who had come out in large numbers, leaving the police station virtually deserted. While the police were engaged in trying to contain the disturbances which flared up at various strategic points in the township, a group of specially deployed students caught an unsuspecting skeleton staff at the police station itself and set the buildings on fire. Elsewhere they burnt down the municipality offices and other buildings associated with the township's administration board, like the post offices, beer halls and the fire department. Some schools and libraries were also burnt down.

There were many whites whose daily business brought them to the township. These included employees of the administration board, commercial travellers and people working for voluntary agencies which operated in the township. Many delivery vans bearing the names of white companies were stopped in the streets, overturned and set on fire. Buses received the same treatment. In many cases their black drivers and conductors scuttled into nearby houses, then retired to their homes or their favourite shebeens to drink the bus company's earnings. Some whites caught in this way were killed, among them a doctor who ran a voluntary medical scheme for children in the township. His body was found in a rubbish bin. Another superintendent in one of the administration board's offices who was watching the battle between the police and the students unaware of any reason why anyone should wish to harm him, was also killed.

A dangerous spirit, such as Sipho and Johannes Venter had experienced in driving through the township, still gripped the streets.

'Sing then,' Sipho said to his children.

'Just a moment, please, I'm coming,' Daphne shouted.

'Start it, Sizewe,' Nomsa said.

'Sing!' Sipho said.

Sizwe and Sandile started simultaneously, on different keys. Nomsa joined in, adding to the discord:

> *Mhla sibuyayo! Mhla sibuyayo!*
> *Mhla sibuyayo! Mhla sibuyayo!*
> *Kuzokhal' uVorster,*
> *Kubaleke uKruger . . .*

'No, no, no, not that one!' Sipho said.

The children fell silent.

'Come on, sing!' Sipho said.

'*Siculeni mange?*' Nomsa asked.

'Just sing, anything. Now go:

> Rock of ages cleft for me,
> Let me hide . . .

'*Asiyazi leyo,*' Nomsa said.

'Okay, if you don't know that one, sing something you know then,' Sipho said.

Sizwe suggested they should sing '*Amabhunu ayizinja*'.

'Not that one either, not that one. Can't you sing anything without dragging in Boers? Okay, just go on talking then. Louder . . . Louder, I say!'

The knocking continued.

'I'm coming,' Daphne said.

'It's okay, Mr Venter,' Sipho said. 'Just follow me and do as I say. This side, please.

Sipho carefully opened the back door and edged out, with Johannes Venter following closely.

The coal-box stood in a corner of the backyard, near the toilet. Sipho had built it himself by joining sundry planks together. It had a lid with a padlock which was locked every night before the family went to bed. When empty the box was large enough to hold two children playing hide-and-seek and therefore indifferent to any temporary inconvenience.

They made for it.

Sipho felt inside with his hands. It was half-full of coal. There were also some dirty rags, old newspapers, firewood and an axe. He brought out the axe.

'Climb in here, Sir,' he said.

Johannes Venter saw the adjacent building and hesitated.

'Why can't I hide in there?' he ased.

'Sir, the toilet would be the most obvious place for any search party to look in,' Sipho answered. 'Get in quickly.'

Johannes Venter climbed in gingerly. Sipho helped to catapult him in, head first.

'Lie on your side.'

He did so. He folded his knees, brought them up to his chin and encircled them with his arms. He could feel the sharp edges of the coal and the splinters of wood through his body. He wondered how long he'd remain interred in there.

Sipho thrust the axe in his hands.

'You may need this,' he said.

'My friend, please, don't leave me buried in this place for long,' Johannes Venter said in a faint voice.

'I'll get you out as soon as I possibly can.'

The lid came over Johannes Venter's body. He sobbed a little and then remembered he must get hold of himself. He tried to fix his mind on his family. When his death was reported to his wife, would she be overwhelmed with grief? How would his children manage being left fatherless so young? He offered silent, incoherent prayers which encompassed just about everybody and everything he held dear. He cursed his fate which had landed him in this dark pit. His company should have placed him in the office. He should have pressed for an early answer to his application for a transfer. He hated travelling which often kept him away from his family for days on end. Not even their clandestine outings to Botswana with Sipho could quite compensate for this sort of inconvenience. He had last seen his family on Monday, no, on Sunday evening really, because he had left very early on Monday while they were all asleep, and today was Wednesday night. Would he ever see them again?

He tried to recall his wife's face but her image had become too dim. His head ached where he had landed on the coal. And then suddenly he felt drained of all strength. A sense of unreality assailed him. It was strange the way his body felt less and less a part of him. His whole body started to tremble. He no longer had the will or the strength to control himself. His head reeled round and round. He thought he heard footsteps receding into the distance. His teeth were chattering badly. He tried to shout, but his breath was leaving him and no sound came out. A deep, deep darkness, such as he had never known before, descended over him.

After shutting the lid Sipho felt pressed. He walked into the toilet and unzipped his fly. Only a few drops trickled out. It had been a false alarm. He flushed the cistern and walked out. He washed his hands from the tap next to the toilet and walked back to the house, whistling.

He stood at the door to listen. There were several voices speaking all at once. A man's voice could be heard above the rest. Sipho sighed audibly and walked in. It was his friend, Eddie, who had come with his girlfriend, Meikie, a nurse at the local hospital.

'*Heit! Fana*' Eddie greeted. 'I learn your white man has decided to live with us in the township. Wish I could exchange places with him!'

'Shucks! Eddie,' Sipho said and flopped into a chair. 'Why couldn't you just tell us it was you? *Kunjani Meikie*?'

Meikie returned the greeting.

'How could I have known you'd gone multi-racial?' Eddie asked.

'It's no laughing matter,' Sipho said.

'Where's he?' Eddie asked.

'Come with me,' Sipho said.

Eddie followed him out.

They came to the coal box and Sipho said, 'It's all right, Mr Venter, it's only some friends.'

He opened the lid.

'Mr Venter, you can come out now.'

'Maybe he bolted out,' Eddie siad.

'He's here all right,' Sipho said.

Johannes Venter did not stir.

Sipho shook him hard several times, then turned to Eddie. 'Lend me a hand,' he said. 'I think the poor guy's passed out.'

They carried Johannes Venter back to the house and placed him on the sofa in the sitting-room. He was covered with soot like a township coal vendor.

Meikie was quickly galvanised into action. She asked Daphne for a basin of cold water. While Daphne went for the water she unloosened Johannes Venter's clothes.

'Careful of breaking the Immorality Act, sweetheart,' Eddie said.

'I think it's just shock,' she said. 'Nothing much to worry about. He should be able to come round on his own soon.'

'What do you intend to do with him?' Eddie asked.

'I don't know,' Sipho answered. 'I thought I'd get the police to escort him home. I guess I'll have to drive him myself. Some kids saw us come here. I'm afraid the story may soon leak out. Will you come with me, Eddie?'

'You must be joking!' Eddie said. 'Ask Meikie what it's like out there. Just a street away there are bonfires all along the road. And it's not just old tyres they're burning. Meikie and I just came back from town by taxi about an hour ago. Listen to me, we've seen a bit of what's happening out there and we didn't like it a bit. Look, I was born in this township. I've never seen it so angry, I tell you. We were held up no less than three times and not just by the police either. They're confining their activities to the outskirts of the township, harassing guys without passes, as usual. It was also reported over the radio that, with the police station razed to the ground, the army has been called in to deal with the riots. But for the time being those kids have established a virtual government in this township. And you ask you me to go and risk my neck out there! Why, I don't even call that a risk. It's outright suicide. Let's talk about something else. Did you hear that similar disturbances have also flared up in Nyanga and Langa townships in Cape Town and New Brighton in Port Elizabeth? All police and army leave has been cancelled. This looks like being bigger than Sharpeville, man. Do you remember how the people scuttled like rats into their holes before those bazookas?'

'But if we can avoid all the roadblocks,' Sipho continued, 'we did it when we drove here, we could probably dump this guy with the police or the army.'

'And be pulled in to show them who the leaders of the riots are? Forget it, man. Besides, you can't even get that far without bumping into the students. Listen, chum, our taxi-driver told us that there are checkpoints on all the roads leading in and out of the township

— and there isn't an infinite number of those, the Boers have made sure of that, for more effective control! These checkpoints are manned by the students themselves, on the look-out for whites and sell-outs. And they are very thorough. Have you heard what they did to Chabeli and Rathebe!'

'Tell us what happened, Eddie,' Daphne quickly put in.

Chabeli and Rathebe were both prominent members of the township's advisory board, 'veteran boardmen' the newspapers called them.

The advisory board's function was to make the views of the people known to the authorities. But few townships residents supported it, so that its elections never drew more than five per cent of the electorate. Nevertheless, the government never failed to point out that the advisory board was the only democratically elected body to represent African opinion. The usual low percentage poll was attributed to the fact that Africans were as yet unaccustomed to the intricacies of democratic procedures. They were still apprentices to civilisation in general and needed the guiding hand of the white man. The alternative, in the Prime Minister's own words, was, 'too ghastly to contemplate.'

When the students had first made known their opposition to the compulsory introduction of Afrikaans as a medium of instruction, Chabeli and Rathebe had been most vociferous in their condemnation of the students. They denounced them as misguided idealists, living in the past rather than looking forward. They were quoted in the newspapers and over the radio as saying that the students were cutting their own throats. They were shutting their eyes to the reality of their own situation and failing to take advantage of such opportunities as their parents had been denied in their days, when African schools were still in the hand of irrelevant missionaries and lackeys of the British empire. They said that the demands of modern commerce and the need to foster better race relations and promote peaceful co-existence in such a plural society as ours in South Africa, with two official languages, rested not only on the Africans knowledge of English but also on his proficiency in Afrikaans. In an interview with one Afrikaans newspaper Chabeli pointed out that the importance of English had been gradually eroded in the last fifteen years since South Africa had left the Commonwealth, and that Afrikaans was definitely the language of the future which it would benefit his people to master.

Chabeli, a former primary school Headmaster, was the Chairman of the local school board to whom the students first presented their petition, so that the board could pass it on to the appropriate authorities. Chabeli called the students presumptuous ingrates who had to be protected from cutting off their own noses to spite their faces. As an educationist of long-standing, he told the students, he knew what was good for them. How did they hope to take their rightful place in a future constellation of southern African states without an education which was at least as good as their former masters? He ended up by tearing their petition in front of members of the S.R.C., a group of elected student representatives from the township's various secondary and high schools who had brought the petition.

The advisory board under the chairmanship of Rathebe, to whom the students went next, treated them with similar scorn.

Rathebe, a bulky man with a drooping stomach, was one of the township's wealthiest men. He owned a string of businesses in the centre of the township. But it was generally rumoured that he was merely a front for some Indian and white businessmen. He made no secret of his support for government policy which was geared towards providing African businessmen with unlimited opportunity for expansion in their homelands, without unfair competition from English-speaking money-mongers. His outspoken views enabled him to win further concessions from the authorities to expand his business in the township. Through the representation of Africans like himself the government had agreed to grant leases of ninety-nine years to a certain category of Africans in the urban areas. He was very often invited to parties for businessmen of all races and entertained very lavishly himself. Only recently he had played host at the township's only hotel to a group of visiting white M.P.'s. He and Chabeli received wide publicity from the news media which referred to them variously as 'township tycoons', 'non-white socialites', 'black moderates' and 'civic leaders.'

The advisory board was in session when the unrest broke out in the township. Resolution after resolution was passed condemning the students, their teachers and parents. 'When we were boys,' Rathebe summed up from the chair, 'it could never have happened. In those days teachers did what they were paid for and every parent knew the folly of sparing the rod. Let it never be said of us that when the moment came we, in this chamber, were found wanting;

that we exchanged our sacred destiny, our sanctified station in life and our duty to posterity for cheap popularity; that we sacrificed our convictions and consciences on the altar of expediency. Let us stamp out these cantankerous elements from our midst, unwitting tools of certain well-known agitators, no doubt, once and for all.'

There was deafening applause from the other councillors.

Late that afternoon reports reached the advisory board's council chambers that arson and looting had broken out in the township, and that some children had been shot dead.

The parents among them immediately thought of their children; businessmen thought of their property.

The board's deliberations were cut short in the middle of an important debate about the site for a new cemetery, many of the members arguing that the site chosen by the authorities was best suited for the proposed African Development Bank and the first African-owned supermaket. The chairman was in the process of circulating the plans, drawn up by members of the African Chamber of Commerce of which he was president, when the disturbing news came. He called for an adjournment.

Chabeli and Rathebe were driving home together when they were caught in a roadblock near Rathebe's shops, where he hoped to check first if all was well. He never got the opportunity.

Roadblocks were common in that area from traffic cops checking on stolen cars, unlicensed ones, cars with no roadworthy certificates, pirate taxis, taxis carrying overloads and mobile criminals of all descriptions.

When their turn came Chabeli and Rathebe discovered that it was only a bunch of school kids, still in their school uniforms.

'What the hell do they think they're up to?' Chabeli asked.

'Exactly what we were discussing,' Rathebe said.

'I'll bloody well teach them who I am,' Chabeli said and stormed out of the passenger's seat. 'You there, remove your little arses from the streets.'

'Look who we've got here, chaps?' one of the students shouted.

'Yes, you know me very well. I don't brook no shit from disrespectful nincompoops like you. Who do you think you are? Just what nonsense is going on here?'

Rathebe, jangling the keys of his new BMW, left the car idling and came out to check. Standing next to Chabeli, he quickly assessed the situation and felt that he didn't like what was happening, not one bit. He hoped Chabeli had enough sense to know when it was time to stop poking one's fingers in and out of the mouth of a growing lion cub which one had been keeping for a pet.

'This is more than our fair share of luck, chaps,' the same student said.

A growing number of students and some onlookers gathered round them.

'Just who the hell do you think you are?' Chabeli asked.

'It's the blokes from the Useless Boys' Club,' some other student said, deliberately provoking laughter by twisting the first letters of the name the advisory board had newly acquired when it became officially known as the Urban Bantu Council — as a step towards granting the township full municipality rights, the government had said.

'Just handle them with kid gloves, old boy,' Rathebe whispered. 'I smell gunpowder here.'

'I'd stop all this bull-shitting if I were you and go home,' Chabeli said. Today you've brought nothing but shame and dishonour to yourselves and your people. Now be off with you all!'

'Listen who's talking about "shame and dishonour"!' another student said.

The others roared with laughter.

'Easy now, old chap, easy,' Rathebe whispered. 'No need to blow off like that. Leave all this to me. I know exactly how to handle this.'

He appealed for silence from the students and then spoke;

'Listen to me, my children. You know us very well. We are your people. If there's anything we can do . . .'

But neither Chabeli's swaggering talk nor Rathebe's pleas had any effect on the students. Rathebe was easily caught as he tried to dash for the comparative safety of his shops across the road. A suggestion to burn his shops, however, was drowned in the general excitement. Chabeli was brought down on his haunches with several blows to his head from a hosepipe.

The two men were made to squat and frogmarched to Rathebe's house, about a mile and a half away. The students clapped all the way to shouts of 'Hop! hop!', while others sang 'We are marching to Pretoria'.

When they ultimately got to Rathebe's house his ample frame was dripping with sweat. Chabeli's lanky body felt cramped all over. Neither man could stand on his feet. The students lifted them to the air and hurled them across Rathebe's high fence. They landed on Mrs Rathebe's bed of roses.

'What happened to their car?' Sipho asked, as he peeped through the window to see if their car was still parked where they had left it.

'A group of kids jumped in and drove around until it ran out of gas,' Eddie said.

'That's what they nearly did to us,' Sipho said.

'And yet you're hell-bent on driving this guy!' Eddie said.

'How's he doing, Meikie?' Sipho asked.

Meikie and Daphne bent over Johannes Venter.

As Johannes Venter slowly regained consciousness, he saw several pairs of eyes peering intently into is face. The eyes terrified him at first. Where had he seen just such eyes before? He tried to place the faces before him without success. He raised his head from the soft pillow and felt a throbbing pain in his head, like some king-size hangover. He felt a scorching thirst. Soft, solicitous hands were pushing him back on the pillow, gently but firmly. There was a hubbub of voices in the strange room. Finally his roving eyes lighted on Sipho's face. He felt a slight reassurance. He vaguely recalled that they were on tour together. But what were all these other faces doing in his hotel room, if that is what it was? And the black women, were they the ones Sipho had promised to organise?

Suddenly an unreasoning fear took a savage hold on him. With very painstaking effort, rather like a man trying to piece together a crazy jigsaw puzzle, he tried to recall the preceding events, culminating in that evening's horrific events.

They were returning from a long trip in the north-western Transvaal. Sipho had to drop first in the township before Johannes could proceed by himself to his own home in Mayfair. How much more convenient it might have been if Sipho, who did most of the driving anyhow, dropped him in town first! But company regulations had to be observed and they forbade Sipho to keep the company car overnight. As the manager had pointed out, Africans were unreliable and always abused the company vehicles left in their charge. There was Sipho's own case, for instance, when he had been allowed to keep the company car once because something, though it was very difficult to say exactly what, seemed to put him apart from the rest of them. And then what happened? The next morning he came to work, without the car, and then tried to sell the manager that cock-and-bull story about the wheels of the car having been stolen while it was parked outside his gate. True enough, the car had been found stripped of all the wheels outside Sipho's house, but only a fool would believe that Sipho himself had not sold the tyres. Only there was no way of proving that. That was the smart streak in them. It needed a white man who understood them very well to harness their native qualities for the good of society. For instance, the manager had decided to retain Sipho. But never again was he to keep the company car overnight. Since then they'd had no problems with him. He was very good at his work, too. Of course, you couldn't expect perfection from them. All the same he was undoubtedly the best of the lot. Not that white salesmen never put company vehicles to private use. But they did so with more circumspection.

To return to Sipho's case. When put on an inventory paper his strengths surpassed his weaknesses, to use the manager's analogy again. As for Johannes, he could never really make up his mind about Sipho. The man frankly puzzled him. Take the case of his qualifications, for instance, which every white man would have displayed with pride. One day after another long trip, Johannes had chanced on Sipho's certificate displayed on the wall when he helped him carry his luggage into the house. Sipho had a B.A. degree from the Bantu university of Fort Hare. Johannes excitedly promised that he would break the good news to their manager, with a recommendation for Sipho's promotion to full salesman, in charge of their whole district. Instead Sipho had begged him, and he had seemed in earnest about it, never to divulge the information to anyone. Johannes thought that there was certainly some grain of truth in what was said about the Bantu being temperamentally unsuited for positions of authority and responsibility. Otherwise how could anyone with ambition and initiative argue that he preferred the position he held to prospects of promotion based on his educational qualifications? It didn't make sense either what the man had said about previously having been sacked from several jobs for being too educated! But then Johannes had not pursued the matter because for his own part he had a certain respect for this man upon whom he had come to rely more and more.

Sipho was officially Johannes Venter's co-driver. Together they did country and covered the whole north-western region of the Transvaal to the border of Bechuanaland — it was now called Botswana, though only heaven knew what was wrong with

Bechuanaland, the land of the Bechuana! But he liked Botswana. They often drove across the border to spend a night or two at the Holiday Inn in Gaborone, just as they had done the night before. You could have any number of black women in Gaborone. Nobody gave a hoot there. And Sipho certainly knew his way about. Johannes Venter thought of how he had come to rely on Sipho more and more in his work. Sipho spoke all the languages of the people among whom they worked; while Johannes Venter could never understand a single word of Bantu; sometimes not even when they spoke English. In the African villages they covered Sipho took complete charge and Johannes Venter did business with the scattered white communities of predominantly Afrikaans-speaking people in the area. But for the African market, the company might as well have given up its north-western operations long ago.

Darkness was setting in when they approached the township. A large hue of red-illuminated the sky. It was like Guy Fawkes's day in mid-June. The jubilant native spirit. Johannes Venter thought. What on earth could they be celebrating?

'What day is this?' he said.

'Wednesday,' Sipho answered.

'I know that, what I mean is, what's all the excitement about?'

'I don't have the slightest idea. Looks like the chaos we usually have on New Year's Eve. I don't like it a bit. Maybe we'd better use the side streets.'

Sipho swung the car to the right hand and they plunged into the middle of nowhere. It amazed Johannes Venter how these people were ever expected to find their way through such randomly laid out and poorly-lit streets. Talk of mushrooms! The matchbox houses seemed to have been simply planted amidst rocks and debris. There were potholes as deep as children's swimming pools, right in the middle of the road. Sipho deftly avoided these and picked his way with the skill of a master navigator. And always a street or two away they could see tall flames and hear wild shouts. The scene reminded Johannes of the Kaffir cities one read about in history or in the novels of Rider Haggard, in those days of glorious savagery under the old Kaffir kings; of brightly illuminated homesteads on festive evenings, when fires were kept alight the whole night through to keep away wild beasts.

They seem to have been driving for ages, into the deep night, across puddles of foul-smelling stagnant water, over piles of rotting rubbish which provided countless interesting smells for the half-starved mongrels that prowled the area, when their car came to an abrupt halt.

Countless little eyes, like the eyes of so many cats, glared at them from the dark.

'What's all this?' Johannes Venter asked.

'I think we've had it,' Sipho whispered. 'Listen, don't panic. My house is only a few yards up the road. I'm well known in this area. It's only a couple of kids, but you'd better let me do all the talking. I can recognise quite a few of them. They often come to play with my kids.'

The note of urgency in Sipho's voice transmitted itself to Johannes Venter.

Their car was surrounded by a crowd of jeering, yelling children. They jerked the car up and down, from rear to front and again from side to side, as if to capsize it.

Johannes Venter's fear mounted. What did they want?

Sipho's voice reached him in plaintive tones. 'Better do exactly as they say,' he said. 'It'll soon be over.'

Many small fists were thrust through the window on Johannes Venter's side.

Small voices piping instructions at him in English: 'Clench your fists like this (difficult to see how in the dark) . . . no, you right fist . . . Now, say "Power!" . . . Louder (somebody'll pay dearly for this) . . . That's not loud enough (Gentle Jesu meek and milk!) . . .'

'Move closer to me, they want to come in for a ride, only they've promised not to take us beyond this street.'

Johannes Venter obeyed without question.

His door swinging open.

A swarm of wildly cheering pickanninnies, singing with so much gusto it hurt Johannes Venter's ears; some on his lap, others sitting restlessly beside him; some packed close together in the back seat; others hanging to the sides of the car, precariously perched on the bonnet and on the roof.

The car, moving at a funeral pace, seeming to sink under the weight of its human cargo, up and down the street, up and down.

Sipho's voice, mingled, with the voices of the little ones: pleading, imploring, explaining, persuading.

Then, as suddenly and as inexplicably as they had come, the

children disappeared into the thick, treacherous African night.

They drove the few remaining yards to Sipho's house in silence.

Once in the house Sipho explained to Johannes Venter that a riot had broken out in the township. The children they had just met were on their way to join their elder brothers and sisters along the township's busy streets.

Sipho spared Johannes Venter the knowledge that several whites had already been killed in the streets of the township. He was to learn of all this, and the reasons for the outbreak of violence, from newspapers and the radio the following day.

Johannes Venter was jolted by a further realisation that he couldn't possibly hope to come out of the township alive that night if he tried to drive home by himself. And Sipho, understandably enough, refused to accompany him. What made his situation even more hopeless was that Sipho wouldn't hear of Johannes Venter spending the night at his house. What was to become of him?

Then Johannes Venter remembered that he'd been thrust into a coal-box earlier. How had he come out? No matter, he was out and alive.

Voices in some strange language reached his ears. Only this time they were soothing, less menacing and more reassuring.

'He will get better by and by,' Meikie said.

'We've only got one hope, ' Eddie said.

'What is it?' Sipho asked.

'We've just got to lie low,' Eddie continued. 'Those students can't be in the streets all night.'

'But they saw us come here,' Sipho said. 'They know he's here. They only need to pass our house and see that car again. What happens if we're raided?'

'They'd have long come by now,' Eddie said. 'Anyhow, maybe that's just a risk we must take. Otherwise, if he tries to drive away by himself, then by my mother, who lies out there in Croesus, he won't get beyond this street. And, as I've already been at so much pains to explain, we can't drive him out of the township, at least not as yet.'

'He's still too weak to be moved anyhow,' Meikie said.

'But he's not sleeping here.' Daphne said. '*Kodwa amabhunu eniwakhathalele ngani nina lana?*'

Daphne again, Sipho thought. What the hell gave her the impression that they were more concerned with Johannes Venter's safety than with their own? If the worse came to the worse, they'd still have to thrust him out through that door to his would-be executioners, if necessary. But that was no reason not to try. He didn't want blood on his hands, not even that of a white.

'What do you suggest?' he asked.

'Keep him here until the streets are quiet,' Eddie said, 'then drive him home.'

'Daphne?'

'*Emalahleni*!'

'Oh, please listen, Daph,' Meikie said. 'We can't send him out there in the cold again. He'd die of exposure.'

'You all think I'm just being a heartless hag, dont you?' Daphne said. 'Have you stopped to consider what will happen if he's found here? I've my responsibility to my family, that's all. I must think of what's going to happen to my children first.'

'Don't misunderstood me, Daph,' Meikie said. 'A mother's first duty is to her children.'

'Exactly!' Eddie said. 'He nearly passed out for good in that coal-box where you want us to send him back. Do you want a dead white discovered in your yard?'

'All right then, if you think you know what you're doing,' Daphne said. 'But I still don't think it's any of my business to look after whites at the expense of my own children.'

She walked into the bedroom, followed by the children. Their excitement and curiosity exhausted, they were now ready to go to bed.

'Actually, she's right,' Meikie said. 'Why must we expose the children to unnecessary risks? Daphne and I and the children can all go and put up at our place, can't they, Eddie dear?'

'Why not?' Eddie said.

'Oh! that's very considerate of you, Meikie,' Sipho said. 'But I'm afraid that won't be necessary. Eddie is right, if nothing's happened to us so far, nothing is likely to happen now. Let's go back to Eddie's suggestion. There are certain problems of a practical nature. We drive Mr Venter to Mayfair when all is quiet. How do we come back? You know, Eddie, I'm not allowed to keep the car.'

'Hold it right there!' Eddie said. 'You surprise me, man. Here we are, ready to risk our necks for your *baas's* sake. Why, man, he'll have to trust you for once. We won't walk back after we've dropped this fellow in Mayfair. You tell him that. Fortunately your car doesn't have the company name on its side. They're burning all such cars which they can lay their hands upon. There was one large Standard Bakery van we passed on our way from town, burning on its side. There were children beside it, munching bread and cakes. I also heard that a group suspected to be thugs broke into a bottle store and made away with most of the liquor. Which reminds me of what brought me here. All this talk about the riots has made me clear forget my purpose in coming here. Meikie, can you bring along that parcel? Might as well hold a proper vigil.'

'It's right here beside me,' Meikie produced a sealed bottle of K.W.V. from her handbag. 'Actually, I don't know why I didn't think of this before, but a stiff tot of this brandy will do him some good.'

She measured Johannes Venter a stiff one and passed it on to him.

He swallowed it gratefully and felt its warmth sinking into his tummy. He was feeling much better.

'Just relax, sir,' Sipho said, 'You're among friends and you need to conserve your strength now, nothing'll happen to you.'

Something in what Eddie said didn't reassure him so much. What new ordeal was in store for him now? What did he need reserves of strength for? He looked longingly at the bottle of K.W.V.

'What have you decided?' he asked.

Sipho outlined their plan to him, but left out the bit about the car, so that Eddie had to remind him.

'*Mtshele ngemoto phela, ndoda,*' Eddie said.

'But my friend and I will have to drive back in the company car. I'll bring it with me when I come to work in the morning.'

'My dear Sipho,' Johannes Venter said, a smile illuminating his face for the first time. 'I can assure you that's perfectly all right with me. You know me, my friend, I don't stand for these company formalities. And I don't mind telling you this right away. I've never seen eye to eye with the manager over this matter of who may or may not keep the car. After all when we're in Botswana . . .'

'If you agree then, well, that's the end of the matter,' Sipho said.

Johannes Venter made up his mind there and then to recommend Sipho for promotion with immediate effect, to take complete charge of the whole north-western circuit, because he, Johannes Venter, was through with it. They'd either move him into the head office or he was going to look for another job. But either way, he was through with travelling, even if it meant having to forfeit some of the forbidden pleasures of Botswana.

Sipho thought what a narrow escape it had been. Supposing his wife had been listening? And there was no telling yet whether she'd overheard them or not. Why did Venter have to blabber so about their visits to Botswana? Sipho never confided his escapades in Gaborone to anyone besides Eddie. His wife hardly knew that he had a travelling document.

'Will you join us for a drink?' Eddie said, pouring out the drinks.

'Theres nothing I'd appreciate better,' Johannes Venter said. 'And thank you, my good sir, for all your generosity and this good lady's, not forgetting your wife, Sipho. I just don't know how to thank you enough, Mr . . .?'

Sipho made the introductions, grateful for the way Eddie had expertly steered the conversation from its disastrous course.

'I guess I'll join Daphne in the bedroom,' Meikie said. 'But, please, make sure you don't drink until you forget to drive Mr Venter home. The students will be out in full force tomorrow. I fear we're on the brink of a major catastrophe. 'Don't forget your business, please.'

Which is what almost happened!

With the brandy nearly finished, Eddie decided to remind Sipho and Johannes Venter that it was about time they left. Both men were so tight that it took Eddie close to thirty minutes to convince them that they had to go. He couldn't have accomplished that much even, if Daphne hadn't emerged from the bedroom to tell Sipho that as far as she was concerned Johannes Venter would have to spend the remaining part of the night in the coal-box; and that Sipho should follow him there, if he liked. That shook Sipho to his senses. But Johannes Venter, who didn't follow the conversation, kept prattling on about the fact that he didn't really mind where they put him up for the night because he now felt very much at one with them. He wasn't one to stand on formalities, he kept on, and Sipho would have his promotion yet, because he, Johannes Venter, was through with commercial travelling, Gaborone or no Gaborone.

It was 3.15 a.m. when they dropped him outside his house—as a precaution they'd put him in the boot—and drove back to the township.

Sipho didn't show up at work that day.

Notes on Contributors

ABRAHAMS, Peter: Born in 1919 in Vrededorp ('Fiedas'), an old slum in Johannesburg, of an Ethiopian father and a 'Coloured' mother. He was educated at St Peter's College, Rossetenville, and at the Diocesan Teacher Training College. In 1938 he travelled about in South Africa and helped to start a school for the poor 'Coloured' people of the Cape Flats, near Cape Town. In 1939 he signed on a ship as a stoker and after two years at sea he worked his way to England. He left England in 1957 to settle in the West Indies. His short story collection, *Dark Testament*, was first published in 1942. His novels include *Mine Boy* (1946); his autobiography, *Tell Freedom* (1954); *A Wreath for Udomo* (1956), *A Night of their Own* (1965) and *This Island Now* (1966).

DHLOMO, Reginald Rolfes Raymond: Born in 1901 in Siyamu, near Pietermaritzburg. His family moved to Johannesburg. After being educated at Ohlange Institute and qualifying as a teacher at Adams College, Dhlomo also went to Johannesburg, where he worked as a mine clerk. Throughout the 1920s he was a freelance journalist for the Zulu/English newspaper, *Ilanga lase Natal*. After the publication of *An African Tragedy* (1928), he began to write for *Sjambok*, 'a kind of *Private Eye* of the time', which flourished between 1929 and 1931. In 1932, not long after the founding of the *Bantu World*, Dhlomo took over its assistant editorship and later served as editor of *Ilanga lase Natal*. He is best known for his biographical novels, written in IsiZulu, of the Zulu kings such as *UShaka* (1937), *Udingane* (1936) and his masterpiece. *UCetshwayo* (1950). He died in May 1971, after several years of retirement.

HEAD, Bessie: 'I was born in Pietermaritzburg, South Africa, on July 6, 1937. In fact there is a sort of tragedy attached to my birth. My mother was a White woman of a very upper class family. Her family were very wealthy and she acquired me out of wedlock from a Black man. This caused such a disturbance in the family they succeeded in getting my mother classified insane and by the time I was born she had been committed to the Pietermaritzburg mental hospital were I was born.' Bessie Head worked as a journalist with the *Golden City Post*. She left South Africa in 1964 and has lived in exile in the village of Serowe, Botswana, ever since. Her publications include: the novels, *When Rain Clouds Gather* (1968), *Maru* (1971), *A Question of Power* (1973); the short story collection, *The Collector of Treasures* (1977); the polemical and historical work, *Serowe: Village of the Rain-Wind* (1981).

LA GUMA, Alex: Born in Cape Town in 1925 and educated at Trafalgar High School and Cape Technical College. He worked, at various times, as a clerk, factory hand, book-keeper and journalist. He was among the 156 accused in the Treason Trial and was arrested in 1956 but acquitted in 1960. During the state of emergency following the 21 March 1960 Sharpeville massacre, he was detained again for five months. In 1962 he was placed under house arrest for 24 hours a day for five years and was also detained without trial, together with his wife, under the 90-day regulation and again under the 180-day clause. He left South Africa in September 1966 for Britain and is the African National Congress representative in Cuba. His publications include *A Walk in the Night and Other Stories* (1967); and the novels, *And a Threefold Cord* (1962), *The Stone Country* (1967), *In the Fog of the Season's End* (1972) and *Time of the Butcherbird* (1979).

MAIMANE, Arthur: Born in 1932 and educated at St Peter's College. He worked on the staff of *Drum* and its sister Sunday newspaper, *Golden City Post*, before leaving South Africa as an exile in 1961. Since then he has worked as a journalist in West and East Africa but mostly in London, first for Reuters and then in radio and television. Several of his plays have been broadcast and published in various languages, as have some of his short stories. He lives in London and works as a television news writer for Thames Television. His novel, *Victims*, was published in 1976.

MATSHOBA, Mtutuzeli: 'I was born in 1950 in the early Soweto of Orlando (East and West), Shantytown, White City Jabavu, Pimville and Moroka. Today's Soweto, the sprawling dirt- and vice-polluted giant matchbox city, was more or less my age when my environment began to register in my consciousness.' He was educated at Lovedale Institution and took a B. Comm. (Law) certificate at the University of Fort Hare. He then worked as an assistant draughtsman at a die-cutting factory. His collection of short stories, *Call Me Not a Man*, was published in 1979 and banned in South Africa in November of that same year. A play *Seeds of War*, appeared in 1981.

MATTHEWS, James: Born in Cape Town in 1929. Eldest son of a poor and large family, his first job was as a newspaper seller while still at school. After leaving school he worked, in turn, as a messenger, journalist and telephonist. He began his literary career as a contributor of short stories to periodicals such as *Drum*. His collection of short stories, *Azikwelwa* (1962), was published in Sweden. He was also in the vanguard of the literary revival in South Africa ushered by the rise of Black Consciousness in the late 1960s. He turned from prose fiction and co-authored *Cry Rate* (1972), with Gladys Thomas, the first volume of poetry to be banned in South Africa. He turned to publishing and formed his own company, Blac Publishing House, in Athlone, near Cape Town. In 1974 he compiled, published and contributed to *Black Voices Shout*, an anthology of Black Consciousness poetry, which was also banned. In the same year, he brought out a collection of his stories, *The Park and Other Stories*, many of them from his first collection. He was arrested in 1976, soon after the outbreak of the 'Soweto' uprising, and released without any charges being brought against him. *Pass Me a Meatball Jones* (1977) is an account in verse of his prison experiences.

MODISANE, William ('Bloke'): Born in 1924 in Johannesburg and brought up in the slums of Sophiatown. For several years he worked in bookshops in Johannesburg and as a jazz critic for the *Golden City Post*. He left South Africa for Britain in 1959 and now lives in West Germany. Theatre is his chief interest. He has featured in many plays broadcast on BBC and has starred in films such as 'The Mercenaries'. His autobiography, *Blame Me on History*, appeared in 1963. He is represented in several anthologies including Peggy Rutherford's *Darkness and Light* (1958) and Neville Denny's *Pan African Short Stories* (1965).

MOTSISI, Casey Moses Karabo: Born in Johannesburg in 1934. He attended Madibane High School in Western Native Township and the Pretoria Normal College but was expelled, before he could qualify as a teacher, for propagating anti-establishment views in the school magazine of which he was the editor. He joined the staff of *Drum* in 1957; was transferred to *Afrika* magazine, then edited by Can Themba, Motsisi's former teacher at Madibane High; and later worked for the *Golden City Post*, the *World* and its sister Sunday paper, *Weekend World* — the latter two papers were banned in 1977, as was *Post* when it was revived. His stories have appeared in several anthologies including *Modern African Stories* (1964) edited by Komey and Mphahlele. He died in Johannesburg in 1977. A selection of his writings, *Casey and Co*, was published posthumously in 1978.

MPHAHLELE, Ezekiel ('Es'kia'): Born in 1919 in the slums of Marabastad, Pretoria. He was educated at St Peter's College and Adams College, where he qualified as a teacher. Dismissed from teaching for his opposition to Bantu education, he became *Drum*'s fiction editor in 1956 until his departure from South Africa the following year. He taught in Nigeria, Kenya, Zambia and America. He returned to South Africa, after twenty years in exile, and now teaches at the University of the Witwatersrand in Johannesburg. Publications: *Man Must Live and Other Stories* (1946); his autobiography, *Down Second Avenue* (1959); *The Living and Dead and Other Stories* (1961); *The African Image* (1962, revised and expanded edition 1974), based on his MA thesis for which he was awarded a distinction by the University of South Africa; edited and also contributed to *Modern African Stories* (1964), with Komey, and *African Writing Today* (1967); *In Corner B* (1967), his best short story collection; *The Wanderers* (1973), for which he was awarded a PhD at Denver; *Voices in the Whirlwind* (1974), political and literary essays; *Chirundu* (1979), another novel; *The Unbroken Song* (1981), from his earlier stories and poems; and *Afrika My Music*, an autobiographical sequel to *Down Second Avenue*.

MZAMANE, Mbulelo Vizikhungo: Born in 1948 in Port Elizabeth and grew up in Brakpan, on the East Rand, and Johannesburg. He was educated at St Christopher's High School in Swaziland; read English, Philosophy and Education (graduating with a distinction in Education) at the University of Botswana, Lesotho and Swaziland (UBLS), becoming the first student to be awarded the MA degree in English by the University; and at the University of Sheffield. He has taught at schools and universities in Swaziland,

Lesotho, Botswana and Britain. He is a senior lecturer in English at Ahmadu Bello University in Nigeria. Publications: *Mzala* (1980, reissued as *My Cousin Comes to Jo'burg* in 1981), a collection of short stories; *The Children of Soweto: A Trilogy* (1982), banned in South Africa two months after publication; also selected and introduced *Selected Poems: Mongane Wally Serote* 1982), *Selected Poems: Sipho Sepamla* (1983), *Made in South Africa: Black South African Poems of the 1970s* etc. He was joint winner of the Mofolo-Plomer prize for literature when it was inaugurated in 1976.

NDEBELE, Njabulo Simakahle ('Jigsaw'): Born in Johannesburg in 1948 and grew up in Nigel on the East Rand. He was educated at St Christopher's in Swaziland; at UBLS, where he graduated with a first class degree in English and Philosophy; at Cambridge University and at the University of Denver. He first carved a name for himself in the late 1960s as a poet. He is represented in many anthologies, including Robert Royston's *Black Poets in South Africa* (1974, originally published in Johannesburg in 1973 as *To Whom it May Concern*). He was also involved in articulating Black Consciousness during its formative years when as editor of *Expression*, a journal of the English Society at UBLS, he emerged as one of the leading literary theoreticians of the Black Consciousness Movement. He is a lecturer in English at the National University of Lesotho. He was the joint winner of the 1984 Noma Award with his collection of short stories, *Fools and Other Stories* (1984).

RIVE, Richard: Born in 1931 in the Cape Peninsula, he grew up in Cape Town's District Six. He was educated at the University of Cape Town, Columbia University and Magdalen College, Oxford. He trained as a teacher at Hewat Training College, Cape Town, where he now teaches English. In 1962 he was awarded a Farfield Foundation Fellowship grant to enable him to study literary trends in African literature of English expression. He travelled through twenty-four countries in Africa and Europe. His stories first appeared in the 1950s in South African periodicals such as *Drum* and have been translated into more than a dozen languages. *Africa Songs*, his collection of short stories, appeared in 1963. His first novel, *Emergency*, was published in 1964 and banned in South Africa. He has also edited and contributed to *Modern African Prose* (1964) and *Quartet* (1965; also featuring La Guma and Matthews). His other books include *Selected Writing* (1977) and *Writing Black* (1981). His stories continue to appear in South African magazines and periodicals such as *Contrast* and *Staffrider*.

THEMBA, Daniel Canadoce ('Can'): Born in 1924 in Marabastad. He was awarded the first Mendi Memorial Scholarship to Fort Hare and graduated with a first class degree in English in 1947. After qualifying as a teacher, he taught English at Madibane High School in Western Native Township. In 1953 he won *Drum*'s short story competition and soon thereafter joined the editorial staff of the magazine. He later became editor of *Afrika* and then the *Golden City Post*. In 1963 Can Themba, with his wife and children, went into exile in Swaziland, where he taught at St Joseph's, near Manzini. In 1966 he was listed, with forty-five others, under the Suppression of Communism Act—which meant that his past, present and future writings were automatically banned in South Africa. He died in exile in 1968. Once described as 'the greatest non-writing writer ever known'. A selection of his stories and journalistic pieces was published posthumously under the title, *The Will to Die* (1972).

THOMAS, Gladys: a housewife from Cape Town, achieved instant fame in 1972, when she jointly published *Cry Rage* with James Matthews. After the ban of their poetry collection, she withdrew from public notice. With the establishment of *Staffrider* in March 1978, the outbreak of the students' and workers' revolt in the Western Cape in 1980, she broke her silence and resumed her interrupted career as a writer but switched over from poetry to the short story, a medium she has found better suited to her talents. She is a regular contributor to *Staffrider*.

Select Bibliography

Section A: Collections and Anthologies of Black South African short stories

Collections

ABRAHAMS, Peter, *Dark Testament*, London, Dorothy Crisp, 1942

DANGOR, Achmat, *Waiting for Leila*, Johannesburg, Ravan Press, 1981

DHLOMO, Rolfes Reginald Raymond, *English in Africa* (Special Dhlomo issue), 2, no.1, 1975, published by the Institute for the Study of English in Africa, Rhodes University, Grahamstown.

ESSOP, Ahmed, *The Hajji and Other Stories*, Johannesburg, Ravan Press, 1978

HEAD, Bessie, *The Collector of Treasures*, London, Heinemann, 1977

LA GUMA, Alex, *A Walk in the Night and Other Stories*, London, Heinemann, 1967

MATSHOBA, Mtutuzeli, *Call Me Not a Man*, Johannesburg, Ravan Press, 1979 and London, Longman, 1981

MATTHEWS, James, *Azikwelwa* Sweden, 1962

MATTHEWS, James, *The Park and Other Stories*, Athlone, Cape, Blac Publishing House, 1974

MOTSISI, Casey, *Casey and Co: Selected Writings of Casey 'Kid' Motsisi*, selected by Mothobi Mutloatse, Johannesburg, Ravan Press, 1978

MPHAHLELE, Ezekiel, *Man Must Live and Other Stories*, Cape Town, Bookman, 1946

MPHAHLELE, Ezekiel, *The Living and Dead and Other Stories*, Ibadan, Ministry of Education, 1961

MPHAHLELE, Ezekiel, *In Corner B*, Nairobi, East African Publishing House, 1967

MPHAHLELE, Es'kia, *The Unbroken Song*, Johannesburg, Raven Press, 1981.

MUTLOATSE, Mothobi, *Mama Ndiyalila: The Stories of Mothobi Mutloatse*, Johannesburg, Ravan Presss, 1982

MZAMANE, Mbulelo, *Mzala: The Stories of Mbulelo Mzamane*, Johannesburg, Ravan Press, 1980, reissued as *My Cousin Comes to Jo'burg*, London, Longman, 1981

MZAMANE, Mbulelo Vizikhungo, *The Children of Soweto: A Trilogy*, London, Longman, 1982 and Johannesburg, Ravan Press, 1982

NDEBELE, Njabulo, *Fools and Other Stories*, Johannesburg, Raven Press, 1983

RIVE, Richard, *African Songs*, Berlin, Seven Seas, 1963

THEMBA, Can, *The Will to Die*, selected by Donald Stuart and Roy Holland, London, Heinemann, 1972

Anthologies

BEIER, Ulli (ed.), *Black Orpheus*, New York, McGraw Hill, 1965

DENNY, Neville (ed.), *Pan African Short Stories*, London, Nelson, 1965

GORDIMER, Nadine and Lionel Abrahams (eds.), *South African Writing Today*, Harmondsworth, Penguin, 1969

GRAY, Stephen (ed.), *Modern South African Stories*, Johannesburg, Ad Donker, 1980

HUGHES, Langston (ed.), *An African Treasury*, London, Victor Gollancz, 1961

KOMEY, Ellis and MPHAHLELE Ezekiel (eds.), *Modern African Stories*, London, Faber, 1964

LARSON, Charles (ed.), *Modern African Stories,* London, Fontana/Collins, 1971

LARSON, Charles (ed.), *More Modern African Stories,* London, Fontana/Collins, 1975

MARQUARD, Jean (ed.), *A Century of South African Short Stories*, Johannesburg, Ad Donker, 1978

MPHAHLELE, Ezekiel (ed.), *African Writing Today*, Harmondsworth, Penguin, 1967

MUTLOATSE, Mothobi (ed.), *Africa South: Contemporary Writings*, London, Heinemann, 1981 (originally issued as *Forced Landing: Africa South Contemporary Writings*, Johannesburg, Ravan Press, 1980)

MUTLOATSE, Mothobi (ed.), *Reconstruction: 90 Years of Black Historical Literature*, Johannesburg, Ravan Press, 1981

RUTHERFOORD, Peggy (ed.), *Darkness and Light: An Anthology of African Writing*, Johannesburg, Drum Publications, 1958 and London, Faith Press, 1958

SCANLON, Paul (ed.), *Stories from Central and Southern Africa*, London, Heinemann, 1983

TIBBLE, Anne (ed.), *African/English Literature: A Survey and Anthology of Prose and Poetry up to 1965*, London, Peter Owen, 1965

Section B: Studies of
Black South African Literature and Society

Literature

BARNETT, Ursula, *Ezekiel Mphahlele*, Boston, Twayne Publishers, 1976

BARNETT, Ursula, *A Vision of Order*, London, Sinclair Browne, 1983

DUERDEN, Dennis and PIETERSE, Cosmo (eds.), *African Writers Talking*, London: Heinemann, 1972.

FEBRUARY, Vernie, *Mind Your Colour: The 'Coloured' Stereotype in South African Literature*, London and Boston, Kegan Paul International, 1981

KLIMA, Vladimar, *South African Prose Writing in English*, Prague, *Publishing House of the Czechoslovak Academy of Sciences, 1971*

MOORE, Gerald, *Twelve African Writers*, London, Hutchinson University Library for Africa, 1980

MPHAHLELE, Ezekiel, *The African Image*, London, Faber, 1962

MPHAHLELE, Ezekiel, *Voices in the Whirlwind and Other Essays*, London, Macmillan, 1973

MUNRO, Donald and PIETERSE, Cosmo (eds.), *Protest and Conflict in African Literature*, London, Heinemann, 1969

NKOSI, Lewis, *Home and Exile*, London, Longman, 1965

NKOSI, Lewis, *Tasks and Masks: Themes and Styles of African Literature*, London, Longman, 1981

OGUNGBESAN, Kolawole, *The Writings of Peter Abrahams*, London, Hodder and Stoughton, 1969

RIVE, Richard, *Selected Writing*, Johannesburg, Ad Donker, 1977

RIVE, Richard, *Writing Black*, Johannesburg, David Philip, 1981

ROSCOE, Adriaan. *Uhuru's Fire: African Literature East to South*, Cambridge University Press, 1977

WADE, Michael, *Peter Abrahams*, Ibadan, Evans Brothers, 1972

Society

BIKO, Steve Bantu, *I Write What I Like: A Selection of His Writings*, edited by Aelred Stubbs, London, Heinemann, 1979

GERHART, Gail, *Black Power in South Africa: The Evolution of an Ideology*, Berkley and Los Angeles, University of California Press, 1979

HARSCH, Ernest, *South Africa: White Rule Black Revolt*, New York, Monad Press, 1980

HIRSON, Baruch, *Year of Fire, Year of Ash: The Soweto Revolt, Roots of a Revolution*, London, Zed Press, 1979

HUDDLESTON, Trevor, *Naught for Your Comfort*, London, Collins, 1956

KANE-BERMAN, John, *Soweto: Black Revolt, White Reaction*, Johannesburg, Ravan Press, 1978

KARIS, Thomas et al (eds.), *From Protest to Challenge: Documents of African Politics in South Africa, 1882-1964*, 4 vols., Stanford, Hoover Institution Press, 1972-77

LA GUMA, Alex (ed.), *Apartheid: A Collection of Writings on South African Reaction by South Africans*, London, Lawrence and Wishart, 1972

MANDELA, Nelson, *No Easy Walk to Freedom: Articles, Speeches and Trial Addresses of Nelson Mandela*, London, Heinemann, 1965

NOLUTSHUNGU, Sam C., *Changing South Africa—Political Considerations*, Manchester University Press, 1982

PHETO, Molefe, *And Night Fell*, London, Allison and Busby with Heinemann, 1983

REEVES, Ambrose, *Shooting at Sharpeville: The Agony of South Africa*, London, Victor Gollancz Ltd., 1960

ROUX, Edward, *Time Longer than Rope: A History of the Blackman's Struggle for Freedom in South Africa*, Madison, University of Wiconsin Press, 1964

SAMPSON, Anthony, *Drum: A Venture into the New Africa*, London, Collins, 1956

TABATA, I.B., *The Awakening of a People*, Nottingham, Spokesman Books, 1974

WHITE, Landeg and COUZENS, Tim (eds.), *Literature and Society in South Africa*, London, Longman, 1984

WILSON, Monica and THOMPSON, Leonard (eds.), *The Oxford History of South Africa*, 2 vols., Oxford, Clarendon Press, 1969-71

Also in Longman African Classics

Fools and other stories

Njabulo Ndebele

Winner of the Noma Award 1983

'And when victims spit upon victims should they not be called fools? Fools of darkness.'

A taut, lyrical and compelling collection of stories, vividly bringing to life the black urban locations of apartheid South Africa.

These are rich and enchanting stories told with the warmth of childhood memory: of the adulation of a child for his trumpet-playing uncle; a teenager's trial of endurance to prove himself worthy of his street-gang; a child's rebellion against his parents snobbish aspirations.

And the title story, *Fools*, tells with painful intensity of events sparked by a meeting between a disgraced teacher, haunted by the impotence of his present life, and a student activitist railing against those who do not share his sense of urgency.

The author believes 'we have given away too much of our real and imaginative lives to the opressor'. These beautiful award-winning stories of township life in all its complexity are his answer.

'Njabulo Ndebele's first book represents the kind of beginning in fiction that will prove to have altered the contours of our literature ... His storytelling is full-fleshed and elegant ... of thrilling significance'.

Lionel Abrahams Sesame

'Brings with it an exhilerating current of fresh air ... solid, vibrant prose'.

E'skia Mphahlele The Sowetan

ISBN 0 582 78621 5

Scarlet Song

Mariama Ba

Translated by Dorothy S. Blair

Mariama Ba's first novel So Long a Letter was the winner of the Noma Award in 1980. In this her second and, tragically, last novel she displays all the same virtues of warmth and crusading zeal for women's rights that won her so many admirers for her earlier work.

Mireille, daughter of a French diplomat and Ousmane, son of a poor Muslim family in Senegal, are two childhood sweethearts forced to share their love in secret. Their marriage shocks and dismays both sets of parents, but it soon becomes clear that their youthful optimism and love offer a poor defence against the pressures of society. As Ousmane is lured back to his roots, Mireille is left humiliated, isolated and alone.

The tyranny of tradition and chauvinism is brilliantly exposed in this passionate plea for human understanding. The author's sympathetic insights into the condition of women deserve recognition throughout the world.

ISBN 0 582 78595 2